Obscured Darkness

Family Secrets Book Two

Rebekah Mc Clew

Obscured Darkness

Family Secrets Book Two

Rebekah McClew

Chapter One
Gone West

As if it wasn't bad enough being chased by paranoid towns' folk wielding pitchforks and torches, the thunderstorm and torrential rain certainly hadn't helped either. I may have been fast enough running however the sudden mudslides, flash floods and the worst part had been the thunderstorms. I may have been graceful at other times; however, one would only need to watch me run in the mud to see me make a fool of myself. It felt so strange to see a flash of lightning strike down from the sky weaving through the air following us until it was distracted by a nearby object and diverted its path. I certainly hated boats, especially when traveling over deep water where I couldn't see the bottom. I knew from where I ran, that I wasn't going to end up on the same boat as Anthony or Charlie.

Anthony discovered a direct path up north would not be easy, I found it just as difficult. Anthony went off east as I had taken off west, as I ran, I was thinking about him and Rose. I just hoped they were safe and alright, also knowing that Charlie stayed behind to buy us time. I hoped he would be alright. This early on I didn't want to lose the father I had just gained let alone my family. I would have to go a lot further before I could take a break or even begin to turn up north. Sadly, the direction I had gone hadn't been a very good choice. The town already feared vampires and many other stories that were being passed around. It seemed like I kept getting driven even further out west to avoid situations. Stopping only momentarily to feed Lucian. I wondered how the others were fairing. I could not wait to be with my family again and have the final reunion I so longed for. Even just to know my family was safe.

Eventually, I came to the mountain area and had not wanted to go much further west than I already did. At some point, I needed to start going up north. With all the thunderstorms rolling through. Waiting in a cave I found seemed safe for the moment, so we stopped. At least in here, I could keep Lucian dry from all the rain. My human self was getting very worn out and needed rest. Not planning on sleeping other than to rest and wait out the worst of the storm. I planned on taking off right away again. Laying down, I positioned our son between myself and the rock wall to protect him. Then quickly fell asleep.

I remembered how easy it was to get lost and hoped I would not lose my direction. At least I knew where we were meeting. It was a matter of getting there. Anthony should be fine. He always seemed to have a natural sense of direction. If I hadn't memorized my estate and the woods around it, I could get lost easily in my backyard. He tried teaching me about reading moss and knowing what direction it was on, based on what side it was on a tree, or how thick it was growing on the ground. The only problem I was having, was a simple fact there was moss covering the ground all over, the ground was so hard, wet, and cold. The only difference I could find had been the moss was growing thicker on one side of the tree versus the other side. I couldn't remember what Anthony said about that little fact.

One problem I learned when asking Anthony or Charley for directions, they were not always accurate. If they said travel south, realistically it meant, go northeast and then drop down south. Or travel to a certain country and go north. So, figuring out where I was, getting to the point where they wanted me, and then traveling from there to the direction wasn't easily done as hoped.

I wanted to get moving before the winter set in otherwise it was going to be harder to cover the ground with snow and a baby. I was already sadly uncoordinated in the mud; it would only be worse on snow and ice. Not something I even wanted to try. At this point, I could only guess where I was at.

I had never left my town, so this was all new even though I did find it a little exciting exploring. I wish Anthony could have been here with me. I wished I could have found a cave a little further up the hill that would have been more concealed by the trees. The cave we were in didn't have any rain coming in other than when the winds picked up. On the side of the cliff, there were several open-mouth caves, so I picked the middle one that was high enough off the ground. It may not have a tree cover, but it would be hard for any human to get to us.

Holding Lucian close. I stared out of the cave thinking about what Charlie and I talked about. I learned a lot about my mother and his family. Being way out here I wondered about a particular story he told us.

The story Charlie told of his sister. The one sister that was given away from the midnight madam stuck in my mind. The girl had been half-vampire and half-human. The only difference with her is that her skin was not pale white or olive color. She reflected a darker pigment. She had what looked like a natural tan, which is why most thought she was all human by not resembling the rest of the family.

Only by the scent, you would know she was still a partial vampire. This could always change as she gets older but as a baby, she looked rather normal. When his family wanted to see how she was doing, they had not known what happened to her. They found the family that adopted her moved far away and died in such a mysterious way. They drowned in the river. Everyone wondered why and how this possibly could have happened, was it that they found out the girl they had was a vampire and they were killed? Only the bodies of the two adults were found. There was a story that she had been left with friends, but no one spoke of them or seemed to know who they were.

Not knowing where I was, I had been the closest to their lost sister than anyone had been in a very long time. I didn't even realize I had been in the same vicinity as Evangeline. Her name was the only thing the family knew of her. The family wasn't even sure if the ones who raised her changed her name or had found out what she was or if she was even safe or existed anymore.

The midnight madam had been her mother and her father was unknown. She was the only child the mistress did not have with the McAllister's father. The mistress had given birth to her other children before her change had taken over completely. Odd that a vampire could have given birth herself since she had nothing to offer a growing infant, somehow unknown to the family she must have been able to nourish herself or possibly didn't need anything during that time which seemed mind-boggling. Then when she was only a week old the family found out who the father was and found out the reason. A special gift that Evangeline possessed because her father made it unnecessary for her to need anything from her mother to survive. Perhaps that was why Charlie's mother never felt any anger toward the girl? She was the only one who didn't appear to need the madam and resembled a normal baby girl. She also hadn't been from her husband; Julie McAllister even formed a strong protective attachment to her, especially when she found the Madam experimented on her. She kept saying if only she could figure out the gene she could force something to come to her instead of waiting for one of the McAllister children to show up with it, not that she ever told anyone what that thing was. Her messing with Evangeline's genes, worried Julie which was also why she kept the family she was given away to a secret from everyone.

Evangeline's birth father was such a rare radiant creature that there had yet been a name to describe him. He was very intelligent, quick, and self-sustaining even though the family knew this, they still didn't quite understand how. He blended in with other humans rather well since he looked very much like them and had very dark skin. The only thing the lady in black would say about him was that he was a cursed man by the name of Kristopher Vondrak.

From Charlie's family only Dreana, Mark, Aidelle, and Anna had not been bitten by the midnight madam. Smallpox ravaged their family while sparing some who had not been so kind to others. Technically if his father counted her as one of his own and not been given away shortly after birth, she would have been the youngest sibling.

So far, the only thing that would tip people off that she was different had been the fact that she aged rather slowly, much slower than most vampires. She was still just a baby when her foster parents took her in believing she was younger than she was. If she had truly been normal, it would have been safer for her to grow up with a human family. The fact she still shared traits from the McAllister family they worried about what traits they didn't know about that would surface when she inherited additional gifts from her father. Hoping since there had been no one there to encourage her gifts they hoped she would be safe not knowing about them. They always feared the worst but hoped in time they would find her and find her well. They had known ones who possessed power however from not ever learning how to use it or never using it at all, the power was never strong enough to use anymore. However, occasionally they are still passed on from generation to generation unknowingly.

With so many vampire hunters out there as of late, therefore I was on constant alert. As I slept, I was alert in case anything was to come near us whether it is an animal or a person.

It was already four days past when Lucian and I were scheduled to join Charlie and Anthony at the cabin way up north however, plans had to change as I ran into one obstacle after another. I only hoped they would not grow too fearful or put themselves in danger by looking for us. I knew I would get us home safely. It would just take longer than I had wanted it to. Only traveling in the dark, and sleeping during the day didn't give very much time. Usually not staying in one place for too long, I felt comfortable here, it was far enough from a town, and no one knew us or knew we were here. It would make getting supplies much easier. The people in this town didn't seem to pay attention to me at all other than to be friendly.

If the scenery hadn't been changing, I would have thought I was running around in circles. I didn't want to keep running and getting into dangerous situations with Lucian, not that I wanted to stay here any longer than I had to. Finding pieces here and there to add to the cave to make it more livable for the time being hadn't been very easy either. Not far there had been a broken-down wagon no one was using. Pulling the hitch and other parts, keeping the flatbed I placed in the cave. At least Lucian would have a dry place to lay down when I wasn't holding him. Even though I didn't want Anthony to risk his life looking for me. I was beginning to wonder if I would need him to find me just because I didn't even have a clue where I was. I didn't know from diverting my path so often if I was already up north or if I had gone south. With being able to run so fast and covering so much ground, I had no idea how far I had already gone. I hoped that by staying here a little longer than most places, I might figure out where I was and get back on track.

I found a dress that had been thrown out. Nothing at all wrong with it, I heard the woman recently replaced her old gowns with new ones. Something I would have done myself except this time I didn't have the luxury of doing it. Taking the gowns out of the bin she threw them in. I took them back to the cave. Altering them slightly with anything I could get my hands on so they would not be recognized. I also found some kids' clothes for Lucian being thrown out behind one of the general stores. Not that he fit them but at least he was clean and covered. The stream over the hill had been warmer than I expected it to be. Trying to blend in the best we could, I hoped we would leave soon.

The only nice thing about this town had been the fact they didn't make a big deal when there was a new person let alone one with a baby. Unless they seemed to already know you, they weren't talkative either. A couple of the older ladies paid attention to Lucian. Smiling and cooing at him. It felt like ages since we had been staying in the cave, even though it was only seven days now. At least if Anthony and I wanted to settle anywhere this would be an easy place to move to. Sitting with Lucian in my lap again I whispered to him.

"Don't worry. We will see daddy and sissy again, as soon as I figure out where we are." Smiling I hugged him close to me trying to reassure myself more than I was Lucian not that I was doing a very good job. I hadn't believed myself much.

It was strange to think that Charlie and his siblings referred to their mother as the madam or mistress. They called Julie mother at times but for the most part and for some of the children who were children of the madam never knew her real name, let alone never once called her mom or mother. Even knowing the truth now of who my birthmother was. I still referred to the one who raised me as my mother. She still was and always will be my mother.

Unknown to me, not far from where I was staying with Lucian, Evangeline was getting ready for her birthday party that evening. Any celebration for any reason was a big deal in such a small town.

Chapter Two
Evangeline

No candles this year, just a large bonfire that filled the night sky. Everyone was sitting around talking and enjoying themselves. Joking about growing up and experiences they had. Comparing their stories and who made out the best in life, even if they said they won they joked about how silly the outcome had been since they were in the same spot as they were several years ago. Knowing if she shared her experience, she would beat them all at the best and worst outcomes in life. Having a different outlook knowing her life was not going to come to an end.

Sitting on the log near the fire you could see the mountains in the background, and the stars shining in the sky above. Being so far out in the middle of nowhere the sky was easily seen here. Some of the mining towns were so well lit that it interfered with seeing the stars until you traveled out into the countryside. Even the sound of the wolves rang through the night sky. A sound I loved hearing.

Just like the previous year, this one felt no different. Turning twenty-two felt like turning fifteen or even turning one hundred. Thinking possibly this would be how I would feel when I turned three hundred and fifty. But then in all fairness, I had turned twenty at least five times now or more not that I bothered counting, they celebrated the day I arrived which they never did know when exactly I had been born. But celebrating my twenty or so birthday was easier since I always looked that age and no one seemed to remember, or they didn't say anything. After growing I stopped at that look in age. Some felt sorry for me that I would never get older, and others thought I was lucky to look young forever.

Two older ladies had been talking and must have assumed they were out of earshot; however, I could still hear them. They were talking about my age and the fact that as the years went by, I still looked the same, so timeless. Then the second lady said the most interesting comment.

"Yes. but wait until the old age catches up to her and she inherits all the problems of aging when her ageless face is full of wrinkles, breasts, slapping against her legs as she walks, and her rear end bottoms out and hits the floor dragging behind her. She's going to look like a worn-out teenager who has been drug through the mud and had the crap beat out of it, but she will still look like she does now only old." It was the oddest but also funniest comparison I had ever heard someone make about myself. When I heard it, I couldn't help but smile, even though the one lady did see me and asked her friend what she thought I was smiling about, if they had only known.

I tried not to think too far into the future since most of it for me seemed to have sad endings. Most were not aware that someday when they died, I would still be living. It sucked to know I would see a child be born and then one day see them in their old age and when they would die. They thought I had some gene in my body that kept me from getting older or that I just plain aged well.

Some day they would catch on and I wondered what I would do? It was hard to keep track when I was little, no one was ever good at guessing my age, so I was able to pass it off better. As a girl most don't ask me about my real age and assumed, I did not want to share it, so they celebrate the one year for me every year. But then the town had been so close-knit I doubted any would have problems when they found out. I sort of thought most knew already it was just not something a person would speak of.

Watching my foster parents, they were always affectionate. Always touching, hugging each other. I could picture them being extremely old and wrinkled and him chasing after her and her loving being chased as she did now. You could tell they were in love. From the way, they spoke to each other, never a harsh word or action. The way he cared for her and the very simple personal things she did for him.

I knew they had a lot of patience when they raised me. Even though at this point I didn't need to be raised I was being handed down from family member to family almost like an heirloom, just a living one. And at times I still felt like a child. As my first set of foster parents did as they inherited me, not knowing what exactly they were getting into. They just knew they loved and respected who they believed to be my parents. People who lived quietly and had kept to themselves other than when people needed help, were the first to offer. Living very modestly it never looked like they had anything; they never seemed to want anything and certainly never expected anything from anyone.

Many people and my foster parents included thought I was very much like my parents in personality and living life. They assumed it must have been a trait handed down through genes. By now I had more money saved up than I would ever need, even though I helped a lot with the town and my parents who cared for me now.

Katherine and Max had been my first foster parents, which made it easier when Katherine gave birth to Hellen. I had a sister and a built-in friend. One I developed the closest bond with. After a time I watched Katherine and Max grow older and then one by one both had passed on. Hellen had met Riley early on and married rather young. Inheriting the farm, they took over being foster parents for me to help keep the secret.

Everyone else from the farm I worked with was enjoying themselves. Most did not live nearby for too long. Many went in search of jobs elsewhere, the younger ones my age goofing off. I never really did get close to them preferring to keep to myself but at times would join in with them when nudged. This was not one of those times. Watching Hellen and Riley sitting next to the fire with their arms looped around each other brought back memories of Katherine and Max, and how they were with each other. There were times I wished I had someone like that. Someone to love, I had only fallen in love with someone once and after that, we broke up but after losing him, I lost my heart and the effort to fall in love again.

My parents had been close to my first set of foster parents. At the time I was only a few months old. They never understood what my parents did except that they were very private and moved here rather quickly and quietly.

Katherine and Max were always willing to answer any

questions I had about my parents or at least what they knew of them. My dad worked with Max for a while when they moved to the area. Their excuse was that they needed a complete change. Then one day they had been traveling on a boat for a side business my father was running and ran into bad weather, later they received the bad news. I had been left behind in Katherine's care until they were supposed to return which never happened. At one point several armed men surrounded their house knocking down the doors and searching every room for me.

Stopping at Katherine and Max's farm they asked if they knew where the baby was, Max, standing next to Katherine protecting her.

"No sir, we assumed the family took their son with them. The cottage has been empty for a long time now." As soon as she offered that information the men looked at each other with questioning looks.

"They had a daughter, not a son, whose baby is in the crib there?" The man attempted to make a move over to where I was laying in the crib.

I was still just a few months old at the time and they didn't have me for too long. Not feeling they could trust the strange men who had come the way they did, dressed the way they were both had the immediate feeling I needed to be protected also, that my parent's death couldn't have been an accident. Stepping in the way Max prevented them from getting any closer.

"That happens to be our daughter, we finally got her asleep and would appreciate that you do not get any closer. I don't want her waking up or possibly catching whatever cold you might have sir. As far as we understood the couple, you're talking about always had their son dressed in blue and called him Mickael, if their son was a girl it's news to us. They kept to themselves and were friendly quiet folk. Now if you don't mind,

I won't put up with being disrespected in my own home, you may take your leave now." The one-man did have a runny nose he kept wiping on his sleeve, ushering the men outside, the last one out made one last comment before they left.

"If we find you lied to us at all or know where she is being kept, we won't go lightly on you." Both men the entire time tried to appear menacing even with the entire black-colored garb they wore seemed more of a joke than serious.

"Sir, I will be respectful or answer your questions but don't ever come into my home again with such ill manners and threaten myself or my family again." Pulling his rifle out he showed the men he was neither afraid of them and would not back down. That had been the last time they had seen or heard from them.

Never seeing what my parents looked like other than in pictures. I had no memories of them. I was immediately taken in by Max and Katherine Weiler when news spread that my parents had died. To them, one more mouth to feed would not even be noticed. I blended in for the most part.

Tired from the birthday celebration I got up and walked out to the barn not wanting to walk to my home since I felt too tired to walk that far tonight, I decided to crash in the barn. Three years ago, I bought the old run-down farmhouse a few miles from my foster parents. Even though I hadn't been old enough to move out, I used it as a hobby to fix up figuring one day I would live there. The one thing I hadn't cared for was keeping up the charade of being young when I would have loved being older and able to live on my own without explanations.

Then last year I moved out. It had gotten to the point where I was not able to hide some things from others anymore and I needed a place I could be myself.

They were happy when they found out I was staying close to

home. They always worried about me. Especially with the nightmares I had when I was growing up. The disturbing pictures I used to draw. Both had wondered how such a small child would even think of things like those since I had never been exposed to anything like that. No one outside the family knew about the pictures I had drawn or what made me different. They kept them rather quiet.

Even in a small town with loving people, gossip is still rather strong and can make it hard for someone to form a life. Besides, they were always worried I would be used, attacked, or even worse killed. Even if someone from town didn't there were always those who passed through. I was taught to be rather private and from there I went rather overboard with privacy. I always treasured being able to relax and be myself when I could.

Sitting in the barn hearing others still talking into the late hours of the morning, I had climbed up into the rafters high above the animals. There was a small niche in the corner I liked to climb into and sleep. At least I would be here early for work in the morning. I never liked walking in the dark alone. I always felt like I was being watched. Never seeing anyone or anything to suggest it, it was a deep feeling I always had. I never shared my feelings with my foster parents not wanting to worry them, but I always felt as if there was something not quite right. I was less afraid of what people would do to me than what I felt the presence of something following me had unnatural, almost supernatural energy. But even for myself, I knew I could get overworked or too imaginative.

After moving into my home, I didn't have visitors but then I didn't invite anyone either. They knew I had an open-door policy as my parents did, but no one was close enough to come visit me.

No one liked to visit my home since they felt sorry for me. I tried to let others know I was happy and was always smiling, which was probably why no one ever gave me a problem. Even though they were curious about where I put the money I earned. The place looked so empty, that most were curious how a single girl on her own could fix it up without any help or experience.

For a single girl, I did not seem to have a visible vice anyone could see. I was never into the overnight parties or even social balls that were being held in the next town over. I wasn't into drinking even though I worked at the bar as well as on my parent's farm. I could have had my debutante ball but chose to be private and keep to myself instead. I wasn't worried if I was never married. This just wasn't one of my concerns. Many did think of me as strange for the simple fact that I wasn't dating or spoke of any interest in anyone. I always heard who was dating whom. I preferred to keep it private when I had met a person. But it had been a long time since then and he has since passed away, sadly he died young, at least compared to my age he was young.

I tended to spend a lot of time at home. No one understood how you could live in a home with no furniture, not even a bed or pillow to speak of. But there were things that others did not know about. I had years of collecting things from different places, however, I kept them in a way that no one would see them, and only I would get to enjoy seeing them. If they only knew of the private room, I built under the very floorboards. I had built an entire house below the existing one. It was easy to convert using the stone cellar that had already existed. I had four large rooms down below even though most of the time I only used one. The existing cottage had been built on top of a rather rocky spot. Carving out a large room down below it was always cool on the hottest of days. Here I spent a lot of time knowing there could never be anyone to watch me there. The original basement was never directly under the house with only access from the outside which I later closed.

I planned on using the upper floors above ground as painting rooms, using any kind of natural berry or natural dies for my projects. Sculpting clay by hand lets them dry out in the sun for days. My front yard sometimes looked rather strange but at least the town understood what they were. And again, some thought this kind of confirmed I was a little strange using a big house just for crafting. I couldn't help it. I liked doing things with my hands. I even learned to weave baskets from a group of Indians much further away. I had run into them when I was searching for stone materials. What I had learned from them was very valuable to me; the advice given helped me a lot.

Feeling a soft fluffy fur brush against me, I could feel Tabitha, our cat had gotten out and must have seen me getting up here. She always joined me either here or at my own house if she had the chance to follow me. Settling in to fall asleep we both slept rather soundly. I always thought it was cute the small snore that came rumbling from the cat. Feeling tired from the day it wasn't a surprise I had fallen asleep so fast.

Morning approached very quickly on the farm, waking promptly before the rooster made his morning announcement. I probably gave this way too much thought, sometimes I wonder if the rooster was either deflated, he never woke me, or just irritated by me for waking him up? Anytime I would open my eyes he would be directly across from me staring at me till I left. Hopping down from the rafter the animals were already outside. At some point, the cat must have left and I had not noticed.

I always kept a change of clothing in the tackle room for the nights I decided not to go home. Hellen would have preferred me to sleep in the guest bedroom or at least my own personal room they kept for me, instead of my sleeping out here. I couldn't help it I felt more comfortable out here. Putting on my work slacks and a white tank top that was stained, at least I wasn't worried about impressing anyone. Pulling my waist-length hair back into a ponytail, I braided it to keep too much from getting stuck in it. Most girls my age wore dresses even if they worked on the farm. But I didn't worry about being feminine. I wanted to be comfortable and wore men's slacks instead. I already was feminine I but didn't feel I had to prove it.

I had a box of pictures I liked looking through, they were supposedly my parents except I hadn't looked like either of them. One particular hand drawn photo, there was a couple in the background that I looked more like. I would spend time looking at the picture of my parents, at least it was what they said but I've been handed around so much its difficult to say if they were or not. I didn't look like my natural parents. One of the family portrait photos had their extremely close friends with them, I resembled them more than my parents. Both my parents were rather pale, their friends had a golden tan with dark black hair like mine. My father had a dirty blonde while my mother was blonde. Their friends had piercing blue eyes like mine, which was another reason I questioned if they could have been my actual birth parents. Both ladies had long hair while my father had a short, trimmed style while their friend had loose long wavy hair. I was positive they were the reason I loved to paint. There were paintings by them that were gifted to my parents with their initials VK-KV. I always wondered why the initials were the same, but lettering was reversed. I always felt emotionally connected to their friends unfortunately I may never know who my original parents had been. My past was very mysterious and no one original was still around to explain it.

My parents stood next to each other, they were rather striking. Their personalities were as complex. My father didn't like the sun and didn't spend very much time in it. He would be found out late at night tending to his garden or crops. He explained that he felt they did better if he harvested them in the dark rather than when the hot sun was out.

My mother on the other hand spent as much time as she could outside during the day, basking in the sun's glow. Many would say she never ran out of energy. She would be gardening bright and early in the morning then go hiking, swimming, painting, and many other things during the day. She even ran a few events for the town children for them to have something to do. Most people had known they were there for at least a year. Then as quickly as they moved in, they left just as quickly. The news of their death spread fast and saddened everyone. The town had been rather quiet for a while after that.

Every morning before anyone else was up in the house I would start work on the farm before the rooster would crow or the sun would rise. Just to irritate the rooster I brought a second one home and put him next to the other one. Shoving the bales of hay from the rafter onto the open flat of the wagon which had been pulled by the ox, my handling this every day was a good excuse. I used to explain why I was so strong. I was even stronger than the guys who worked on the farm. My foster parents were worried if I would be feminine enough. They wanted to make sure I didn't forget to act feminine since I fit in with the guys too well. Even to the point, they would forget they were with a real girl when joking around.

From my youth I was enrolled in charm school and etiquette lessons. One of the things I enjoyed the most had been to dance. I would attend many socials and dances if there had been a partner available. I loved the music as the trends changed. Others simply loved dancing with me since I was so graceful and never once stepped on their feet. It's not like I didn't like being girly or dressing up, it's just that it didn't fit on the farm when I was working. And I wanted to work hard and not be dainty about it. Even though I still caught the attention of the other guys when I worked, I was still graceful even if I didn't notice it myself. I was still very attractive even when I was wet and dirty.

Taking the ox out of the barn with the flatbed attached. I directed him to the field to feed the other cattle. As I dropped each bale of hay, I still liked watching how the animals would follow behind eagerly waiting for the food to be dropped off. As the sun started to rise and the rooster finally started waking up I had at least half the chores already finished.

I wanted to get this morning done early, I wanted to check out the new wolf pack and see if they were integrating or getting along with the other wolves in the woods. Only changing my slacks, I put on a pair of pants I cut the legs off to so I could move easier if I needed to climb. The curtain to the house moved to show signs of others waking up. This morning I finished more than my chores, taking off jogging towards the end of the property and then as soon as I was on the trail. I ran even faster. Careful not to run into a full run or at least as fast as I could in case someone else oddly was up this early and walking on the trail would possibly see me. I was always careful and kept alert for others when I would do something abnormal by other standards.

Once surrounded by the woods. I shot off even faster following the trail up to the top of the hill. Normally if I were to walk this with Hellen, we would make it halfway up the hill and must come back down to make it home by nightfall. The mountains were seen in the distance from the house and always looked a long way away however, with my speed I could make it there almost in no time. There were smaller hills closer however I liked the tall peaks in the far distance. This is when I loved running the most, feeling the wind whip my hair behind me. Feeling so free nothing else gave me this rush feeling.

As I ran a few smaller animals barely had time to move out of the way, running past the edge of the cliff and further past the watering hole the animals would congregate at to drink. I kept running even further into the forest which started to feel like a jungle with the ground getting wet and swampy. Vines and bushes started intertwining between the trees making them even thicker. Then there was a spot where there was nothing but knee-level water that I had to run through that was filled with willows. And even better my favorite trees were growing here in the deepest part of the swamp, the weeping willow. I hadn't seen it anywhere other than here. Riley had made it out here once but never wanted to come out again. However, he wanted to see the great large tree I kept telling them about.

He thought that it might have been from travelers possibly European or Asian and at some point, must have dropped them and they acclimated quite well to the swampy area. There had been at least nine of them that I counted. One was closer to the edge of the swamp on the further side where the water started to recede a bit and get firmer. Climbing up into the tree I could get a good view of the wildlife from up here. Even watching the wolves come in to catch their prey in the swamps since it would slow some creatures down. Most of the animals were used to me being there. The ones that still didn't trust me. I could still see from a far distance.

One thing I noticed this morning had been something very different. I was used to the animals being uncomfortable around me until they were used to me being in the area. I came here a lot to watch them but also to collect some of the seeds from the willows. I tried to grow them near my home but for some reason, they would not grow.

After a while of being a regular here in the woods, they started trusting me that I wasn't going to hurt them. Except for this morning, I only came across a few small animals closer to the house. Once I was closer to the mountain the animals disappeared. Even the birds were nowhere to be seen. Through the swamp I hadn't seen one fish, not that they had far to go but it was so quiet here in the swamp. Normally I could listen to the birds and once they would quiet, I knew the wolves were coming. I didn't even see a single wolf. Was there a larger predator I didn't know about? Was something scaring them off? After waiting for a while longer. I gave up and went running through the swamp again except this time heading to the watering hole.

Heading off slightly in another direction to get there faster. I ran up the side of the mountain dodging trees until I came to the part of the hill that came to a peak and stopped. I could look over the side and see the watering hole from up here without disturbing the animals below. There wasn't a single animal down there. This was strange. Climbing down the side of the rock to get to the water. I looked around to see what might be scaring the animals away. Getting down close nothing looked out of the ordinary. Except for one very minor thing, but I didn't seem to think it should make a difference.

I could see a dark piece of blue sticking out from under a few leaves' half in the water and half out. Getting down now near the watering hole, leaning over and picking it up, it looked like a woman's bonnet. It even had an odd scent. It didn't smell like the clothing Hellen had but then it had the same scent as mine. I had left clothing outside before and it never would get the same scent as mine and I know this wasn't mine. I had never seen another woman back here before. Occasionally when the guys would come back here and get drunk or go hunting but I never actually saw a woman come here other than Hellen when she came with me. Taking the bonnet, I placed it up on the rock in case the owner came back for it, at least this way it would dry and be seen easier.

At least no one was expecting me today. Hellen was shopping with Riley in town for goods for the farm and she wanted to pick up fabric to make new dresses. Heading home this time I took my time now that I wasn't in a rush. Even on the way home, I noticed, that there were still no little animals or birds around. This didn't make me feel too good. It's not normal not to have animals around. It wasn't until I was closer to my house, I could see Tabitha smashed up against the door as close as she could get. Something seemed to have scared her also. When I was within reach, she bolted from the door and leaped into my arms, and snuggled almost under my armpit trying to hide from whatever scared her.

Taking her inside and looking around to make sure there wasn't something inside waiting, I went down to my bedroom to relax. From the way things were going. I planned on heading off for the farm early that way I could see if the animals on the farm were also having problems, they seemed fine when I left. But then maybe whatever it was went through the swamp, then the woods, and went past our homes. I might have missed it since I was going the other way. Laying back on my bed to rest I loved looking at my ceiling. I had painted a picture of every family member that I had a memory of. Even four people who I never knew who they were, had been just as the physical image in my memory as the others had been, so I had added them. Then after a while, I drifted off to sleep for a while.

Getting up early as I always did, I expected to see Tabitha curled up on the chair or the floor waiting to go out. She was still smashed as close to my side as she possibly could get. Whatever scared her did a pretty good job at it. Deciding to walk to the farm. I wanted to observe and see if there were any changes outside. Tabitha refused to leave the safety of my home. As I got up and was leaving, she climbed under the bed covers hiding. The weather seemed fine. It hadn't even rained the night before but still no animals. Walking up to the farm house, I could see Hellen in the window moving around as she was setting the table. She was up a little earlier than normal, so she had gotten a lot of her shopping done early in town as well.

The next day hadn't been any better either. Tabitha the house cat stayed under the covers all night even into the next day refusing to leave still. On my way to the farm, I still hadn't seen any animals, they were still missing. All the animals from the farm were inside the barn. Not one of them was outside. Not even the dogs. One dog looked a little strange with a long black bushy tail coming out from behind him until I saw that it was one of the cats hiding; apparently, it felt it was safer hiding behind the dog. As I rode out on the wagon with an ox that did not want to go out but finally did when I forced it. Not even taking one bale of hay off the wagon I noticed not one animal followed me out, none of the horses, cows, or pigs. All of them were still hidden in the barn. Then I started wondering where the chickens are.

Heading back to the barn. I left the wagon in the main room with all the animals so they could just eat it off the wagon. Leaving grain in the top rafter where the chickens and rooster had finally migrated, I headed for the house. I wanted to find out if Hellen heard anything strange going on while she had been in town. We could have been in for a storm since they will act strange when the weather changes. The only problem had been the weather was nice out. We did have a bad storm a few days ago except they hadn't even acted this scared then. Something must have them spooked.

Once the barn door was closed, I noticed on my way out that a carriage sat out in front of the house. As far as I knew they were not expecting anyone. No one I ever saw before and it hadn't been here when I first started, they must not have been here for too long.

Too busy right now to be concerned with it not that I was in a sociable mood right now. Being careful in case anyone was watching me, I walked past the house figuring I would talk to Hellen once the strange guests were gone. Heading over to the neighboring farm one out of sight of Hellen and Riley's house. I ran full speed. Lacey was about to have her third baby and her husband was short-handed, so I volunteered to help. I headed straight out to the pasture area. Doing this so many times before I had it memorized, there were no surprises. So far, I had already been helping for over a week.

Even the cattle here were used to following behind the flatbed as it rolled past them, and I pushed the bales of hay off the end. As the last bale of hay was dropped, I worked myself back to the front of the ox to get him to head back into the barn. None of the animals on this side seemed to be scared. There were even more birds than normal over here. I noticed one of our barn cats was here and slinked away when he saw me. Whatever it was it must have been on our side. I had already taken care of the chickens and collected all the eggs. Closing the barn doors, I walked out ready to wash off my hands. Once I was done and said goodbye. I walked back over to Hellen's house. As I was getting closer, I could see the carriage was still resting outside of the house.

Long before I was ever near the house, I could still see in the window of the living room this far away, I could see my foster father was shaking hands with the strange man. He might have possibly been in his late forties or early fifties. It was rather difficult to tell since he looked so well kept and very handsome. The only real sign had been that his hair looked like it was graying a little. Standing in front of the window now as I looked at that exact moment, he turned his head making instant eye contact with me before he even looked anywhere else. It was as if our eyes caught each having a conversation with each other we were not aware of before he broke the connection. That's when he turned back to my parents finishing his conversation. I walked into the house trying not to interrupt them since I was hoping to hear what they had been talking about now.

Making sure not to offend or interrupt. I went into the washroom quickly to wash my hands and then stepped out to see him sitting in his carriage again staring in my direction. I was hoping to meet him when I came out except, he seemed to be ready to leave. Strange he shows up when the problem with the animals hits and in all my years here I had never seen him before. Trying not to get too crazy about it, I doubted he would be the reason the animals are disappearing or afraid, after all, why would they be afraid of a human?

"Who was that? I haven't ever seen him before. Is there something wrong?" Looking at my parents, they didn't look worried or concerned so I hoped it wasn't anything serious.

"A family friend of ours knows Andrew and some of his workmates. They are traveling rather far and needed a place to stay. They were fascinated by the mountains and wanted to explore around a little. Apparently where they live there is more flat ground than mountains. They're not in a hurry. They don't have to be at their place by a certain time, they wanted to explore and get to know the area then when they are ready, they will take off." Just as Riley finished his comment Hellen took over immediately.

"They promise not to get in the way too much. They said they followed something out in this direction and were hunting. I hope you don't mind but I let him know that if any wanted a tour or help around town you would be able to help. I trust they will be in capable hands with you, even Riley agreed. Even though we would both like to see you dress like a proper lady while they are here."

"Should be okay, will be interesting meeting new people, haven't had much here for a while. I'm done early with my chores today and helped at Lacey's farm also, looks like she's still pregnant, and should be ready to pop any day now. So, I'm heading home. I don't work the next few nights at the tavern so when should I expect them?" Not giving my mother a response about the dress, I hoped I would not have to get into that again.

"They will be here first thing in the morning. Andrew came up before the others to make sure everything was set. They let us know a few weeks ago but we haven't had time to talk with you. In addition, we know how tired you have been and didn't want to cut into any sleep time you may be able to get. Should be early tomorrow morning, it will depend on when the rest of their group gets here. Not as early as you are used to getting up but I have Hank taking your chores in the morning so you can concentrate on the guests, I want their first visit to be a very good one. I know you're better than anyone to keep them safe. But remember just try and act a little normal. You know how you can get at times and it creeps people out. Don't want them leaving early just because of their developing nightmares from being here. I love you but be on your best behavior."

"Don't worry I'll be as normal as I can." Smiling my usual devilish grin I would give at times when I was being sarcastic. Even still the words that I didn't say I'm sure Hellen would have figured out without being told.

The privacy factor and how odd people get when strange things happen. I didn't have to say much since I knew far too well what could happen if they found out. As far as my foster parents knew about me, I had a sense of when things would happen before they did. But even then, I kept further secrets that I developed as I grew older. Doing this only because I knew the little gift, I had scared them at times even though they tried not to show it. I loved the fact that no matter how much I caught them off guard they tried their best to be supportive and loving.

Always curious but cautious when meeting new people, wondering what they will be like or how many I will have to watch after? Walking as quickly as I could heading toward my home before the night set in. Not that I minded except not knowing what was scaring the animals over here. I wasn't in the mood to run into whatever it was. So, I was happy to be home. There were times I felt drawn to being in the dark. I felt so free and able to do anything I wanted. And at other times it was nice to be out in the sun when others were around.

Mainly because I loved being in the sun at times none of my parents seemed to worry since they assumed from stories they had heard about vampires, at least they thought I wasn't one. So, they treated my gifts as if they were good ones. Even a little amount it was nice to have others around, although most of the time I preferred solitude.

I knew everyone in the area. No one would even be interested in breaking into my home. Everyone thought I didn't own a thing. Some thought I might have been waiting to decorate the place when I was to meet someone and get married. It was not something I was thinking about. I was always most comfortable in my own home. Besides no one ever locked their doors in such a small town, there was never any reason to.

Obscured Darkness

I walked to what would be a master bedroom. Directly in from the front door there was a large staircase that led upstairs to the second floor. None of the floors had been finished just a rough wood floor. Even upstairs the rooms hadn't been roughed in yet. From looking at it, one would assume the house was just built, however, it has stood like this now for three years. The old farmhouse was a great structure. However, inside it was moldy from neglect and the years that water would leak into the house, and unfortunately, a raccoon died in here. It had to be completely gutted out and redone. The outside was rather sound and had been built sturdy. I always loved the fact that half the house was built using stones for the base and sides.

To the right was the large master bedroom. The only way anyone had any idea which room was supposed to be for what. I would use charcoal on the floors to leave initials of what the room would be like with the future on the floor. Friends and family always figured it would be covered up eventually with granite, marble, or a nicer-looking wood. Most of the rooms were filled with paper. Either from stories I had written or paintings. I loved sculpting art projects however most when they saw them, they always had that odd look on their face like they were just humoring me when they said they looked nice. I knew they didn't like them, but it was nice they tried to find at least something about them they liked. It was interesting hearing some of the comments. Some liked them because they were round or bright and cheerful or one said it looked so different almost like three animals collided with each other.

The large bathroom was wide open to the bedroom only thing that stopped one from looking directly into it was the large stone hearth that you had to walk around on either side to get to the large bathroom. The fireplace continued straight upstairs where later I hoped to put up a wall and have the fireplace be seen from either direction. Right now, I could go up there and walk through it. I liked having my bathroom inside rather than outdoors in the old outhouse. It was so much easier to keep clean. I had been told many times that I was crazy, but it worked for me.

Most of the town used outhouses. I was the first to have an indoor bathroom for my private residence even though several castles and other areas did have them. I couldn't help but cringe going into one, I may have been used to them, but they smelled so fowl and I was always worried about what was going to be waiting for me in there, either a large raccoon to a small spider. Odd a spider landed on me, didn't exactly bite me too well. It died rather fast, I guess he had to learn the hard way. Not that anything could harm me, but I still didn't care for the nasty-looking little things.

The plumbing fixtures had white glazed enamel and the toilet with nickel material. The floor was covered with white marble. I planned on using this in all the rooms. It took me a while to get it here. If I could get the wagon to move fast as I did, I would have all the pieces of stone here. I followed Victorian etiquette for designing the bathroom. The slabs of marble I would bring home were too hard to lay flat so I would crush them to tiny pieces, lay them out and then glaze over the top for the shine.

Other than the bathroom and kitchen being finished, the house still looked like it was under construction. Opening the closet door, I walked in and closed it behind me. Anyone seeing me would assume I was lost mentally, especially since there was nothing in my closet not even clothes hanging up. It had been my private entrance to my private rooms.

Chapter Three
Demon Hunters

Morning came quickly as it always does. Dressing in what was my favorite to wear, I put on my blue jean skirt and dark blue t-shirt, and originally it had lace arm sleeves except I had torn them off. I hurried out to the farm as fast as I could only to slow up before I came to close, so no one would see how fast I could run.

I looked through the window as I passed and could see everyone sitting at the kitchen table eating breakfast. Even John was up. Usually, he did not get up till noon. He was a preteen and one of the youngest foster children that had been taken in. Since summer he had been sleeping in every morning. One thing my second pair of foster parents loved were children but could not have their own, so their home was open not just to the neighborhood but to any child with no home.

After opening the door to the house and entering the first to greet me was my foster mother Hellen. No matter how hectic things could get she always kept up with everything and everyone. She seemed very happy having extra people to cook for. Hellen was always trying to feed me something telling me that I was too thin and might wither away or worse be carried away with the wind. Even if I did eat a lot, I never managed to gain weight.

"Come dear eat up, looks like it's going to be a long day today. John will occupy the two teens, but you can show the adults around. Some are busy this morning and a few are waiting around the barn area.

Speaking up Andrew said, "Actually I believe I am the only one available this morning. The others will be busy until later, I'm guessing around noon. You don't have to show me around, I'll stick around the house today if it's okay. I doubt you want to spend your time with an old man." While saying this he smiled looking sincere.

Looking directly at him I wasn't going to let him get off so easy. "I'm sure you don't want to spend time with a young kid, after all, you might not be able to keep up. I wouldn't want you to feel older than you already do. Feel free to borrow the walking stick near the door." Standing there staring at him with a smirk on my face. Even though I didn't believe he was that old. Odd he seems to have an issue with age. Why did he seem to think he was so much older than me? Walking over next to his seat I leaned over just a little to whisper to him.

"Do you need assistance getting out of your chair? We all know how difficult that can be at your age." Leaning back, he smiled, he knew he had been challenged.

"I think I might have underestimated you. Okay, show me something interesting and I'll show you how well this old man can keep up." Standing up and walking over, he opened the door and held it open for me as I started walking out.

Before I could get out of the door Hellen was standing near it and whispered to me, "be nice, I know you, make sure if he says something you don't like or acts rude you don't ditch him in the mountains."

"I do that once and you worry I'm going to do that every time?" Smiling at her I knew she understood more than that.

"It's been four times; just make sure you bring this one back." Slapping me on the butt as Hellen closed the door behind us.

Looking Andrew over he hadn't looked older at all. Other than the way he dressed was the only indication that he was older. If he wore different clothing he could have passed for my brother. It looked like he was wearing his grandfather's clothes.

"Bareback or on two?" Looking at him to answer I was curious if he would walk or ride when we went. At least on horseback we could go further and take the regular trail.

Looking like he was thinking over my question not that it was that difficult. Andrew finally spoke, "I've been riding enough so I think I would prefer walking, I have to work tomorrow so I would like to be able to stand on my own two feet." He smiled as he answered sure I was going to give him a hard time, even though he was smiling more because he realized that I got the point.

'Don't worry old man I'll be careful with you; I'll even walk slower just for you." Letting a light laugh I kept walking but now deliberately slower.

Walking for a while, the ranch finally began to fall from view as the mountain in the distance became larger.

"Are we walking to the mountain?" Looked at Evangeline curiously just how far they were going to walk. He may not have been out of shape, but he wasn't interested in just walking around. Maybe she was taking it easy on him and not doing much to keep it simple? If she only knew the truth, he thought shaking his head.

"Why are you worried? A little too much for you?" Smiling, giving him a hard time again.

"I could walk all day little lady."

"Good to know but no, we would have to cross into the woods, I don't mind going in there, but I won't take others, too many things to avoid. And right now, the animals seem to be acting strange, not sure if there is something, they're not used to but better to avoid it until I'm sure it's safe." Keeping my voice monotone and not to add any feeling to my explanation, I looked at him and asked,

"Curious how you know my parents?" Looking at him for a moment but continuing to walk and talking to him as we came closer to the stream, "this is one of the places I like to visit and share with others. Our family would spend time away from the farm here. There was a gazebo near the stream with the fire pit we used quite often."

Thinking for a moment Andrew didn't want to share the real reason he was here. Even though he was good at making things up at a moment's notice he hoped Evangeline would believe his story, even though this time he thought this might interest her a little. Just to see what she thought of it.

"I happen to be a scientist of sorts. I like to explore myths and stories and see if there are any truths to them at all. We happen to be following tracks that were believed to belong to a certain creature and hoped to catch it to see if it was real. My friend Tony Barnes used to live near town, and he said he knew the Weilers, he was sure I could stay here so I sent a note for permission and here I am."

Obscured Darkness

"Have you found any interesting creatures?" Looking at him now with interest, curious what they might have been after.

"There are more things out there than people realize, most have been around for so long they either blend in or are hidden quite well. The group I have been with has been at this for generations. I have only been with them for a short time. It's fascinating to see how they work."

Taking a moment to take in the look on Evangeline's face to see if he was boring her before asking her.

"If these creatures blend in so well, why not leave them alone, especially if they are not harming anyone." I wanted to find out his mindset.

"You do have a point however if we did not find them and left them alone, we might never learn anything about them," he hoped this would satisfy her questions, "I don't have a guide yet but I will need one so we don't get lost in the woods. If you're not busy that would help. I know you said you don't take others in there, but it would help us, we plan on going in the woods anyway and if anything happens, we are armed. Your parents seem to be under the impression that you know the woods rather well. Anything I need before we go? If you're interested do you think we could get a start on it tomorrow morning? That is if you don't have other plans?"

"If you wanted to get a faster start on it, we could go tonight. Your right I don't like to take others in the woods, mainly because of the wild boar and a lot of other critters. I just don't like to risk the chance of others getting hurt, especially when I climb a hill or follow a footpath that others are not used to. Nighttime is the best time to go up there by the water hole, where most of the animals from the woods around here go to get a drink. If it's a creature then that's the best place to look for it. I'll get what we need for safety and getting there, but you bring what you need to do your job just make sure to pack light if you can it's quite a way up. Not sure what animal you are looking for, but all animals eventually end up there."

"Sounds like a good plan. We can head back and I'll round everyone up. We can be ready in a few hours, so tonight should work."

"Great, then meet me in front of the main house and we will go from there, depending on how many come we can borrow the horses, we can ride up to the mountain at least and leave them down below once we reach it. That should cut some time off the walking till we hit the tip of the woods."

Both Andrew and I started the walk back, both talking about the wild boars and comparing interests. I shared what had been happening with the hunters trying to cut down on the population and the attacks the town had endured. Not that I shared what had happened to stop them which personally when I think about it, I managed to gross myself out. I never thought it would be something I would be capable of.

Scaring the boar away with gunshots or even making other loud noises didn't help. The kids were not safe in town if the boar decided to come running through. For a while the population exploded so bad that even the hunters didn't cut their herd back enough. Hellen was afraid of my going out into the woods in case I were to get caught by a large group. It had been rare to only spot two or three. The groups had been killing livestock and destroying several of the local farms. One morning when I woke up, I found all our chickens slain along with our pigs and most of our cows badly injured or half dead. The population had gotten so bad that they were getting violent with everything. The right side of the barn was destroyed along with the fencing. Something had to be done.

I was walking in the woods when a single one decided to

attack me. Even though my knife had come in handy it wasn't enough against this thing, then there was such an insane urge that came out of me that I had no idea that I possessed until then. Almost on instinct I swung myself upon its back and sunk my teeth into it draining it of its blood. It went so fast and I hated to admit I liked the taste of it. Oddly enough I hadn't felt hungry for weeks after that. I didn't even have a scratch on me. Later I tried it with three more and was just as successful, and then I went for the large herd. I waited until most were at the watering hole when I pounced on them. This time I did get slightly injured. I could only handle so many and move so fast, there was a large group of them. When I came back, I tried to clean off the blood from myself and clean all the scratches. Hellen freaked out when she first saw me.

"What happened to you? I knew you weren't safe in those woods, is it the boar? I don't want you going out there alone, I know your old enough I just want you to be safe, I won't be able to handle it if I know you're going out there alone." This had been the first time I decided to lie to Hellen which I was surprised she didn't pick up on or either she didn't want to know the truth. After the problem had been taken care of even years later, I never told her what stopped the boar.

"Don't worry it's not the boars, there was a new hole formed out by the swamps and I fell down the side of the mountain because I was busier watching something else than what I was doing. Besides this time when I went out, I didn't see one boar. I'm thinking oddly enough they've moved on."

Ever since then I decided to start holding back and not filling her in on every detail when normally I would have told her everything. It felt odd keeping it from her but then I also felt freaked out that I liked the taste of animal blood. It was almost as if the animals on the farm knew what happened. It had taken a long time before they would trust being around me again. Even I didn't feel safe with myself. I had to be extra careful not to do that again. I was always worried if I would ever lose control and do it without realizing it. It felt like such a head rush almost as if I weren't thinking even though I knew what I went to do and had picked my target, just during the actual craze I lost all train of thought other than to move from one to the other. Since I hadn't told her there was no way I was going to tell another person.

If Hellen were nervous about some of my gifts, I know what she would assume from this and be terrified. She feared that I would be a vampire and I wanted to do everything I could to keep the fact that my life kept pointing in that direction from her.

Leaving Andrew at the house I stocked up on ropes, water, and snacks. Packing a rather large backpack to carry supplies to make sure there had been enough for everyone. Just in case I packed some of my weapons. Even if he said they were already set I wanted to be covered also, putting my favorite hunting knife in its holder just under my sleeve. With the wind being a bit chilly tonight, it would be a good excuse for wearing a long sleeve shirt which I changed into once I was back at home. I didn't want the others to be nervous about how I was being armed however taking chances was not an option either.

Nothing should go wrong however it was always a good idea to be prepared just in case. I had a total of nine different knives stashed on me, mainly throwing knives. Not that I needed those, but I liked using them. Besides I should be seen using those than doing anything else someone would get too curious.

This would have been better during the daylight now they have to watch out for the other animals in the woods. It would help me if I knew more specifically what animal they were searching for.

A few years ago, when I had been walking through the woods I came across a rather strange person. It looked like a young boy covered in dirt and grime. He had been lying on the ground with no heartbeat. At first, I thought he had been lost, gotten injured, and died. There were no indications of an animal attack or blood anywhere.

He laid there perfectly still. As I stood over him watching him for a moment, his eyes opened and he sat straight up. I jumped back a little when I reacted; when I spoke to him, he knew exactly where he was going. All he told me had been "You should have been scared when you thought I was dead and ran away; they know when you're dead and when you're not. The only way to live is to keep ahead of them. Watch your back. Someday they will figure it out and be after you." Half understanding him and still being shocked since I had never seen this before. Before I could say another word, he shot out of sight, something I had never seen anyone else do other than me. Only confiding in Hellen about it I had said I must have been dreaming. Or did not understand what I had seen, however, I never spoke of it again after that.

The walk hadn't taken up very much time, I was bored waiting. I decided to head off for the tavern. I liked working there and I wished I had taken an earlier shift instead of taking a few days off. Not many people were in the bar at this time of day, which usually filled up much later in the evening. The tavern used to be an old house turned into a bar. The couple rented out rooms upstairs, live music always playing even though the tempo picked up much later in the night which is why I loved working then. Occasionally I would get into it and dance on the stage with the guys.

Sitting down on the stool at the bar I noticed a group of men in the far corner with their backs turned towards me. I couldn't see who they were, but their voices were rather deep-sounding. I heard Andrew's voice so he must have joined them and was hidden in their huddle somewhere.

Grabbing a mug from behind the counter, the owner rarely cared if I came in and helped myself if I poured a few drinks while I was at it. Serving the other two at the counter while I was there, I sat down and drank my beer. Not something you saw a lady do too often especially alone but then people were used to my quirks. But then things were much more relaxed here, we got away with a lot more in a small town than if we had been in a larger town with the proper social circles. As I sat there, I tried to listen to their conversation. As soon as I did, they were no longer talking in a language that I understood. It was almost as if they knew they were being listened to. Whatever they were talking about they didn't stick around for too long after, Andrew was the last one to speak.

The others stood up walking out leaving Andrew sitting there to finish eating. I wondered if he was keeping an eye on me now. I could remember what the men were saying except I had no clue what they were talking about. Getting up I paid for my tab and Andrews since he was the only one left. Picking up a bowl of prunes I walked over to his table placing them in front of him I said.

"These might help you later old man." Setting them down he smiled at me as I turned and walked away. I wanted to find out what they were talking about and I only knew one person who was fascinated by language, he lived one town over so if I was going to get there and make it back in time I had to get moving. Andrew's group was waiting outside of the bar. Not wanting to tip them off. I walked slowly heading in the direction of my home. Once I was out of their sight, I kept walking toward the woods. It was going to be much faster cutting across, up and over the mountain, and straight across the field until I reached the other town. At least Thomas lived on this side of the other town so I wouldn't have to walk through his town also.

Once I had the chance to take off, I looked around to make sure no one wandered out this far. As soon as it was clear I took off in a shot barely touching the ground running fast to get there as quick as I could.

Outside of my family, Thomas had been the only other person who knew and confirmed what I could do. He was standing outside of his house when he saw this blur coming toward him. Standing still he waited since he hadn't seen me in a while, he must have wondered what brought me back. He used to live in our town until he was offered a job over here. The town he lived in now was much larger than ours.

"So, what brings you to my side of the slope?" Smiling I knew he was happy to see me. Even though I know he still felt creeped out that I looked the same while he continued to age even though it was rather gradual.

"Your expertise is why I'm here, I need to know something, but I don't understand the language and I was hoping you might be able to translate it." As I was talking to him, he sat down on his chair on the porch, setting his cob pipe down. Thomas loved to travel and experienced learning languages the best way a person could. He had learned it firsthand.

"I can't promise anything, but I can try to help." By now Thomas had been used to my unusual help requests that they rarely surprised him anymore.

Sitting in the chair near him. I recalled exactly what I heard the men saying. At least I know if there was anything creepy about what they were talking about he would still tell me if he understood what they said. I hadn't decided how I would explain why I wanted to know. So far at least he wasn't asking. Waiting for a second to make sure he was ready I spoke slowly and tried to pronounce it exactly the way I heard it. At least I was thankful for that gift. I may not be able to copy their voices, but I could remember things I heard exactly. I was always blessed with a great memory. Even though there were times things had been said years ago that Thomas said to me when we were younger, he wished I would forget. Even if I told him I had I knew he didn't believe me, but he was happy to know I wasn't holding it against him.

"Here's what they said, "parlare in italiano mi pare che qualcuno sia in ascolto. Che cosa faociamo con la ragazza, se troviamo la creatura? Qualcuno puo rimanere a proteggere l'essere umano, il resto ottenere la creatura abbastanza lontano e distruggerla. Una volta fatto il suo ci spostiamo. Staro con lei.' And that was it." Smiling at him hoping he would be able to explain it Thomas had a strange look on his face almost a look of panic.

"Who said that, and do they know about your gifts?" Leaning forward he looked panicked almost white as a ghost himself.

"Hellen and Riley have guests visiting. They are traveling through and are staying for a few days then they plan on leaving soon to go wherever they're heading. They don't know about my gifts at all, they don't even know that Hellen and Riley are not my real birth parents. Why? What did they say, you look like you've died yourself?"

"Be careful around these people they may be hereafter you or if they don't exactly know what they are looking for if they find out it could end up being you. I'm assuming they were speaking Italian and I am a little rusty, but this is what I get out of it. And I quote 'speak in Italian I think someone is listening. What do we do with the girl if we find the creature? Someone can stay to protect the human; the rest get the creature far enough and destroy it. Once it's done, we move on. I'll stay with her.'

"The last person to speak was Andrew, he must have said he would stay with me. They wanted a guided tour through the forest. I wonder what creature they want to hunt down and kill since they never said anything about it to me?"

"Probably the same reason you don't tell them you have a gift. Has there been anything unusual lately? Something to support their reason for being here. Have they said what their profession is? Hopefully, they are not demon hunters; we had a few pass through here a couple of days ago."

"Andrew said he was a scientist of sorts. If they are demon hunters, I'll have to be extra careful. Thank you for translating it for me, I have to hurry and get back or I would visit longer. I 'don't want them to get suspicious and find out I came way out here." Getting up Thomas was just as fast to get up.

"Look Evangeline, they may not have caught me and who knows maybe I am who they are looking for, but I have a feeling it's not a creature with fur they are after. If it means keeping you safe you can stay here with me" I know he meant well, and I understood his fear of what people would do if they knew. Especially in his town now it wasn't safe.

Even though he wasn't totally like me. He found out when he sneezed and fell through the wood floor without making a hole in it, he wound up in the stone basement of his parent's home. He was quick and could walk through objects. Not all objects but for the most part, some of it wasn't stone. He knew his mother was a shade and passed it down to him. He managed to teach me a few things he did, except we hadn't known if I was the same or a rather similar creature.

"I think they would realize something was up if I weren't there. Besides, I can keep an eye on them and find out what they are after. If I stay here, I put you and myself in danger. If it turns out they are after either one of us I will come and get you, we can find a place to hide. I promise I will be careful, but I would scare Hellen if I didn't come home." Hugging Thomas, I knew he didn't want to let me go. He watched me run at top speed, and even far enough away I could still hear him say, "be careful and walk as soon as you're close enough."

On one of my trips years ago, I first met Thomas when I was running through the woods. Instead of colliding with him while I was watching the wolves, I ran right through him. So far, he had been the only other person I knew that was different like I had been.

Time had not passed fast enough. Even getting to the house to meet up with the group. I hoped they would be too tired and want to wait till morning. Sadly, this wasn't the case. They were all standing by the front door all eager and ready to go.

Keeping up in stride they walked for a while in silence. I thought maybe the beauty ahead might have silenced them as it always does me. No matter how often I would see it, this had always been my favorite view, the full moon out casting a pleasant glow over the tops of the trees. Walking through the woods. I did happen to notice that even the birds were absent today again. I would usually hear them in the distance except they were scarce now. I decided I wasn't going to offer any extra assistance finding this creature they were being so secretive about especially since it could be like me, and I certainly wasn't going to help them kill it. The words of that young boy kept coming back to me almost haunting me. I always wondered what happened to him.

Obscured Darkness

Everyone followed me as I led them up the mountain. We followed the path to the watering hole. As they came close to the lip, they could see the animals that had already come here to drink. I noticed none of the three men had any form of rifle or hand weapon with them. I was curious what kind of hunting they meant. They seemed rather disappointed when they were not seeing what they hoped for, sitting there for several hours being silent. As the night went on, the chillier it had become. I even noticed the others starting to shiver. Occasionally they would speak to each other in a whisper in Italian not that I understood what they were saying but I almost thought they wanted to head back, they were stubborn hoping whatever they were searching for would show up.

There were several different breeds of animals that had come and gone for the past several hours. However, none of them seemed to be the ones they were looking for and they did not seem too eager to part with the information as to what exactly they were looking for. At times I even wondered if they knew.

"Let me know when you are ready to head back. We have a long walk ahead of us. I don't think we will be seeing too many more animals now. Most are sleeping during the day, or you get the basic little critters."

Standing up I started to put my things back into the bag I brought along with me. Never once did I need one of my knives but then I was glad I was ready just in case. Even the guys I brought up here gave me the creeps enough that I was thankful to have brought a full arsenal with me.

Taking the suggestion to head back from Evangeline the others started to pack it in also. Lining up they worked their way down the path. Halfway down the side of the mountain, I noticed there was quick movement along the side of the cave wall to their side. I wasn't sure what it was but wasn't sure if I trusted the men that were with me to go check out what it was quickly. Since they did not seem to want to share the description of the creature, they hunted let alone what they planned on doing with it once they found it, except for what I knew from having their conversation translated. Like me, it could be unique and need to be protected as my foster parents had protected me. Since they hadn't noticed it, I figured there was no reason to point it out to them.

I mentally took a note of where I saw the movement planning on coming back later when I knew they would be busy, that way they would not follow me or get in my way. I would still have to be careful since someone could still see me on the side of the cave wall noticing something extremely unusual about me as I climbed it. The simple fact that I could stay on the sidewall with it as flat as it was. There were no holds, but I could get up the side with no assistance or problems. There were a few large open caves on that side that were shelters for many different animals. But this time the scent I had was unlike anything I ever encountered. It smelled a lot like the bonnet that I found which I also noticed when we were at the watering hole that it was gone. I decided I would keep close-lipped about what I was looking for. Curiosity had caught my attention and I wanted to find out where that scent was coming from.

Once down the mountain after several hours closer to the farmhouse, the men started talking about when they would try going into the woods again opting for a different time. That's when Andrew came over to speak with Evangeline. Andrew waited for the others to be out of sight getting drinks in the house.

"How often do you go into the woods? And do you ever see anything interesting? I was rather hoping we would have seen something last night since it was dark and what we are looking for travels by night."

"What might seem perfectly normal might be interesting to someone else who doesn't normally see it. I don't pay attention to how often I go into the woods other than I have been here a long time, in that time I've gotten to know them. And why do you think what your hunting is in our woods?" Looking at him accusingly.

"At first we were way off track but then were alerted that it would be headed this way so we tried to get ahead of it the best we could. We know it will come through here or already has but we need to find a trail of some kind. We feel it might have decided to stay put and we wanted to find out if it was still here or not."

"Why is it such a secret? Why won't you tell me? I can't help you find what I don't know what I'm looking for?"

"This is very serious so don't laugh. You may not even like what I tell you," not sure if he should say anything Andrew hesitated for a moment before speaking, "is there a quiet place we can talk where no one will bother us? The other guys don't like me sharing any information like this." Taking a deep breath, he waited for me to reply.

"I know of an empty house we can talk at; I'll grab two horses and we can ride out there, it will be faster. The house isn't that far from here." Bringing two of the horses over we hopped up into the saddle.

Not that I needed it but Andrew felt like helping me. Taking off in a fast stride on the horses Andrew followed me. At least this way I didn't have to worry about how fast I was going since it was all the horse's speed. I had decided to take him to my house. Not that I was going to show him my private room. Tying the horses up to the tree in front we sat down on the porch.

"Is this far enough for you?" Settling in and getting ready for what he might tell me.

I was curious why he was telling me if his friends didn't like him telling others?

"Trust me nothing could ever be far enough. What I'm about to tell you might be upsetting but there is a reason. I don't personally do it for the same reason the others do. It wasn't exactly my choice to get tangled up with them. We help towns eliminate abnormalities, creatures that are dangerous to people. I have helped take care of the harmful ones, but I must admit. I don't agree with the others about killing what is not harmful to others just because it has the same abilities as something that does kill. After all, if I did agree with the group then we should kill all humans, after all, some are capable and do kill so why not judge all the same way? I'm merely here to try and prevent what I can if it's not dangerous. And that part, I shouldn't have told you. They don't even know I have sabotaged a few attacks."

"Maybe you're telling me because you feel guilty and for some reason, you feel you owe me an explanation? Or a long stretch. You possibly don't feel any threat from me and you possibly trust me?"

"No, I don't feel guilty and I agree for not knowing you I already trust you; your personality makes it easy. We are searching for a creature that resembles a vampire and it was last spotted near here. When our mutual friend told us, that we had to visit here and that there was something extraordinary that we could not pass up we had to come. We almost were wondering if he meant there were more vampires here. Maybe this one came here for another reason? In our travels, we have come across all kinds but have not been able to catch one yet. We have caught many other creatures however the vampire seems to elude us. This one seems slower than normal almost like it's being held back by something, it's why we are hoping this one we might be able to catch and possibly learn from it so that we will be able to catch others like it easier."

The way he said they might be able to catch made me cringe. I still tried to hide what I felt. Even now I felt in danger being this close to him now and I could tell what Thomas would be thinking right now. If he knew he would be calling me an idiot. What would he think of me if he knew my gifts? I was never classified however I could be considered a creature myself since I matched much of their descriptions.

"I'm pretty sure I haven't seen one of those around here or at least I would hope I would notice the difference. I don't know anything about vampires." Looking at him curiously now waiting to see what else he would say.

"There are so many legends and myths about them. It's hard to tell what is real and what isn't. Most terrorize and kill humans for food. They drink their blood to survive. Some even look like you and me. So far there seem to be different types of levels. We haven't dealt with them long enough to know the differences too much. The ones who look closer to us, are known as hybrids or half breeds. It's not always easy to pick them out from a group other than how they smell, act or catch them in the act. It wasn't until recently that we found they don't all drink blood. Some survive off animals and some who do not touch the blood of any kind." Now Andrew was fidgeting with his hands, as he seemed nervous.

Instead of looking out in front, he looked directly at me as he said this. Which made me wonder if he had any ideas about me at all and possibly knew my secrets?

"Personally, growing up my best friend seemed perfectly normal, he was able to do things that I never could. He climbed, ran, and threw things faster. He never ate anything at our house.

When I would spend the night, we had munchies and I seemed to be the only one eating. He always had a hard time sleeping. So, I never saw him sleep. Later we found out that was a normal trait for them as well. Then we noticed he never got older. He always looked the same age. The whole family never aged. Then someone caught his older brother feeding off an animal in the woods. The town condemned them to death. How could we allow them to kill humans so they could live forever?"

"How could you kill your friend; he couldn't have been that bad if he never harmed you? Their feeding off animals is no different than average humans who go out hunting with a rifle to kill animals? It sounds like they treated you like family." I stared at him in shocked disbelief.

It had sounded like he was telling me of a small rodent he killed; there was not the slightest hint of emotion in his voice at all.

"Things were different then. He was a monster; he could kill so many people so taking his life to save others was worth it, at least at the time I thought so. I didn't have a choice he had to be stopped before he did do something. He was a demon. These creatures are here for one thing and that's to kill, when a person dies, they should die and that should be the end of it. Any creature with mystical properties is a demon and needs to be stopped."

"I hope you don't believe what you're saying. The fact that I am carrying so many knives on me does make me a threat. I brought so many weapons to protect myself from you and your group. If I don't have mystical powers, I could still kill does that mean that I need to be stopped? I could be specially gifted with weapons does that change my status?" Watching Andrews's expression to see how he would respond to my asked question.

"That's different you carry those to protect you. You're a

very sweet human and nothing more than that. There is no potential danger. Besides, you were with us earlier why did you bring so many knives with you? Did we make you feel we were going to harm you? I'm sorry if we worried you or made you feel you were not safe." He didn't like answering my questions.

"I'm not afraid of the animals it's man's paranoia and peoples' stupidity. Besides, I took five men out into the woods to hunt something they wouldn't tell me they were hunting, so I was more protecting myself from them than I was the thing they hunted. I have another question; how do you know that not all vampires feed off humans? How do they become vampires to start with?"

Taking a deep breath before Andrew answered. "At first, I found vampires fascinating until I found out some of them fed off humans, and then one made a mistake and killed a friend of mine, I wanted to kill them all. If you are bit by one, they can either kill you or make you into a vampire. Somehow some can breed but we don't know how they manage to do it. Their bodies are dead. They come in all shapes, sizes, and ethnic backgrounds. We don't know how they started other than from rumors and legends."

"Have you killed any?" The thought of anything being killed or even myself worried me, if he knew how different I was, made me feel ill.

"We have tried stakes but after being stabbed they keep moving, it's only temporary until we can behead or burn them. We shoot them with silver bullets which are usually reserved for werewolves, however, there is a further belief behind this. When Judas betrayed Jesus, he was rewarded thirty silver pieces. His betrayal became a curse to the undead or unholy similar to crosses or holy water. They burn when splashed with holy water however when shot with a bullet, a regular vampire would die.

Not a half-breed, they do not bleed or leak anything but are just as strong as ever. Only half breeds bleed but we can kill their human side, but not the vampire or creature side of them. We have sprinkled or even doused them with holy water and it's like bathing them. We have done burnings and we watch their flesh strip away from the bones, but they never turn to ash, or at least not until some are forced into the natural light, we have been finding them adapting. We have tried so many other ways to kill them. The one we killed when I was with the group, we ripped out its non-beating heart and stabbed it through with something as simple as a deer's antler that had been lying on the ground. We did everything we could think of, burned the organs, and separated so much of the body that it was almost unrecognizable. Then before we understood what step we took that worked, all the parts of the creature poofed into dust and blew away. The monster died immediately." Andrew was rubbing his hands as he spoke.

Not looking for anything I couldn't help but notice the long black stretch marks on the palms of his hands. Even though the fact they were dark black, made me even more curious about them.

"What happened to your hands?" I was hoping not to be too personal except I had never seen those markings before.

"I wish I could say they were a tattoo of some sort. It was more from an accident that I had. They didn't get infected except the skin had died and turned black. At times, my hands get sore when it's cold out." He stopped rubbing them and faced them palm down on his knees.

"Strange kind of accident since they almost look like veins going from your wrist to your fingertips." All I could think that might have died were his veins from the way it looked but then would he have feeling from them if that happened?

"You're a bit too nosey, now any other questions? Hopefully, ones I can give less gruesome answers to?" Smiling at me I wasn't sure if he meant for me to ask more questions or for me to stop, at least to stop with the questions about his hands.

"Is it possible to be a vampire and not know it?" Now curious about the thoughts running through my mind.

I was seriously beginning to wonder if I might be one. It would explain a lot, but I did not crave blood so how could I be? But then I never tasted human blood as far as I knew. As far as the animal blood I only craved it while I was doing it.

"Now you're making jokes, I need to get some sleep and from your questions, I would say you are in severe need of it also. I'll put my horse away when I get back. I'll see you later or tomorrow? I have somewhere I'm going to stop at first. Goodnight." Leaning down he kissed me on the forehead and stopped for a second, almost as if he regretted kissing me goodnight.

"What perfume are you wearing?" He was curious about my scent.

"I don't know. A friend made it for me, it's in a clear bottle and meant for bathing rather than misting on." Acting relaxed, I hoped he had bought my story since I wasn't wearing anything.

"If I hadn't known both of your parents were human, I would assume you were exactly what I was looking for. Tell your friend they need to change the scent. They could get someone seriously hurt wearing that scent. Smiling he turned and walked away heading toward the horse. I kept sitting on the porch watching Andrew ride away until he was out of sight. I felt more stuck in place when I realized how close I had been to almost being caught. To keep the cover that the house had been empty. I rode not too far behind him leaving the horse in the barn. I had stayed in my room for a while, then when it seemed safe, I slipped back out into the barn.

Staying out of sight in case any of the group decided not to sleep or had seen me earlier, I was trying to put together a plan of my own when I heard Hellen coming into the barn. Peering over the edge of the loft. I had been wondering about a few things.

"Hellen, I need to ask you a question if you have time." I wasn't sure if she would have an answer however I could still ask. Climbing down from the loft I knew it would be easier to speak face to face rather than have her straining upward to speak with me.

"I always have time for you sweetie, you know you can ask me anything. I'm an open book." Curious about what I might be asking she sat down on a single bale of hay that was laying on its side in the barn waiting for me to start asking questions.

"Do you know anything about vampires? Has the town here ever had any?"

"Wow, that's not a question I expected. As far as I know, we have never dealt with anything like that. But all those are just myths, vampires don't exist. I think it's an excuse when someone doesn't want to believe the worst in someone, so they try and make them out to be a monster. I think it's a way for a person to believe why a good person would do something so bad when they don't take responsibility for themselves. Why would you be thinking of something like that?"

"I know you will tell me the truth. I'm not supposed to know this, but I talked with one of the men that came here. The men that are here said they are hunting a vampire that supposedly came this way. They think it is hiding in the woods. Their friend led them to believe there was something else here, he thought they would find interesting. I kind of got the feeling he meant me. And whatever creature they are looking for I think it is in the woods. I know I saw and smelled something different than normal and I don't know what it is. I think it's why the animals are acting so strange. But I didn't want to tell them until they told me what they were going to do. But Hellen, the thing that worries me is that I match their description of a vampire. I match the same scent as whatever it is in the woods. Andrew came close to classifying me tonight when he noticed my scent as being different. He would accuse me if he knew you were not my biological parent. He thinks the perfume-scented bath mix I have is in poor taste by someone that doesn't know what they're doing. Other than the bloodthirst. Am I? I know I'm not normal. I can go underwater and not need to breathe. I barely sleep, my skin is as cold as a corpse and my heartbeat is rapidly faster than any other human that it almost sounds like it's not beating. As far as I know, I don't crave blood."

Now panicky feeling knowing there were hunters here. I could end up on the list, is that what Andrew meant that there was something he could not miss here? Was I the main reason he was sent here to figure out and maybe kill?

"We know you're different and we have tried to hide it. We don't know anyone else like you. We know your parents were not like you or they would not have drowned. We even thought of the possibility that they were not even your parents. Especially from pictures left behind in the house. There is one couple that you have a picture of that looks the closest to you. Or at least the young man does. Besides, I know for a fact you bleed when you get injured, you were an expert at that when you were little, which brought me close to a heart attack on many occasions. But I don't think vampires bleed, there has never been a mean bone in your body. Your father and I have always thought of you as our angel and nothing sinister. The only thing truly different about you is how slow you age. It could be a birth defect. Same as my parents they cherished you so much they did everything in their power to protect you. I don't think I like the idea of you hanging around them if they're crazies like that."

"I'm okay, they won't bother me besides the one is nice, and he's fun to joke around with. He seems more like he's still learning about it, kind of looking for an adventure. But I'll still be careful around them. I'm very careful about how I act around them or anyone for that matter. I'll make sure I'm even more careful around them now, I don't think I'll be taking them up on the trail, if they want to explore, they are going to have to do it on their own. I'll use the excuse I have to work or something, I can always take a few shifts."

"If you need anything else, I'll be in the house for the rest of the day, I have a lot to catch up on. Especially the cooking, they seem to be rather hungry men. Bye, sweetie. And remember just be safe." Standing up she stood near me, gave me a quick kiss on the cheek, and left for the house.

Chapter Four
Gone in Search

Walking past the house I could see no one in the kitchen assuming everyone was still sleeping. Never putting my knives away, I felt somewhat safe checking it out myself. Making sure no one was watching me take off. I hurried up the pathway we had taken earlier except this time I took a slight detour so I would end up on the end of the mountain cliff to the side. From there the view of the caves on the mountainside should be visible enough from the ground.

Off the trail, the shrubbery and vines became so dense, that unless you knew your way around it would be easy to get lost. Not sure where the instinct came from except, I found I never wound up lost in the forest no matter how hard I tried. Not much activity during this time of day. Most creatures preferred the darkness to be active. Besides, it was also much cooler at night.

At the foot of the hill, I looked for a foothold to start. It didn't take me long to start scaling the high wall. Most of the sidewall had been completely flat except for the occasional tiny piece of stone sticking out which had been just enough to use. Halfway I checked the first cave. Nothing was in it except a frog that was hiding under the leaves in the far corner. Then moving onto the second cave in the wall. I stopped before getting there. There was that scent again. I could smell it even stronger now along the sidewall heading in. Listening I could barely hear anything except the faintest breath and two heartbeats that beat as rapidly as my own. Moving up to peek in. I could see movement in the furthest back dark corner of the cave and then it stopped.

Now standing in the mouth of the cave I tried to keep my voice as soft as I could. Hellen used to tell me I had the voice of an angel. The last thing I wanted to do is make whatever it is feel threatened or backed into a corner. Not entering the cave, I sat on the edge in case I needed to make a run for it.

"I mean no harm. Please do not be frightened. If you can understand me, please let me know. My name is Evangeline. Rest assured you are safe with me." Not sure what language it might speak, I hoped it spoke English otherwise I was going to have to bring Thomas here to translate.

I was sure when he saw me, he would be thinking something other than the need for translating. Not moving one inch still trying to hear what I could, trying to detect what was in the far corner hovering. Then a pleasant-sounding voice very similar to mine answered.

"I am not fearful of you it's the others that I am. The ones I saw you with earlier. They wish us harm. They have already separated me from the rest of my family but hopefully, I will find them soon."

The sound was like nothing else I ever heard before, it was almost as if I was speaking with myself. As if the echo of my voice answered back. Now stepping out of the shadow Nichole showed herself in the brief light cast in the cave. This was not what I expected at all. Holding my breath for a brief second, I could not believe what my eyes were looking at. I felt they were deceiving me. The first thing I started to think had been some gas must be getting released from in the cave and I was hallucinating, if anyone were to see me, they would wonder why I was speaking with myself? She was breathtaking. Of all the people I knew, no one looked like her.

"The guys I brought up here earlier, I don't know them other than they know a family friend, and my parents wanted me to give them a tour up here so they wouldn't get lost. They didn't tell me directly at the time, but I found out the creature they said they were looking for is a vampire. Are you a vampire? Are you what people are so terrified of? You're so stunning. You don't look like what I would have pictured a vampire to look like. It's hard to believe you could do anything as they accuse you of."

"Looks can be deceiving but yes I am what those men hunt. I come from a line of vampires so I can only assume I am also. I have only gone this far because I have not been able to get back to the direction I need to be going. My family will worry soon. But I cannot risk traveling during the light or I would be seen even more easily."

"How would they know? Do you turn a shade of blue or pink or something?" If this woman would know how to tell what a vampire is then maybe I could get my question answered if I was one myself or not.

She had such a sweet-sounding laugh it even made the baby she was holding look up at her with his full attention.

"Nothing like that, I look like you, humans that are alive have a very distinct look to their skin and scent. My scent gives me away the most. The paler you are, it's easier to stand out however the more pigment you have, it becomes more difficult to tell simply by looking. Not meaning to be morbid, however, when a person dies, their blood pattern is different. There are tinges of purple, grey, or other pale tones which are most often noticed on the feet, knees, hands, and lips. Another change with vampires is if you were to put a piece of marble in the sun you would see how smooth it is with a hint of color hue in it, most don't have lines or wrinkles. That's not to say some don't have wrinkles, a lot of it depends on when the change took over or how it affects you. I wish I had wrinkles, it would show I was finally maturing, to show I lived. My skin has hardened but if I had been changed later with natural lines in my skin then they would have stayed there.

I could not take my eyes off her. If I had not known, I would have guessed she could have been my sister.

"How many vampires are out there? Why have I never known or come across any before you?" I didn't want to bring up Thomas since he was trying to blend in but then he had told me he wasn't a vampire and that he was a shade. He never liked being compared to a vampire mainly because of the legends and stories that surround them. I hadn't wanted to make an opinion until I had met one and found out the truth.

"I am only learning that myself. I grew up being a half-breed which is why I blended in for so long then others found out and that's mainly why I had to flee with my family. There are so many rumors and legends about vampires. If we could only get an actual chance to show we are perfectly normal, very much like everyone else just with a few gifts. I doubt people would be so afraid, except we don't normally get that chance. Like at my wedding so many found out the wrong way and I regret that but many times there's nothing you can do about it. And I must admit just like any human some vampires are not good either. I trusted a human and found out how wrong I was. I only recently found my father who has been teaching me who I am now. We had to split so my husband has my daughter and I traveled alone with my son. I don't know about vampire life other than what I have been exposed to so far. My husband and children are half-breeds like myself. My father however is a full vampire. As far as I know, each vampire is different, some vampires can be quite sadistic and cruel, so people have the right to be afraid. However, my family is not a threat. How did you know I was here? I'm surprised you're not afraid of me."

"Earlier today when I was with the men looking for you, I noticed your scent and movement, except that when they would not tell me why they hunted you at the time. I kept it from them. To be honest I am afraid of them and not you. I have gifts that I conceal. My foster mother told me that I must have come from an angel, but I wish I knew my past. Now the hunters have come discussing special creatures. I am even more curious because the way they describe you is the same traits that I have."

"What do you know of your family? Have your foster parents told you very much or know about your beginning or gifts?" Nichole looked at her with interest wondering if this would be the same, Evangeline. Would they have kept her name after all these years?

"My foster parents have always answered any questions that I've had but they were limited themselves. Most that I know is that my parents just showed up here. They said they wanted a quiet place to live for me to grow up. They were here till I was a few months old. Then according to Max my foster dad at the time, he said that my father came out to the ranch and told them they had a business emergency and couldn't go into details but had to leave immediately. They asked Katherine and Max to watch me until they could get back. Then they find out that the boat they had gone on sank. They were assumed to have died from drowning even though the bodies seemed mangled which doesn't happen from only drowning. This is why some believed they were killed with intent or they never actually made it to the boat, saying they drowned was an easy way of covering it up. Hard to say what happened. So, I have been raised by Katherine and Max and then later by their daughter Hellen and son-in-law Riley. My parents supposedly called me Evangeline and they loved the name, so they kept calling me the same. I'm guessing that if my parents had the same gifts I do, they would not have drowned so now I'm wondering if they were my parents? I just don't know?"

Nichole no longer had any doubt who Evangeline was now. Without the explanation or pictures confirming it, she looked so much like her father Charlie which would have been Evangeline's older brother. Thinking about it for a second if this was her father's sister then she had finally found who would be her aunt. She even looked younger than herself. Interestingly since she had been born much longer before, Nichole couldn't help but feel excited finding her even if she hadn't set out to do it. Evangeline looked like the rest of the family members in the picture she had taken from his house. She knew as soon as she had said who she was when she came into the cave, she just wanted to have it confirmed first. This had to be her!

Many times, since Charlie first told me about her being given up, I wondered how her mother would be able to do that. Did she love her? Did she wonder about her or curious at all if she was safe? Did she watch over her as Charlie had with me? I guess I would never know since I will never be in her position to know what she was thinking or going through. All I knew had been that I would rather die than give up anyone from my family. They both had the same mother, the midnight madam, and having separate fathers they would be step-siblings except they looked more like each other than some of his siblings who were full blood-related.

"I believe I can help you find who you are and re-introduce you to most of your family. My father had a sister named Evangeline; she was given up as an infant because of his mother. Julie was not a vampire or half-breed. She thought the child was normal because of the way she looked. She gave her away to get her safely away from the family. She was afraid that if she were human, her life would be changed without asking what she wanted. Julie was against others being turned into vampires. She preferred them to die with dignity as she felt life intended. It's one of the reasons she separated herself from her family. She didn't want to risk the curse not that the madam would have changed her. The others wanted to keep in touch with her still except the family she was given to disappeared with no warning. No one saw the baby since then. How old are you?"

"I recently celebrated my twentieth birthday again, but my foster parents are in their seventies, so I think I am really in my hundreds. When I hit twenty the first three times the town had burned down when the lightning storms were so bad. A lot of families could not make ends meet so they moved. Living on the ranch far enough away from others made my age easier to hide. Very few are from the originals from here that know the truth, but no one has ever said anything. Other families that have moved in since the town has rebuilt itself have accepted it. How do you know my real family?"

"I know your brother; he happens to be my father." Pulling out a picture of the McAllister family there were all the children even Evangeline in the center just before she was given away. She looked so much like everyone except coloring of her skin.

It didn't take me long to register it all. With a rush of excitement, I felt a slight bit overwhelmed but then also curious beyond what I had ever felt before. The desperate need to know what happened to my family, to learn about my past. The desperate need to understand who I was and if this person could help me figure that out, I wanted the chance to do that.

"I know of a safe point you can hide at. I can lead the others in another direction and join up with you if you will let me. I want to know my family and finally understand what makes me different. Just let me say goodbye to my parents then I will join you. I can help you get out of here."

Describing where the safe place was located and how to get there, we formed a plan on when to take off and how both would get out without hopefully the vampire hunters figuring out what was going on, or that Evangeline herself was indeed a half-breed also. Now all they had to do was wait a few hours until they could make their move. If they all slept at the same time it would have made all this so much easier. Unfortunately, two stayed up in case anything was to change. Even though they said it had been because they couldn't sleep, I still had the feeling they were standing guard.

In my room, I started packing a few things into a small bag, small enough to carry over my shoulder but not enough to attract attention that might give people the idea that I was planning on being gone for a while. Only taking what I valued. Then in the side zipper, I put my prized pictures of my family and friends. Feeling a momentary weakness stopping myself from crying I knew this was best. I knew they would be alright without me, but I would miss them. It was better to leave now than when heartache hit and I outlived every one of them.

Obscured Darkness

Desperately wanting to speak with Hellen and Riley. I wasn't sure how to tell them. I did not want them to feel abandoned by me. They have done so much already for me and there was no way I could ever express how grateful I was for them, or how much I appreciated their protecting me. Not knowing if they would talk me out of it or not. I couldn't bare the idea of saying goodbye let alone the possibility of them telling me not to go, if they did, I did not feel I would have the strength to leave.

The feeling in the pit of my stomach pulled at me so tightly. I would miss my family here. I lived here for so long that it had become my home and knowing generation after generation attached me even more. Hoping after I was gone maybe someone else would move into the little house I fixed up, to keep it from falling apart again. Perhaps one day another would move in and call it home.

This had been the one gift my parents left me when they passed on. One thing I always wondered when I had been fixing up the old house. Since it was so dilapidated how could it have gotten this bad when my parents had not been gone that long or did they ever really live in it? But then I wondered if the men searching for me at the time, possibly tore it apart looking for something maybe any kind of a clue that I still existed?

As much as I would miss my current family, especially my bond with Hellen, I wanted so desperately not to be the only one like myself. I wanted to know if I had family out there and if there were more like myself existing. If it turned into a trap, I would accept the consequences but for now, I had to find out.

Deliberating on how to tell Hellen and Riley. I did not want to tip off the hunters to where I was going in case they were to ask, and I felt it safer that neither Hellen or Riley know where or exactly when I was leaving, giving us enough time to get a safe distance ahead. My only real fear had been my concern for Hellen and Riley. I wanted to make sure they would be safe once I was gone, the hunters were still here, and I didn't want to risk them revolting against my family.

As soon as I finished writing my letter, I sealed it and hurried to the house to leave the note. Hellen had gone for the day and Riley had gone into town with her. Making sure no one had been awake in the house. I walked into Hellen's room and slipped the letter so that it would half stick out from under her pillow. Neither had been expected home right away and the guests were not expecting another excursion for a few more hours, they wanted to try nightfall again however they made it clear they wanted to search on their own this time without Evangeline, which made it easier so I would not have to explain why I was not going to show them around again. For me, it worked out in my favor this time. I was confident that Hellen would find the letter later that night.

Waiting so long was making me nervous. Keeping myself from pacing the floors I tried to keep myself busy with chores around the house. Even though I had none of my own now I finished some for Hellen.

The first to wake had been Andrew then shortly after a few of the other men had gotten up. Three went ahead and traveled in their direction. Andrew decided he wanted to stay behind and spend time talking with Evangeline. This made it harder trying to find a way to ditch Andrew, and not make it look like I was taking off somewhere he would want to know about. Then before the last of the three took off. It dawned on me exactly what I had to do. To give them exactly what they wanted.

"Andrew, may I please speak to you before you go. I heard something that might interest you. I don't know how accurate it is, but I heard from our neighbor to the west of us that there was something rather strange on his property late last night. A few of his animals died and he wasn't sure what did it. He said it a rather strange form; he wasn't sure if his eyes were playing tricks on him or if he saw the real thing. It moved too quickly and he wasn't quite sure. It may be what you are looking for; I thought I would let you know what he told me."

Staying relaxed hoping they would fall for it. And hopefully not catch any quiver in my voice at all that might give me away. Smiling and noticing their approving nods they began to plan their course of action. With me still standing at the door it appeared they had taken my word for it, even though I heard one whisper to another. "Odd for it to risk traveling during the daylight, it's either desperate or a fake move." Taking off immediately in the direction described I was happy for them to be gone. Andrew took longer before he left.

"So where are you going today?" I wasn't sure if he noticed my bag I was hiding or if he was trying to start a conversation.

"I'm working at the tavern today, just doing a different shift than my usual and then I'll be staying at the farm next door. She's been having contractions, so I wanted to be there to help out." I figured he couldn't argue with that explanation it seemed logical enough.

"Then don't forget your overnight bag. Reaching behind the door he grabbed my bag and handed it to me." Smiling and nodded as I took the bag from him still trying to keep my cool.

"Thank you, I would have forgotten it. I may not live far but it's still a pain just to come back for a bag.

"I'll see you later. I should get going. I have to catch up with the guys." I watched as Andrew left heading off in the direction that the others had gone in.

I had started walking slowly away from the house, than when I could no longer see Andrew and was far enough away from the house. I had a few things I wanted to pick up from my house on my way so I walked quickly keeping an eye out for anyone who might be watching. Grabbing my other bag, I left it on the side of the porch with my other personal items. I ran for the woods. I knew that Nichole would be waiting for me at the abandoned shack on the far edge. The shack used to belong to Kendrick. At one time had been my best friend even close enough he had been my boyfriend until he said he could not handle the truth any further. He had not wanted to think about the fact that after he died, I would still be here. He first knew me when I had been raised by my first set of foster parents. Mainly he wanted to protect me. As odd as it may have sounded, he wanted to stay away from me so he would not attract attention to me as he aged, and I did not. It had been a painful choice and not one he was even sure was a good one, but he felt he had to do something even if it meant losing what he loved most. What was even stranger and I would have loved him anyway, as he had not wanted me to watch him age getting older.

I still loved coming to the old shack. I had so many wonderful memories of this place, which is why I had chosen this as our meeting place before we were to take off. In a way, I wanted to not just see it one last time, but I also wanted to say goodbye to it.

Trying not to take too much time once I was out of the eyesight of Hellen and Riley's home, I no longer worried about watching my speed. Rarely, I would run this fast. I let myself run as fast as I could carry myself. Passing through the forest at an alarming rate even scaring some of the animals as I whizzed past them. The cabin had only been four miles away.

As I was getting closer, I could pick up on the scent of Nichole and her son. They were waiting there as Nichole promised they would. But at the same time, I had a strange scent I picked up on. I knew the others had gone the other way and no longer sensed them, but something still felt wrong. Either way I felt once we took off, we should be ahead of whatever I sensed was wrong. The only time I smelled that scent had been from Andrew. He had a different smell even though he said he wore it to confuse creatures into trusting him, that's why the others with him didn't hunt him. I couldn't help but not believe his story unless he was trying to test me with it. Or there was something more to him than he let on.

Chapter Five
Path to Self-Discovery

Nichole had been waiting patiently in the cabin swaying Lucian to relax him. She was finding it hard to take care of a baby that insisted on not sleeping, accepting gratefully the new change of clothes that Evangeline offered. It felt wonderful to finally be wearing clean clothing, especially after collecting clothing from garbage cans and traveling in the mud and rain for so long that she felt like a mess. Even after no one used it the makeshift shower still worked. Taking only a brief nap she looked around the cabin while the baby had been occupied by a woodblock toy. There had still been personal items left behind.

The cabin had been left exactly intact as the last person who had lived in it left it, a dinner plate on the table with a glass cup next to it. Dust and cobwebs covered everything. There were very faded letters stacked on the reading desk. Reading one she saw that Kendrick had written a goodbye letter to Evangeline. She felt bad that Evangeline had to go through losing a loved one and knowing this would not be her last. She must have felt so alone not knowing who she was or why she alone would still be standing. No one to speak to about it that would understand her. Nichole had always been curious about herself except she learned to accept it. She did wonder if it would have affected her more if she had known much earlier on or if she would have tried to find her birth parents earlier if she had known?

Evangeline packed food for both, even bringing baby food with them. Not that she was sure if the baby ate regular food or goat milk, so she brought both. Just in case they found food was not available. I wasn't sure if they would want to eat these since I wasn't sure what vampires ate. Nichole thanked her for the bread loaf and ate it. At least Nichole had a normal side to her as well as I did.

While Nichole waited for Evangeline to join them, she had looked over the small map Evangeline had drawn from the little she knew, at least now she knew what direction they need to head off in. Then not wanting to prolong the wait at the cabin they took off. The next town over there had been a carriage waiting on the side of town for them. I had sent Thomas with a note to give to the livery stable there. He promised if he ran into Hellen and Riley that he would not say anything. Thomas was in favor of my going if leaving with Nichole meant getting me further away from the demon hunters. I was careful not to let Hellen know what I was planning even though she was rather smart herself and had her way of figuring things out.

Not wanting to draw too much attention but not wanting to let any time slip by even if it had been daylight still. We planned on traveling by carriage until we could leave the carriage and horse's a few towns over when the sun would start going down.

We could outrun the carriage, but this would be easier to hide in and not alert anyone to anything unusual. There were only the two main towns they had to go through, after that it had been open woods to the north.

When we reached the stable as I half thought might happen. Hellen and Riley were there waiting by the coach driver. Even without saying a word I had never been able to hide anything from them as I had done with so many others. Thomas was standing next to them shrugging his shoulders to show he didn't know how they guessed something was up. They had an odd expression. I had never seen them show before. As Nichole and I carefully walked up to them trying to note the surroundings to make sure nothing else was wrong. Hellen had been the first who walked up to me.

"I knew someday something like this might happen. If she is like you then you will be in better hands. If you find it's not what you want, you always have a home with our family." Reaching out Hellen pulled me to her and hugged me rather firmly trying to keep back her tears that did not want to be hidden.

"I know you will be happier. Not that you were not happy here. But they will understand you better and be able to protect you more." With a kiss on the cheek, she stepped back.

Thomas was the last to hug me goodbye. "I know you will be safer but don't think for one moment I won't still worry about you. If you ever need me, you know where to find me."

"We want what is best for you. And we will always keep a room for you." Riley was the last to hug me, then let me go.

He opened the door for both Nichole and me to get in. They stood on the side of the street watching the carriage stroll away with the driver up top as Nichole and I were sitting safely inside. I had watched Hellen and Riley until they were no longer in sight. I had waited for my tears to dry before I could speak.

After being in the carriage for a short time I wanted to ask questions right away. Not wanting to be rude and just blast questions however not wanting to sound too uninterested I finally asked Nichole.

"How large is the family? What are they like? Do all vampires look like us?" There were so many questions I wanted to ask and others I did not know how to even put into words.

I wanted to have so many answered but I didn't want to be rude and ask questions that would be invasive. Nichole seemed rather calm and very patient with me with all my questions.

"I grew up very similar to the way you did. My mother died after I was born. However, I was raised by my aunt who I had believed was my mother for a very long time. The one I believe to be your brother is my father. He made a promise to my mother to allow me to have a normal life and he did. I grew up believing I was normal even though I knew I was nothing like anyone else. Throughout my life, he was always there watching me just giving me my space to grow up on my own." Taking a moment before she finished speaking again, she hadn't talked about this in a while.

"In an unusual way, Charlie introduced me to my husband who is also like both of us. We are half breeds. My father is a full vampire. I still have more questions to ask him myself, but I figure I have so much time now to find out. One of the things he told us about his family had been about the sister he never had the chance to get to know. He told us how a sister of his was given away. She was the youngest of the family. You would be from the same mother, a half-sibling since you both have different fathers. They have ideas about your father, they know who he is and a few things about him, except no one, knows what happened to him or if he's still alive. But no one knows for sure what he is, however you would be considered a half breed, you would have inherited something from both parents." Stopping again for another moment to make sure I was still following along Nichole wasn't sure how I was going to take this part. If you're not familiar with it, it can be creepy or just plain scary.

"Your mother that had been dubbed the midnight madam was later killed by the town's people out of fear. They called her that name because the only time they would see her is when she would sneak out late at night. She didn't care for the sunlight and she preferred to keep to herself and people didn't understand that. They feared what they didn't know. When she was buried, they assumed it might have been when she became a full-fledged vampire. She always hated being a half-breed. She didn't trust anyone to change her that might not try to control her. Therefore, she waited. At the time she didn't know if she died, she would cease to exist or if her vampire side would take over. After being buried when the town watched to make sure she went into the ground. Later she pulled herself out. I haven't seen very many vampires or half-breeds. I was about to meet the rest of my father's family; they were to meet us at the cabin up north. As far as I can tell looks are subjective. Certain things change however you still look pretty close to what you did before you died or in our case very well preserved."

Stopping for a moment Nichole shifted Lucian so the sun would be shielded from his eyes. Even with the shades down a little bit of sun was shining through.

"You look so much like the pictures of his family. It's hard to believe you wouldn't be the sister they have looked for. We had an incident that made it safer that our family to leave and start over elsewhere. It comes to a point you can no longer hide who or what you are. I had no one around when I was growing up who knew who or what I was. I just knew I had to hide it, keep it secret. Then my other mother I think finally realized it also, she was quite depressed when she finally realized I would not be the daughter she hoped for. I had grown up thinking I was like everyone else just with a few extra gifts. Not that I ever admitted it out loud. Just watching others and seeing how they react. I knew I was different when I had to hide my gifts and they did not since they did not possess what I did. I finally gained a father even though in the back of my mind I sort of knew he was always around. At least it was what I hoped and later I found out it wasn't just a feeling. That it was true he was still around. Charlie can fill you in more about vampires; most of what he knows is from others he has met and from his mother and family."

There were many long stretches between towns. The carriage seemed extra slow after our fast burst of running earlier, almost the same as moving in slow motion. In most of the towns, we were able to pass along the side of the town rather than go through. One town we guessed must be suspicious of strangers since so many stopped and watched as the carriage rolled through. Even though they could not see past the drawn shades on the windows that strange feeling came back to me. At first, I thought it might have been that I wasn't so used to so many people being suspicious. Even though this time Nichole let me know she was picking up on the same feeling as I had been.

"We need to ditch the carriage. There's something that's been following us for a while and it's getting too close, we need to outpace ourselves from it. I was hoping it would stop but I think it intends on catching up to us." Nichole reached out from the window and tapped the outside of the carriage.

Coming to a halt, Nichole got out and informed the driver they would finish the rest of the way on foot and that we were close enough, that he could start heading back. Both stood there for a moment watching the carriage rumble back down the path before taking off. With Lucian secure in her arms we took off north again as fast as we could. Covering so much more ground than we were previously. It had felt like hours before we stopped again. Not that either had been tired; it had been time to feed the baby. I couldn't help it, but I loved being able to break out into a full run and not stop let alone have someone else that kept up with me. Nichole was faster than I was.

She had gone much further west than she originally planned. She had started in another country, even her boat ride here hadn't brought her to the correct place. It seemed as if fate was determined she end up where I lived to find me, even if it wasn't her original plan. Once crossing the border heading north, we had to veer east quite a bit before we came close to the direction we needed to go. I had never gone this far from home before, but the scenes and places became an adventure. Not being the only one who also possessed the talent had been exciting to me also. At least Nichole understood me. For the most part, we had turned it into a racing game between the two of us, running across grass plains then through swamps barely touching the ground or gracefully and barely touching submerged stones as we crossed various brooks and streams.

Listening for others making sure not to run into anyone we slowed down a bit. We heard something, so we decided to walk a little not to catch attention. Even though someone might have found it odd that two women and a baby out in the middle of nowhere were walking. Briefly on the way we had encountered another pair of vampires. This was a first for both Nichole and me. They were rather confused when they realized they were hunting half-breeds. It was the first time they encountered this. They had traveled many places around the world, yet this was the first time they met half breeds that were living on their own. Most they had known had not lived long. Mostly for living among humans and being caught. It was far easier to kill a half-breed than it had been for a full vampire, both had been equally strong however full-fledged vampires usually had more time to be used to their skills, while half-breeds are used to hiding and not fully using their gifts and not usually knowing what they were fully capable of and being caught off guard.

As we came closer to the cabin neither Nichole or I could shake that nagging feeling that we were being followed. Neither could sense who or what it was. We didn't think it was a vampire, but it did seem human. At least the vampires we had been followed by earlier had already taken off but what human could have kept up with us? However, the scent on it almost seemed like whatever it was tried to distract us by dowsing itself with the scent of another to make it unrecognizable. For a short time, it disappeared but now it was back almost as if it was heading them off and finally caught up again. It was too hard to believe that it could be who I thought it was. Shaking the thought from my head, Nichole kept moving forward and leaving Evangeline behind to keep guard to see what might be following or rather what was about to pop out in front of us. Then I caught a glimpse of what it was and stopped dead in my tracks but waved for Nichole to continue.

Standing still for quite some time but looking in the direction the figure had moved it stayed there possibly hoping it would not be seen. I kept my eyes on it where I originally saw the bushes move and the dark spot located. I made it known I was waiting for the figure to make itself known. Even though I knew what my fate may be. I waited for him to come out of the darkness and confront me.

"How long did you know?" That was all I asked knowing he

was not that far from me to hear.

I knew what he did for a living. He already let me know that. I was beginning to wonder if he was going to ever carry through or if he was second-guessing himself, or worse waiting for the others to join him.

"I have not known for long; I was following the other girl you are with. I did not know you were with her until now. Hopefully, you realize she's a vampire and it's not safe for you to be with her. You might be her last meal. Are you with her by choice or force?" The way he was standing I could tell he was still trying to decide what he wanted to do.

"I'm with her by choice. She's not a threat. No more than I am. What made you follow us? Did you figure out that Hellen and Riley were not my parents?" Still standing in the same place I was curious if I were about to find out exactly what he did to what he considered to be demons.

"I really should have guessed, it does make sense, the others never noticed it. I always felt you were hiding something, especially the lame story about your friend making that scent. No one duplicates that scent unless you get it off a dead vampire or a creature of some sort. The thing I find most troubling is that I did not follow my heart. I should have gone the other way, the way you told me because that way I would not have followed you here. Once I noticed you were with her, I was hoping to find you were not with her by choice. It would have been so much easier. The others are not that far behind me. After heading off in the other direction, we swept up north since we caught the trail and Keith did not believe your story. He felt it was too convenient. He was right after all. He usually is. I was hoping we had found the other one, I never expected to find you."

Walking up close to me Andrew stopped and was standing a few steps from me. Placing each of his hands on my shoulders the expression on his face was of concern and worry.

"I can stop myself, but I cannot stop them. I do not fear you, but they won't care. They will know you're a vampire or at least helping her, since you're here willingly they will consider you a threat for helping a vampire. Being able to keep up with her will give you away and they will kill you feeling justified. I wish I had known. Maybe there would have been something I could have done."

"If you knew I was a half-breed I rather doubt you would have acted differently. The only difference is that you would not have gotten to know me. Besides, it wasn't until recently that I had a name for myself. I grew up thinking of myself as just having extra abilities." Still not moving but knowing that Nichole was not far off listening to our conversation stashing Lucian in what she hoped was a safe spot. Neither of us wanted to lure them to the cabin except Nichole had known her family sensed her and would be here rather quick.

Chapter Six
Caught

Intent on listening. I could hear the faint echo of the other men. I knew it would not be long before they caught up, we could not lead them to the cabin and risk the lives of the others but then we also needed their help. For a brief second, I felt a wave of panic, I could sense three other figures with Nichole. One left after arriving and seemed like Lucian's scent disappeared. Not until I had a waif of their scent again that I relaxed. They also had the vampire scent. The only one I now worried about was Andrew. I did not want to see him harmed however I could not run away from him now. If we had run before, they would have kept following us. I wished Thomas was with us because he would have known what to do. I didn't want to harm Andrew anymore than he wanted to with me. Even though he may not have a choice once the others join him.

Obscured Darkness

"I could try and spare your life and say she took you by force, it would be the only way I could save you. At least it would explain why you have the strong scent on you. Even if I defended you without explanation or didn't cover that you're a half-breed then they would kill me also. You have to convince them that you are human."

"I can't do that. As odd as it may sound to you, she is my niece and the baby boy is my great-nephew. I can't pretend to be something that I am not anymore. However, I also do not want to hurt you. I will defend myself and my family, but I won't hurt you." We both kept intently staring at each other as we heard the footsteps of the others approaching.

Slowing down in front of us they had a bewildered look on their face, curious about the situation seeing Andrew speaking with me and no vampire in sight.

"How did she get here? Is she one of them? Did they already change her?" One of the men asked while getting off the horse and walking closer.

"I was about to ask you the same question, how did you get here so fast or am I to assume you have some special gift you're not telling others about? Besides, it takes much longer for them to change someone, even you know that." Andrew Looked at them accusingly and was trying to figure out what to do next.

"We traveled by horse, we almost lost you, but we could guess you were heading north so we took another path and caught up. Our guess had been correct. However, I do not see any horses that you are using? I believe we will have two vampires to kill tonight. I'm sorry brother but you know the rules. No exceptions for anyone."

The second he said that a person I did not know but could only assume was Charlie stood close beside me. He looked so much like me. Without explanation I could feel it, he felt like family. Then seeing his face, it was confirmed. I could see Anthony standing beside Nichole. I felt a little better not being alone but felt awful if anything were to happen to my new family. Even though I was curious if the demon hunters even had an effective way of killing a vampire? Not that I wanted to find out.

Andrew had still been standing in the middle of the two groups. He almost looked like he was standing there in pain trying to make his mind up. He could easily prove to the others he was human or surprise us all and find out he's not. Then at the last, he looked directly at me. Slowly he walked over to me standing not too close in front of me.

Charlie leaned in and whispered to me, "if he starts fighting or when they do, tear in with your teeth and hands. I know it sounds horrible but don't hold back, this is your life you're saving."

The idea made me cringe; it was the worst thing I had heard but I understood it would be needed since the others did not seem to want to give up the fight. But then I also wanted to hear what Andrew wanted to say, there was something he was painfully trying to fight back.

"I am so sorry, I don't want to do this, and it's against everything I have come to believe in. I can't do this again. I convinced myself once I watched the hypocrisy and saw what my father and others have done, and condemned them for their actions. I convinced myself that it was the right thing. I can't do this to you or let them harm you. Please trust me as I ask you to do this. Bite me, I know I won't change immediately but they may not trust it. I am already a hypocrite."

He reached out with his arm offering it as a sacrifice; he winced as he said it. This was not what I was expecting. Even Charlie seemed surprised.

"I can't do that. I can't make you something that will put you in danger also, the venom would never spread fast enough, it would only put you in danger and you might not be able to protect yourself." I was curious unless he was hoping for something.

"I know that, and you know that except they still don't believe or accept it. I was hoping to pretend to change and then they would think I was a vampire like you. I could protect you. Do you have to change me with your mouth? After all, it is where the most germs are?"

"You're not worried about the venom I would inject you with, but you are concerned about the germs in my mouth?"

"Yeah, I guess that is a little unreasonable to focus on that?" Andrew looked like he was searching his mind for any idea that could come to him even if it were an absurd one.

"Don't be foolish Andrew. Take off behind us. You will be safe for a while there and since you're not a demon they can't trace you. You can still walk away Andrew. Please, there is no way of making this easier." Standing there I pleaded with him to find some way out of this even if it were to save Andrew.

"I can't walk away either. I can't keep watching or knowing this is going on, especially to you. I have had the privilege of getting to know you and you do not deserve this. I hoped you would never have to witness something like this." He had a look of shame and confusion on his face.

Walking away now facing his back to me but keeping himself distanced between the two groups. Not sure in his mind if it would work. It usually happened when he was terrified beyond any experience and this feeling he had now was close to how he felt then. The fear of losing Evangeline and having to keep fighting for the lives of others was getting harder than what he could deal with on his own. It was easier when it was just the three of them except, they keep adding more to their group every day. Andrew could only hope it would work again.

"Before you descend upon them and fight. I must state this first. If you do manage to kill them then you must kill me also. I have been a hypocrite for quite some time. I've warned off a lot of the creatures we hunt. There is a reason we are not more successful. I don't believe we should kill all we find. Remember when that vampire attacked me when I was alone and you wondered how I survived. You even checked my vital signs so many times trying to make sure I had not been bitten. I was never bit. I am not a vampire. However, I don't think it's possible to ever really know what we all are. Something within me reacted and reached out as the second it jumped at me. If I am human and something can be dormant in all of us, then do we not have the responsibility to all kill ourselves? Or are some to survive because we no longer believe in the survival of the fittest? Are we truly the ones who are meant to survive? Do we deserve to rid the earth of its children who may have been here longer than us?"

"You know as well as I do, these are demons and they must be destroyed now move so that we may correct what is wrong. If it comes to it regardless if you are human or not, we will kill you to get to them, we will deal with your betrayal later." Mike had been the one to respond to Andrew.

There had been eight people that Andrew currently traveled with. There were reasons they had not killed any vampires and the sad victims that they killed were ones that did not take his warning. However, he never thought for one second that Evangeline would have been one. He should have picked up on the signals but for some reason, he did not want to believe that of her. She was so innocent and childlike. He couldn't help but feel so strongly enough to want to protect her from this wretched world of demon killers and creatures that existed.

Watching his friend die he could never get over it, he could never stop the screaming he heard as their family was wiped out, even the ones that had no vampire traits in a case for fear they might develop them later. Then his hypocrisy when he found he had a problem and had to hide it from the very ones he traveled with, the very ones who would kill their brother for their belief.

Standing there he allowed the frustration, anger, and fear of what was about to happen to build up inside of him hoping for the same results. If it didn't happen then he would have to fight. Andrew certainly felt the same desperation he had from before. Sudden hot and cold flashes kicked in, not until he felt the ground tremble beneath his feet, did he finally get the confidence that it was going to happen.

"Last chance, get out of the way or you die with the demons." Hissed one of his old comrades, Andrew only grew more confidant by the second.

I'm not moving." Andrew stood still holding his place to show his determination.

"You're not leaving us any choice." They started walking with their weapons ready in hand looking as determined as Andrew had.

"You're going to have to kill me also; I am a demon of another kind. Don't know what kind but you're about to find out there isn't a name for everything." As soon as he uttered the words the ground trembled even more underneath them.

The wind rushed warmly past them hurling them back onto the ground. The air around Andrew had become extremely hot and strong wind whipped through the woods as all of them watched him in amazement. The sky was blotted out while everything was dark. Andrew had begun to blend in with the air surrounding him, not becoming the wind but as black as the night sky. His black clothing soon became more like camouflage around his body. The only way of seeing him still had been the veins in his arms and neck. Deep crimson red as they blazed in their host body. Only his silhouette could be made out. His hands raised halfway out to the sides and his palms rose upward. The deep grooves on the palms of his hands lit up. From his wrist to his fingertips, he shot out a blasting fire blaze to the sides of his old comrades.

"I am sorry I have to do this, but the killing has to stop. You cannot even be reasoned with and I have tried for years. Just like the very man you seem to follow you yourselves have indeed become the monsters." Andrew said his parting words as the blaze of fire around his old group rose higher. The light from the blaze itself made Charlie stand back flinching from the stinging from the light of the fire. Neither Anthony or Nichole seemed to be affected by it.

It felt as if a powerful storm brewed for their very own eyes to watch. As the temperature rose so high, we all backed up to get away from the scorching heat. We had to move so far back that we were now on the tip of the hill. Watching from atop the hill the entire blaze engulfed his old comrades. Not a single voice could be heard from the wind whipping around furiously keeping the fire controlled. Then as they burned to ash themselves Andrew dropped to the ground. Not that it was a matter of feeling tired from what he did, He hated killing. Even stopping those who would kill others he hated stopping life of any kind, he hadn't felt it was his right to decide who lived or died.

Andrew knew he could not leave them after a few warnings knowing they would be running forever from them. He didn't feel he had a choice. He knew the demon hunters would never quit. The others never had to leave their protective stances as we watched in amazement what was happening before our very eyes. Something none of us had seen before. The entire family joined once there was news of an impending fight. Not that they were needed since it was against eight humans. However, now seeing this happen they felt their number hadn't been needed. Not that any of us could get over what we had seen. We were not sure what to expect and it certainly hadn't been this.

I walked away from the protection of my family walking over to Andrew. Placing my hand on his shoulder he still felt extremely hot from the fire ring. I knew it had been hard on him to do this. I didn't know if I would have had the strength to kill if it had come to it. Placing my arms around him doing my best to comfort him even though I know it could never take away how he felt about what just happened. It wasn't something any of us would be forgetting.

Barely above a whisper, Andrew said, "I wish there had been another way, but I know they never would have stopped. They would keep hunting not just us but others also. How much longer could I have hidden my gift before they found out? When that vampire came at me, I didn't flame out like that. I disappeared long enough to scare her back into the light from it. Not that she could see me. The room was already dark and I went pitch black." Standing up still looking at the ashes of his old friends he couldn't shake that sickening feeling in the pit of his stomach.

"Come with us." I offered hope that my family might be able to help him also.

Now that he had his gift that was out in the open something my family had never seen before, maybe he would be more comfortable living with those who would never judge him? Besides, I thought I would love to have Andrew around since I felt much closer to him.

"I appreciate the offer Evangeline; I would love to stay with you, but I have some people who I need to find. I owe favors that I need to take care of. There is someone who is waiting patiently for me and I need to find her again. Now that it's safe. I promised her that when they were gone, I would come and find her. I hope you understand. You will be safe with your family. Maybe someday our paths will cross again. But it's time I started taking care of things I put off." Leaning into me giving me a reassuring hug, and then placing a light kiss on my cheek, I stood there watching him.

Andrew waved goodbye to my family and slowly walked away. Charlie had come down next to me placing his arm around my shoulder giving me a reassuring squeeze.

"I'm sure he's going to be alright. It's time for us to go also." The rest of the family that had remained all trickled back to the cabin.

We hadn't been too far from what Nichole had called a cabin and she seemed as surprised as I had. But then if it were to fit a large family, I should have guessed it would have been larger than what I was imagining. It had not looked like a traditional cabin at all.

Seeing this, place both Nichole and I were amazed by it. It had been anything but the humble little cabin that I was expecting. From the side of the mountain, all you could see was a single-level shack. Brown trim boards that were fading and peeling, nothing that would invite a stranger to check it out. It looked rather poorly taken care of or abandoned single-floor house from the outside. Broken windows and faded window shades, parts of the wall looked like it was falling apart. Dark green moss was even growing on the north side of the wood and the roof had been covered with it while vines grew along the whole sidewall. Getting closer there were no gaps in the wood. It was well sealed showing this look was intentional. The view from the inside had been different. There were at least four levels to this cabin. Most of which had been underground, only one floor above the ground. It looked like a mansion built into the mountain.

Both Nichole and I followed Charlie into the cabin. Inside it was even more impressive. White marble with black streaks throughout almost like lightning strikes covering the entire floor, cream-colored valances, otherwise the windows were uninhibited. If a person were to simply look past the outside exterior of the house, they would be amazed at what they found inside. Most went to the second floor where there was a large room very much like the one upstairs only it had a large dark green built-in couch that wrapped around the exterior of the room only cutting off where the doors either led to a room or the large winding staircase leading to the next floor down below.

The second floor mainly had three rooms that came off from it. With two bedrooms and an office, the second floor had been decorated to be an entertainment room and doubled as the family room. A baby grand piano sat in the corner and a rocking horse along the wall. There was a table in the center with a few books, the game of 'quoits' a game like horseshoes or ring toss. Also, there was a deck of cards along with dice.

The third floor had four rooms off from it. Three were bedrooms and another office. Two of the bedrooms had a mini office and a mini sitting room. As the floors went deeper into the mountain or lower the rooms had more space branching out in either direction. Nichole and I followed Charlie as he showed us our rooms. Anthony already had two cribs set up in their room on the third floor. I had the room next to theirs. Charlie didn't have a bedroom; he only used an office on the second floor which he shared with his sister Lorah. It appears the older members of the family claimed the second or first floor. Only one room other than the main room had been on the first floor. It was a small office that Bethany and Dinah both used. Not that any of them needed a bed in their rooms. They saved those for the family members who still had their human side alive with them.

"You may want to come out and greet our guests. We have a bit of a party planned on short notice. We figure having all the family here was reason enough for a gathering. Not something we have had in a long time, but we want to celebrate this." Charlie went on to make sure the others were all grouping outside.

If anyone would have seen this, they would have to admit it was an amazing site. One that some of the older family members would have been used to or had seen before. Nichole, Evangeline, and even Anthony stood back near the cabin staring in awe as the guests began to arrive. In a site, they never dreamed they would have seen. Lorah and Dinah had been the main planners. Both could never turn down a chance to throw a party and had been the main ones who first had a hard time when the parties ceased in their old home. They used to get quite involved in planning them with their mother.

Nichole and I stood there for a long time watching everyone. This had been the first time we had seen this many that were like us and it felt so good to know we were not alone, that we had a family. I could tell she felt as overwhelmed with excitement as I was. I never wanted this to end.

The backyard had been transformed into a garden paradise with a makeshift wood plank floor on the ground with benches around for watching when the dancing started up. The gazebo had even been pulled into the mix. The moonlight that was now peeking through added the perfect lighting for the evening. It looked like a magical enchanted night. White lace streamed through the trees and draped on the outside of the cabin covering the outside's dank appearance, and oil lamps lining the ground separating the different areas.

As they stood there, swishes of wind would shoot past them only to slow up in front of either Charlie or one of his siblings. Handling the formal introductions and greetings, many of them went to the dance floor. It was such a sight to see. I hoped I would never forget. I had hoped to gain a family. However, I never knew such a world existed.

Standing there watching as Anthony and Nichole introduced themselves and the babies to the others. I knew I would never forget how thankful I was to be here. I wish Hellen could have seen this or that Andrew could have been here to witness all of this. To be a part of it.

What had looked like a simple owl coming down to perch passed the tree limb, as it slowed and lowered closer to the ground changed its shape slowly. There had been what looked like a flock of owls slowly coming to join us. As they gracefully switched form they continued to walk as humans not even missing a step. Neither Andrew or Nichole seemed to be surprised, however with this many coming at one time they were still in just as much awe.

Even off to the side, there had been a set of red foxes that transformed just as elegantly as the owls had. I noticed they seemed to come in pairs or single. Not many came in groups unless they were family or a coven of some sort. Of course, there were werewolves, they looked the most magnificent. Some were huge and others were rather dainty in size. Both men and women they transformed into.

The one form that seemed to surprise me the most had been

the smoke that showed up. At first, I thought a rather thick and dark fog rolled in. One side had been so dark that the light no longer made it through until it started breaking apart. It had not even appeared to touch the ground. Then shapes came out of the fog, almost as if they were either stepping through time or space using the fog as a transport. Then instantly I wondered about Andrew. Would he be able to do that or be something like them? Then at once, you could see who and what they were. They took the form of humans. Each creature had been just as graceful as the next.

One of the women who transformed out from the dark fog talked with Charlie, both being engrossed in their conversation. I could only hear parts of it.

"Lily, where is your husband? Will he be here tonight?" Charlie had an expression on his face I hadn't recognized before and the tone of his voice sounded sarcastic.

'He's somewhere; he had been standing near me when we were in the West Indies. I'm sure I'll run into him again." Both laughed. This didn't seem too strange to them. They seemed rather lighthearted about it.

The music was blasting rather loudly. Not sure where the music had been coming from, I walked around all the guests to the further side. Along the way occasionally I received hugs either from family members or friends who had known the family for some time, they were happy that I was back and safe. As I walked also caught some conversations, some of which ended abruptly as I neared since they were talking about Andrew. They were surprised he had not been killed since he killed so many others. Then finding out he had a unique gift of his own.

Finally reaching the other side there were several people. If they knew how to play an instrument no matter what kind they joined in. The music sounded so soothing to the ears. Occasionally they had a strong beat and faster tempo; however, everyone playing with each other kept right in line almost as if they had been doing this for centuries.

It never seemed like guests were going to stop coming. Over the next several hours' many new ones came and went. Some left the party several times at a time for whatever personal reasons, some of the creatures seemed normal however I never thought I would see a chipmunk of all things become something. This world was far more interesting than I ever believed. How mistaken I had been when I began to wonder if I was the only one like myself. Now, this was opening my eyes to so much. I would never doubt the concept of another type of creature or gift again. Compared to some of these I felt so plain and small. The additional talents also amazed me. Just what some of them could make music from and still be in harmony with each other.

Still standing on the side hoping no one was minding that I kept watching everyone. The couples are out on the dance floor dancing with such fluid movements. I must have looked like I yearned to dance myself. One of the wolves came over to me now in human form. He was very handsome, tall, and muscular with dark hair. His stance seemed a little intimidating, but his voice was so calming and sweet. I almost felt entranced by his voice. Let alone his smile was so inviting.

Not saying much, he invited me to dance. Not waiting for a response, he took a hold of my hand and led me out onto the dance floor with the other perfectly matched couples, and began to dance with me. I have never danced before other than simply pretending to dance in one spot almost hopping from one foot to the other according to the beat. I could tell he has danced before as he led me around the dance floor. The music was a much faster beat and we twirled around the dance floor much faster.

He was a very good dancer. With no dance experience, he could have made anyone look good. He led not just like an expert but somehow, he got my body to respond to the moves that were needed for the music even as it changed. From the slow tempo to the faster we kept up dance after dance. I was loving it and getting into it. Occasionally I could see the look on Charlie's face. He looked happy I was finally looking at ease and blending in. Most of all we're happy to have me back in the family. Even the others who were my sisters and brothers welcomed me rather warmly.

Occasionally, I would see Nichole and Anthony dance past us in the other direction. Both babies were being passed around not just to family but also to friends. This felt good even though at times I could feel a twinge of guilt, feeling bad that I left Hellen. She knew I needed this, and I loved her. Hellen knew I would be okay. I would have to send her a letter and let her know how I was doing.

The man that danced with me never took his eyes off me. At times I wondered what he was thinking. Was he curious or know something about me?

As we danced, we eventually wound up by the side of the dance floor. Stopped for a moment as other dancers went whizzing past us. This was unlike any dance I had ever seen. No human I ever knew danced this elegantly and fast let alone this style.

"I hope you don't mind me asking you this question. But do you by any chance feel something familiar or recognize me? I would understand if you did not, but I was curious."

Stopping to think. I was sure I would have remembered a man who was a wolf. No matter how he looked, since I never met another creature or someone with unusual looks before. I only knew two men who loved to dance that were good at it and that had been Max and Riley. But neither were as good as this gentleman.

"I was never in a capacity that we would have talked but we did meet a few times. I wish I had known who you were, but then again family situations were different than so this perhaps would have been the best time. Either way, I am happy to see you again." He stood there smiling happily as everyone else had been.

"When did we meet before? I don't ever remember meeting a human wolf before. How did I not pick up on your scent?"

"Would you have been paying attention to the scent of a wolf when all you thought of me had been an animal, at the time when you did not know who or what you were looking at? I knew from your scent you had a vampire smile, but it was confusing since I also smelled human blood which is why I hid my true form from you for so long. Each time that you wandered into the woods. I kept an eye on you. There were other creatures out there. Did you ever wonder why you had such a healthy fear of the woods? Or why the other creatures would leave you alone?"

"I knew I felt like I had been watched but I never knew why. I loved the forest but at night, it felt like too many eyes were on me. But then again as nighttime set in. I also felt the most comfortable. I could be more myself. Others that I knew didn't usually see as well as I had in the dark."

"Yes, and one of those times you were yourself. I saw you race across the woods, I had to follow you. I knew no human could run that fast. I followed you to that old shack. The man who lived there knew what you were; he never spoke of it. I even had talks with him but I found he learned more about our world than he wanted to know. But he fell in love with you. I used to come to your back door at the house of the people who raised you. There were a few who were your parents. The first couple that dropped you off, then you seemed to get passed around after that, always seemed strange to me that you aged so slowly.

The thing that first caught my attention had been the scent and the fact I barely saw you age in front of me, and then you stopped altogether. One of the times I watched you. I remember very clearly when that other wolf almost attacked you. That was the night you fell asleep on the forest floor. You were so young but naïve about the dangers of the woods."

"Oh, my gosh that was you? I remember laying down to watch the stars. I was more tired than I thought I was. Then I fell asleep while watching the stars. The next thing I remembered was waking up to the growling of a wolf. It lunged at me, and the other wolf came from behind me attacking it. I thought after it was scared off, the second would come after me. I was ready to try and outrun it, but I remember the look on his face. It looked friendly. Almost scared. Then it took off. That was you?" I looked at him in amazement as I realized just who he was.

Not changing his whole form, he transformed his face momentarily then switched back. Charlie had been watching and wondered what the transformation had been for until he saw the look on my face. Then he understood the reason. The look of familiarity on my face had shown even with a smile.

Until this moment even though I was happy to know my new family, it also felt good to have a connection to my old family and old home. Nichole and Anthony were still dancing. Something this family and others seemed to be into. Also, there had been several who were talking to each other and occasionally looked in my direction or that of Nichole. We both seemed to be the main topic of conversation. Not something I was used to. I was used to being more private even though I couldn't help enjoying being around everyone.

As the night went on the group did start to dwindle. With some staying inside while others made their exit. Lewis had still stayed. We talked for several hours inside. We had gone to my room for a little privacy. Sitting down on the bed we talked about the old town and the people there. He even pointed out a few townspeople who knew about me, but mainly stuck to themselves since they were trying to stay quiet. They were fearful and worried about what might happen to me when they found that the demon hunters followed me out.

"If it's okay with you. I can bring back a letter for you to Hellen. I can let her know that I am a friend and that you missed her. Then also I can let some of the others know about what happened to the demon hunters. If I also have your permission, I would love to see you again." Lewis sounded like the perfect gentleman, always asking for permission before he stated or did anything, with the most perfect decorum. I never felt more relaxed with someone before. I didn't even want him to leave. It almost felt like we talked for an entire day.

Even Nichole leaned in to say goodnight when she was putting the little girl Rose down to sleep, she was already asleep in her mom's arms, at least she didn't have to encourage her to want to sleep. Lucian wasn't interested in sleeping, so he stayed outside with Charlie for a little longer. We lay on the bed for hours talking and comparing experiences. Eventually, we found we ran into each other more often than either of us realized. I found out that he was good friends with Thomas for a while. In addition, some of the things we did out of kindness even affected each other.

I always wanted a relationship like my foster parents had and I found myself not only feeling as an immediate part of my new family, the way Lewis and I spoke I felt comfortable, safe and as if I was reconnected with family. I won't deny that I was physically attracted to him, the fact we both shared several experiences, and I missed home much less with him here. I wasn't looking for a relationship. Except I think at this moment I was open to so many new experiences with my life changing so much, it felt natural. I first fell in love with a wonderful, patient, loving human. I learned what I wanted in a partner and how I should be loved from the way I was raised. I wasn't one to instantly fall in love and I certainly had plenty of offers growing up. Part of me was lost forever and still was when my first love died but I felt that amazing feeling of being with another person. I didn't need him, but I wanted to be with him. My soul felt healed.I didn't need time to know how I felt or what I wanted. At this very moment, I knew I was ready again to allow someone else in and fall in love.

Looking at him with no doubt in my mind. I knew he felt the same way. He lingered each hour explaining he would be leaving soon yet dawdling and not wanting to leave. I didn't want to lose his company either. Eventually, the pull had become so strong. I felt like I could burst if he made another excuse for staying longer. I didn't want to give him up. I had even started making excuses about why he had to stay longer.

"Will you do me a favor, one even greater than giving Hellen a note for me?" As I sat up on the bed so that I could see the expression on his face better. I could feel the emotion emanating from his body.

"I would do anything for you, my love." He stated without even needing to think about it.

"Will you stay here another day with me? I don't want you to leave quite yet. Maybe when you do go, I will go with you. I love my family, but I don't want to spend a day away from you. Besides, it would be nice to see Hellen again, and then I would be safe traveling with you. We would work our way back together."

"As long as you want me here, I will always stay with you, besides, I don't have a home that I need to go back to. You're my life now. I always felt connected to you, and I can see why. It's not just fated to bring us together again. There is a reason for everything. I have been my happiest when I am near you or watching over you. Even when we did not speak, I could feel you. It had been hard when I saw you in love with the human, but I knew you were happy. That alone made me happy. I didn't want to interfere, even though I still stayed around to make sure you were safe when you went into the woods. Except it also hurt when I saw you hurt. I know how much he meant to you. After so long, I didn't know how to introduce myself since I loved you so much. I thought I would scare you if I showed you who I was. Especially since I seemed to know so much about you already and I wasn't sure if I were what you would want, I only wish I had known you were Charley's sister. I knew it would be hard not knowing what you were, but then I always wondered if I could have made you feel more comfortable if you had known about me? Then your guard would have been down and who knows how the situation with the demon hunters would have turned out? I'm not your first love which was Kendrick, but I hope you can accept me?"

"I don't know how I would not be able to accept you. I loved Kendrick so much, it was heart-wrenching after he died. I never thought there would be a possibility let alone allow myself to think that way, of having a future with anyone. I would have accepted you if you had chosen to present yourself to me. I want this as much as you do. Stay here. I am sure my family will approve. I want you to stay my love." Laying down next to him, leaning as he put his arm around me pulling me closer to him.

"I promise I will never leave your side, my love." Laying there for several hours with the music from the outside slowly wafting in.

As it grew softer the ones who had been playing slowly stopped and were leaving. Then finally no music could be heard in the bedroom anymore. Then as it had stopped, Lewis began to hum the first slow tune that we danced to.

Chapter Seven
Keeping Promises

Always making it a point never to break a promise, Andrew had yet to break one and he certainly was not going to start now. After several days of travel from such a cold climate to an even colder one, the snow became so thick he even wondered if he would find the spot that he had to dig up. The trail had been easy to remember, heading through the woods following the hill to the top into an almost clear opening. With the water just on the edge of the cliffs, the fog certainly did not help him see any better. Sadly, there was nothing for him to listen to, to let him know if she was close to where he was trying to find her.

There was a private and very small cemetery at the top of the hill. Only one large building stood towering in the center. Standing in front of it he paced out about twenty steps forward. Once he hit the end closer to the farthest side of the cemetery where the hill began to slope, he planted his shovel downward and began to dig. Wanting to get it done before the new caretaker found him or saw what he was doing. Not wanting to answer questions or run into more demon hunters. Andrew wanted to get the task over with as fast as he could. He kept digging until his shovel stopped with a sudden force. He knew he found something, he hoped it was what he had been looking for. Clearing a large area, he waited a moment.

The demon hunters had been so relentless when it came to chasing after her. Never losing her trail and figuring out her personality they were able to keep up, always one step behind. With far too many near misses it was getting difficult to keep her out of harm's way, let alone not allow the others to see his gifts as he tried to protect her. They would not be shaken that the easiest thing to do had been to make it appear that she was killed and buried. Till now she sort of hibernated until it would be safe for her to come above ground again. It was a good thing she hadn't needed any air to survive under the ground. Personally, Andrew thought to himself he would have felt at least claustrophobic but at the time there wasn't anything else he could do. It was much easier to hide one person than it had been to stand against the hunters to protect a single person.

There was a slight mark on the casket, positive this was the right one. Andrew tapped on the casket waiting for a response. His answer was soon given. The top of the coffin sprung off flying. A small figure sat up reaching its delicate alabaster hand out. He took hold and pulled her up. Not that she needed his help but mainly out of regard.

"It's safe; the group I was traveling with is no longer. I didn't wish to kill them. I hoped at some point they might be swayed or reasoned with. Sadly, it was not going to happen. A situation presented itself that could not be safeguarded. I have done away with them. I promised I would come for you when it was safe. We need to get going before anyone else shows up here. This is something I prefer not to have to explain."

If anyone had seen her here, they would have assumed she was morning the dead. She wore a black lace gown that complemented her features. Charlotte had re-risen from her grave and was thankful to be out amongst the living again, even though she was not living herself. She had her reservations about Andrew, but she took a chance. He could have killed her that night she attacked him to protect herself. They had hunted her and planned on killing her. He let her go. He saved her life and here had done it again. As the fog rolled, they walked, disappearing into the rest of the night.

Not having too much planned other than to set a few things straight. The first would be to help find Charlotte's sister. When Andrew first came across Charlotte and her sister Claire, they had been separated hoping it might confuse their followers. Andrew had been rather good at tracking and predicting the natural direction one would choose to go. Therefore the group left the other sister to follow this one, she was much less predictable than the younger one had been. He had hoped because of this she might be clever enough to outsmart them and they would lose her trail.

That night Andrew sat back on his bed to relax before they took off again. It had been broad daylight and very few fugitives they were after ran during the daylight. Setting his boots off to the side of the bed, Andrew pulled the foot tub over. Days like this, if he started questioning himself, he knew he was a human when his feet ached this much.

Barely moving he could see the curtain hanging from the window swing forward slightly. A dark figure moved rather fast but no definite confirmations. However, he felt if this is what they were after this was a rather bold move for it to make. Pretending to be preoccupied with the water in the basin, keeping a vigilant watch for the corner in case of any movement, hearing the creature's breath, it stayed in the corner perhaps hoping I would forget it was there or maybe felt safe and not react when needed.

"I know you're there. If you give me a moment, I would appreciate speaking with you and perhaps saving your life. You won't get this offer from my traveling comrades." Still sitting there but now slowly taking his feet out of the water and letting them drip dry on the towel he placed on the floor. Andrew had been hoping the creature might trust him enough to at least let him speak to it, still no movement but then there had not been an attack yet.

"My group hunts your kind and they know you're here. However, I like to prevent the kills if it's possible. I only have one main question for you. Do you hunt humans?" Not that he felt this was a determining factor of why one should live. Right now, life was precious to preserve. The lives of so many mortals so that one vampire or creature could live forever was a rather high price to pay.

Still no response. Andrew grew tired of waiting. Thinking this would be one more fatality to add to the now growing number. The more creatures killed the more arrogant the group had become and the more flawless from blame the group had acted. Andrew stood away from the bed. He slowly turned now facing the creature. She had on her black lace dress leaving very little to the imagination. Her skin looked so smooth and flawless. Not even able to guess at her age Andrew felt convinced she had to have been a vampire. She showed all the characteristics of one. It had been hard to make out her skin color since she blended in with the shadow so well. Her skin at times looked like cinnamon. She looked as black as night when she stepped back into the shadow. No wonder why most would never see her in the woods. She blended too well. The only thing that seemed to give her away had been her strong scent of iron.

"I can give you two options. First, most don't care for. It's death. The second option is to let me hide you, but first I must make it look like I killed you, so they won't keep looking for you. I can help them lose your trail. If I were to pretend that I didn't see you and try to get them to move on they would just come back here or pick up on your trail again, which we have already done four times now."

"Why would you do this for me?" Her voice was so alluring and angelic sounding that others would never hear it as a voice of a demon or anything other. If most did not hunt humans Andrew was sure they would be viewed like angels just without the wings.

"I've seen a lot of injustice and I don't feel it's right. We all at some point must make that choice for ourselves, even at times when it means our own lives to save those of others. The groups I travel with are not above killing mythical creatures, or anything else that possesses particular powers that they feel a human would not possess. Anything that might be deemed a demon."

"How can I trust you? I've been lied to before, and I am sure it won't be the last. I have lived this long with no help, what can you do for me that I cannot do on my own?"

"The sun is out rather bright now, there isn't a place you could hide without being seen by my group. I can see to it that you live at least one more day. You have no reason to believe me but then why not? At this point, you have nothing to lose if you do choose to trust me. If I wanted to kill you, I could have called them at any time. I could have done it myself." Andrew walked over to the fireplace and scooped up some of the soot that had been lying on the stone floor into a cup. Now standing in front of her getting ready to explain what he would do except he was interrupted by a knock at the door.

"Andrew, who is in there with you?" The doorknob wobbled but never opened. Andrew had locked it.

Whispering now Charlotte asked, "they don't allow you company?" Smiling slightly at him now.

"No, actually they don't. One of our main rules is that none of us date or mingle, it's not safe with what we do and if another were injured because of our job it would be inexcusable. You don't have much time to choose, is it going to be life or death?" Still holding the cup firmly in his hand.

Hoping she wasn't making a mistake she made her choice. Not sure what he was going to do with the ashes until she saw him break off the leg to the chair. A streak of fire shot along his arms almost as if the fire traveled through his veins and out his fingernails lighting the chair leg on fire. Making a long blaze from the window he lit the entire side of his room on fire, creating a wall of fire that no one could have seen through the door.

"Go out the window now. This side of the building should be slightly shaded for now. Wait for me in the woods." Giving her an order before he spoke to the men on the other side.

Waiting just long enough to make sure she made it out first before he finished his plan.

"She's in here. The room is on fire. I can't get out." Now linking the fire along the side to the window the only area that had not ignited had been near him in the corner of the room. The others slammed into the door repeatedly until the old door simply gave way. Stepping through the fire, allowing his clothes to set ablaze, he had to act as though he was in pain, being dowsed not long after. Someone else had seen the woman leave but assumed she made it out safely. Not bothering to say a word assuming they knew about her the man carried buckets trying to put the fire out. Several others joined in a long line dowsing the flames until it was completely out. The small corner of the room never was touched, except for the cup that he spilled out onto the floor. One look at it and the others in his group relaxed assuming she had been consumed by the firelight.

"Guess the only thing we can do now is to try and find the trail of the other. We want to get a good look at you first. Since you didn't respond right away, we want to confirm she did not bite you." After being searched they seemed to be convinced Andrew was okay there had been no bite marks.

No marks other than the scar he received when he was little. His friend's sister before she died commented to him. "Not all are bad. Maybe you will learn yourself if you finally see yourself as an impurity." She scratched him across the inside of his arm down to the palm and all along till the tips of his fingers. It burned for days. Not sure why she did that. He felt you had to get bitten to be affected. Then a few days later after that moment he understood why she did. She gave him a rather rare gift. One he finally learned was a gift and not something someone should be condemned for having. Andrew's only regret had been not knowing the truth in time. Always wishing he could have saved the life of his childhood friend from being condemned as a demon along with his family.

Letting the others know he was going to the cemetery to make sure that the woman's body had been buried properly. Only one had come with him. This all would have been unnecessary if the one person kept their mouth shut. Sadly, the truth tends to come out of drunken mouths. The man who had seen her spoke of her in the tavern where the rest heard him.

Andrew spread a rumor rather quickly that she had been seen in the light and looked like she was not well, heading for the graveyard. Andrew paid the digger at the cemetery enough money to keep his lips shut. She lay in the bottom of the box which had been made into a secret compartment. The open viewable half had been open for others to see and the only part made of pine. A body from one of the other graves had been taken and placed on top but not before it had been charred to a point. Closing the top and watching it get lowered into the ground. It had been placed only so many feet above her friend who had been killed a few days before by another group of demon hunters.

Andrew promised her that when it was safe, he would come back and reunite her with her sister as soon as he made sure she was safe. He had come across so many other men and women, however, this is one of the very few times he felt obligated to come back. But then she was also the only one he ever watched be buried and knew still existed. Sadly, I couldn't deliver on the second part of my promise yet. I still had to finish that part.

Lately, Andrew found himself drifting into memories of the past quite often hoping to avoid the choices he made then and hopefully never to repeat them, having a carriage ready to transport the two of them. It would safely conceal her face during the daylight hours and from those who might recognize what she was.

The first stop Charlotte wanted to make had been to her home since she hadn't been there in so long. She hoped that Claire might have come there once she was safe. After traveling for a while by carriage they found the horses could only go so far before the driver said the weather had been too cold and dangerous for them. Getting out on foot both Andrew and Charlotte took the very few items they had with them and walked through the snow. The cold hadn't affected Andrew since he could warm himself at will. Charlotte never noticed the cold since her skin had already been ice cold. Anyone out this far would have been very much like us or too busy getting to where they needed to go to notice anything about us, other than the fact we were dangerously underdressed for this kind of weather.

There had been no trail to follow other than the ledge of the mountain they followed with a row of trees on the other side of it. Halfway up they could see the mansion come into view. They had probably only walked slightly a few hours at the most. At least they did not have to worry about any towns this way. Most towns were built not far from the waterways, or at least near some sort of transportation area. Up here it was so remote that nothing could get through. No fear of others seeing them or being around them. At home had truly been where Charlotte could be herself.

The large gargoyles looked menacing as they loomed over the front steps. Walking up the stone path that lay covered in the deep snow. Some jutted up a little from breaking from such frigid cold weather.

Before they were close enough to the door it slowly opened to reveal a man standing there dressed quite nicely. With a big smile on his face, he warmly greeted Charlotte with a hug.

"I rather figured you might never come back here. With a lot of rumors floating around, it's diffficult to tell what happened with you and your sister. I was passing through so I thought I would stop here before I moved on. Good to see you back, where is the little sis anyway? I didn't think you would be back without her." Mathais stepped away from the door walking toward the parlor room with Charlotte and Andrew following behind him.

Mathais sat behind the piano and began playing a tune, switching between several different slow melodies. "If you need any help finding her, I will offer my services if you felt you need me. Is he human or vampire?" Mathais Nodded in my direction.

"Not entirely sure. He has an unusual gift. He controls fire and wind, at least from what I can witness from him. He also shadows as I do. He has never been bitten or born from a vampire line. I think he might be an original, however, he did get the gift from a young girl before she died, and she managed to infect him. We should be fine. If you're in earshot, I will call. Did you hear in the rumors where they said she might be?"

Mathais stopped playing, turning around to face the others he thought for a moment. "Most of us have been avoiding the towns for now since they seem to be in an unstable frenzy of their own. Many creatures had been sticking closer to the colder climates away from the shipping and carriage trails, with fewer people and towns to compete with. The last rumor I heard was that she went to the far east and got herself trapped. Having a human side is a rather nasty downfall, would have been better if you killed off that side. She was drugged and is now in an asylum. It is possible to be crazy but I'm sure not for what they are holding her for. If it's true you're not going to want her there for too long."

"Then first thing in the morning we will leave for the east and see if we can find her. I won't need sleep however I need to get a few things before we travel in case, she needs something."

Getting up quickly from her chair. Charlotte walked to the towering staircase that pretty much dwarfed the parlor. The whole room looked as if it had been built around the staircase making it the main centerpiece and not the actual art and instruments. There had been one large u-shaped balcony in the center with stairs coming winding down on either side of the room. The staircase looked and felt like it was made from marble. Much of the house had been built with stone and marble, a very secure and expensive-looking structure. From the looks of it being different ages, it had shown she had been around for quite some time.

Charlotte grabbed a large leather bag and began filling it with a few items of clothing, and a few pieces of food that would survive the trip. Figuring Claire might be hungry when they found her. A few first aid pieces since her sister still had been half-human. She used to be half-human herself until her acidic vampire half took over completely. Some would survive the process and others would simply turn to dust the second the transformation had been completed. Always being puzzled by this she wasn't sure why when she had been bitten why she didn't lose her humanity altogether as most had. Her host parents explained venom worked differently with some vampires and could even take years or decades to spread depending on how they did it.

Not wanting to delay too much, Charlotte made sure she had all the supplies she might need to bring with her. Momentarily she had a sickening feeling in her stomach. Glad that she had Andrew with her to help. She wasn't sure what she might be dealing with, especially if the humans or whoever is holding her sister discovered who and what she is.

The night had not passed on very quickly. At some time during the night, Mathais left. When he said he was going to stay for a short visit he meant it. Before he left, he told Andrew he was going to make a brief stop out east so he would be in the area for a short time. Just in case he was needed he wanted to be made available. If he were needed all she had to do was say his name out loud and he would be there.

Chapter Eight
Claire

I know my life keeps moving regardless of if I am aware.
I feel I am no longer moving forward I have not fallen behind.
As if I could grasp my hand and I might be able to hold on.
Not knowing what to hold onto or when to let go.
Such an inward feeling I feel so lost.
Still, hopefully, I find myself soon or no one else will.
The drugs enjoy consuming me.
Even when it's a heart that never beats.
Everything I see reminds me of you.
I swear your face appears in the shadows.
So many choices to be made.
So, few to be chosen from.
Fear of causing pain.
Fear of holding back.
Fear of never risking.
Fear of never trying.

Obscured Darkness

My heart wrenching in pain.
No longer the simple choices of childhood.
Fear of emotional isolation.
Fear of being loved.
Fearful to trust.
Afraid to be trusted.
To open completely to have it not returned.
Making the wrong choice.
Making the wrong move.
When am I right and not wrong?
Having one to connect so close.
Beating together as one heart.
Fear consumes and protects me.
A little voice whispers.
Don't worry do not fear.
For what you fear most
Will not come near.
With a playful laugh
All things will become clear.
There is time for things to pass.
And in a short while, things will improve
Anxiety and pain will be put away.
Look for new hope every day the breath of life!
Fresh and new
Will come knocking on the door for you.

Claire had been found writing this message on the wall of a tunnel in her blood hoping her sister would recognize the blood scent. There had been enough to pick up the scent for several miles, even when it dried it would be picked up on even further out. She had written it knowing her sister would not only know it was her blood but also what mental state she was in. The demon hunter who managed to fool her, the very one who enslaved her now, at this point she wasn't sure what was real and what had been made up in her head, she felt so confused.

Claire could hear her cursed name "Maggie" they had given her at the hospital being spoken. She had been injected with so many shots she could barely move. This had been one of the rare occasions she hated having a human side to her. Other than seeing white coats approach her, she temporarily blackened out, partially for losing so much blood and the mixture of so many drugs in her system. The one who held her tested her to see what drugs would do to a half-breed. At some point, he figured her out and wanted to be able to duplicate the process among other things.

The doc always renamed his patients in case they would get lost or die. This way if anyone had been reported missing, they would not connect the two and know he had been holding them against their will. In addition, another way he would brand his patients so that people would know they came from the asylum had numbers on their arm. Even I was stuck with a number tattoo.

"Too bad the old hospital had to close; it would have been safer for her to stay there. The longer she stays with us the worse she gets. I'm wondering if she's having withdrawals from her medications since she's sweating and shaking so much? The old doctors seemed to know how to reach her mentally, we can't seem to break into her head. Her old doctor passed away however I think it's his son that has taken over."

"Why did the Maple house close anyway? It had a good reputation and then there were those pathetic stories that went around. Do you know what happened there?"

"It's a tragedy, several of the doctors were found dead. They think two of the patients were involved but as for the rumors, it's hard to tell. This is one they suspected. She ran away again, and we were the first that caught her, so we are doing a routine check on her at the request of her doctor. There is always some sort of truth to a rumor and whether they were abusing patients or not we might never know. Right now, there's no one to regulate them. The second suspect has not been caught; this one was only caught because she was so doped up on drugs."

"Looks like she's in for more testing than normal, I'll up her medication amount and hope it helps."

"How long has she been in the current Maple Institution?"

"Sadly, not long, but if she has been there, she has managed to escape at least four times. Would have been nice for her to have a different outcome or at least a better one than her mother had."

"What do you mean by that? I guess I don't quite follow?" Leaning against the desk with his back now towards Maggie.

"Her mother had been a patient herself and somehow got herself pregnant by a visitor or one of the times she broke out herself. At least that was the explanation the doctor gave us. Maggie has never been quite right, probably from all the medications her mother was on, she never had a chance. She grew up at the Maple House Institute until it had been closed recently. She's been moved to different places but was to stay at the new facility for now. The doctor's son changed the name to Mable House, not sure why he chose to change only the first name and didn't make much of a change, its eerily similar. Even though it doesn't seem any different from the last one." Leaning over the counter he continued to sign medical information papers for Maggie.

Maggie had been laying on a cot half in and out of consciousness, she tried committing suicide earlier except she was caught by the caregiver of the hospital she was at, at least this had been the story they told her. She didn't know when she was in her world or theirs. Her own made sense while the story twisted and turned so much; she didn't know what the truth was anymore. Maggie could hear the conversation they were having about her and disagreed with everything they said. The person they spoke about hadn't been her. As doped as she was, she knew she wasn't like that, she wished she could have long enough to let her head clear. The older doctor tried hiding the fact that she would never die. Therefore, he passed her off as a daughter of a patient.

The doctor himself was not dead and neither did he have a son. He found what would make him immortal. The whole reason he held onto her. The only problem had been that I refused to bite him. He couldn't understand how I could have been bitten and be permanently marked with the scar and still be half-human. Even I didn't have the answer to that one. As he withdrew the venom with test tubes it didn't react the way he hoped. He wasn't trying to turn himself into a fully-fledged one.

Watching one of her caregivers talking with the doctor, her eyes kept flitting open and closed. Not sure if she imagined it or not, she tried to sit on the gurney without the others watching her. They had been deep in conversation when they turned and saw the straps were no longer on her. They had been unhooked hanging from the sides of the bed and she was gone again. Security had been called in with all staff searching for her.

There had been so many parts to the hospital but then it had to care for such a large area. It would be easy to get lost here. Trying not to be noticed, Claire stepped into a room as a few doctors walked by searching for her. She hadn't been off the gurney for too long by the time they noticed she escaped.

Stepping back out into the hallway she put on a white jacket that had been left in the last room. Hoping no one would notice her right away only glancing and seeing the coat, she worked her way down the hallway which seemed to have no one in. Almost turning the corner, a man with white pants and a beige top saw her heading quickly in his direction. Stepping into another room hoping he would run by; she hid in the dark corner of the room at first.

Grant had been surprised she didn't lock the door behind her. Standing to one side he pushed it open with his elbow, ready to stand to one side. After all, he didn't have any weapons on him let alone own a gun. Grant only knew a little of Tae Kwon Do, at least what his friend taught him. Not that it would save him from a bullet if she had gotten her hands on a gun. Scanning the room. Everything seemed to be intact. He knew it would not have been difficult for someone to get in here except it had been one of the few rooms that did not have a window so there was only one way out.

Taking a slow step into the room he could see the lunchroom, everything seemed to be there, the door to the private bathroom off to the right with the door open. He walked over and peaked in, no one was in there. Then slowly walking back to the other side of the lunchroom he could walk directly into the sitting room away from the tables. Nothing seemed to be out of place other than a wrapper on the table. Taking a closer look, it wasn't his. Half startled his immediate reaction as he turned and punched in the direction that he heard the sound, stopping as soon as he saw who it was. He never made contact thankfully the object moved from his striking hand.

Half slurring the words trying to act soberer than she had physically been. "Big shocker I can do that also. Here's your name tag and a few other things you left. Well, sort of left it; I took it out of your pocket. I'm borrowing your jacket since I'm cold. Don't follow me. You don't understand what I'm trying to get away from." Slumped against the wall trying to sound convincing I hadn't heard anyone out in the hallway. Opening the door and closing it Grant didn't try and follow me until I was at the end of the hallway heading outside. He stood there and watched as I left.

Another doctor passed him asking if he had seen anyone come this way. Explaining he came from this direction himself and he hadn't seen anyone. He then told them he couldn't get into the lunchroom because the door was locked. Grant locked the door on his way out. A few others assumed she was in there; they started breaking down the door as Grant walked away from them. Frustrated once they were in the room not finding her, they kept searching.

People in white coats looked like they were frantically searching around the hospital not just inside but also scouring the grounds trying to find her before she escaped too far. They underestimated how far she could go in such a short time. Only a few ventured out to the street. Not that you could see far with all the trees blowing over the road from the strong wind. Needing to be careful enough not to be noticed, I could have escaped and made a clean run for it again, but I knew the others would never be safe. I had to find a way of making it safe for the others also. There were four others still in the old building locked up and I knew I had to save them. There was no way I would have committed suicide, not when I promised I would get them out.

Walking along the road a horse-drawn omnibus slowed down on the cobbled street next to me. Assuming I was just another drunk which seemed like a lot of his passengers were lately, he thought nothing of it at first until I gave him the address of the place I wanted to go. I told him how I just wanted to go home and sober up. 1152 Evergreen way. Still not in my right mind I slipped into one of my favorite dreams.

After traveling for a while, the carriage driver stopped the carriage and got down from his seat. He could see I had fallen asleep again. Not wanting to wake me and feeling in no hurry he sat in the seat opposite me and watched me rest feeling I must need it. Then he also hoped maybe with a little bit of rest I might be able to make a better sound judgment call on not being left here at this place. In my current state he didn't feel I would be safe alone. Why would a lady want to stay here? Even more curious he was wondering about the outfit I was wearing. Taking his jacket while I slept, he laid it over me to keep me warm. When he saw me starting to stir, he hadn't wanted to upset me being alone in there with him he started talking to me right away.

"Miss, are you sure you want to be left here? There hasn't been anyone in this place for a while now. This place has fallen apart so much it should be condemned." The carriage driver sat patiently almost expecting me to change my mind and climb back into the stagecoach.

"I know what I am doing. I'll be fine; I used to live here before it was closed. I plan on fixing the place back to its former glory. This was once an amazing building full of history and beauty. But sadly, was used for very evil things. I plan on making sure those things never happen again. Don't know how I am going to do it though. I need to start at some point, thank you for the quick ride here and concern." With that, I waved goodbye to the coach driver and began walking towards the old hospital. I knew that was a flimsy and sad excuse but the way I was feeling so ill was the only thing I could think of.

"I swear my passengers keep getting crazier every time." Closing the door to the carriage behind her, he stared after the woman wondering if she was in her right mind.

He was curious if he should try and help or do at least something? Looking at the dilapidated old hospital, why would anyone come here to fix it up let alone pretend it was their home? Picking up the reigns he took off for the nearest town to make a report on the woman. Not sure if she was an old patient or a woman who lost her mind. He felt bad leaving her there, but if there had been something wrong with her, he did not want to risk dealing with it. He reasoned to himself that after a while she may sober up on her own.

Stopping in the very small hospital that appeared on the edge of town. "Hey, I don't know what your policy is on this but one of my carriage passengers was loopy, she might have a legit reason for being there, but I think she needs to be checked out. It's like she's living in another world." Thinking he was doing a good thing by making sure she was protected he was turning her over to the worst people possible.

"Thank you for informing us. We will have one of our attending doctors come and check it out." After the conversation, the coach driver didn't want to stick around. One last thought of the old place sent a shiver up his spine.

Determined and stubborn even though she was very weak feeling she managed to shove the Iron Gate door open. If she didn't have so many medications pumping through her, opening the door would have been no problem. Opening the door, I saw that not much had changed. Perhaps several layers of dust collected, but the furniture looked as beautiful as it had when it was new, it just needed cleaning. Walking into the main room stopping in front of the check-in window before you could get to the patients' rooms. Grabbing a small waiting room chair and slammed it into the glass, having to break the glass that separated me from the lock on the other side of the door. Climbing up over the counter I could unlock the office door but sadly the main door through the hallway had been bolted shut.

Old lace curtains still hanging on the walls with thick dust clinging to them, many unraveling from being uncared for, and several portraits of the girls who worked at the old place wearing their old nurse's uniforms. All the girls were either sitting in chairs, couches, or standing. All wearing Victorian-style gowns with hair swept up or off to the side for the portrait. Looking at them you would never know they had been nurses; you would have assumed it had been a private residence. The doctor liked more of a relaxed atmosphere. Not that any of the staff ever stayed for very long, usually by the doctor's choice. He seemed normal until he found the one downfall that destroyed him mentally. The ability to live forever changed his personality. Before he seemed humble then after he turned evil desiring control and power. Even though the few of us that knew about his change wondered how long he had been like this. He was very good at hiding his true self only when others knew the truth he didn't hold back. His true personality came out. We had assumed he was like this as a human only it became like an infection and became worse when he had changed. None of us had known about his real change we could only assume. He wasn't a hybrid like many others.

The wind picked up while a storm began brewing. I could feel the cold wind blowing in with cold drizzling rain. I hoped to find something or figure out some way of stopping the doctor from infecting any more or harming the others. Now that he had gone power hungry believing he was now invincible and leaving a bad name for vampires and other creatures that existed.

Unfortunately, throughout history, he is the one that people would remember since the good ones do not make names for themselves or they would be found out. The unwritten law that was understood by most had been to keep their secret at all costs, to keep it from those who feared the unknown or from those who would misuse it to harm and control others.

Walking into one of the rooms trying to remember where in

the hospital I was at now. The only thing that had been in the room was a coat rack and an empty chair with a bookcase in the corner. However, for me, it could have been anything I wanted it to be. Lost in my delusion the image came to life. I could have sworn I saw another person in the room with me.

"What are you doing here? I've been here for a while and have yet to see another person come out this far to the coast."

Startled, I quickly turned and slipped being caught by the hard floor.

"I'm here to fix the place up. I have history here. I purchased this place recently and didn't know anyone had been entering it." I knew I lied to this person, but I did not want to give myself away since I was still very drowsy.

Even being out of it. I still had it ingrained into my mind that I needed to protect myself.

"I assumed it was abandoned. After all, most do not want to be in here after they know what it was used for. I have family history here also, probably more than most." He walked over to the floor and sat down next to me looking very comfortable. "Tell me about your family or how you're connected." Resting his hand on my knee.

"I would be more comfortable if your hand was not on me." Shifting slightly so he would get the hint to take his hand away.

"Sorry I made you uncomfortable I tend to get relaxed when I'm here." Taking his hand back he stood up and walked over to the old rocking chair still perched in the corner with what looked like a very old baby blanket laying over the top of it.

"You remind me so much of one of the ladies who used to live here. You could have been her twin." Picking up the folder that had been on the dresser near him he got up and handed it to me.

Taking the folder from him and opening it up I noticed some

of the pictures, they were the same as the ones I had seen on the wall but only from a different angle.

"How were these done? It looks like there was another person handling pictures," It looked like he was holding my suitcase I used to own except he was opening it to take out the pictures I collected I kept in it.

"My pictures came from my side of the family, when she was here, I don't think others knew her real talent or she might not have shared it with anyone? As the professional must have drawn their portraits she saw the same profile and drew it herself." Watching him with interest I hadn't remembered seeing him working here before. Why would he have my suitcase? It had been destroyed when we took off running. Slowly images of Charlotte started clouding my mind making all of this seem so confusing.

"Sorry, where are my manners, I should have introduced myself to you with a bit of information that will help, as he reached out to shake my hand, he was about to say his name and then as suddenly as I had seen him, he vanished as if blending in with the air around them.

Just another illusion that didn't exist, this was not only confusing but also made it so difficut to accomplish what I was here for. If I could keep my mind, I could be free from this place soon. Sitting in the dark with the oil lamp on the floor, I sat there shivering in the cold. So, fascinated and enthralled by what the coat rack had been saying to me.

There had been an oil lamp in the corner however I decided to keep it unlit for now. Mainly to prevent anyone from seeing in hoping the figures I saw in the darkness are not there. Knowing if I saw them in the daylight will only confirm I had either lost my mind or there is truth in what I saw.

Laying back on the cold hard floor I let my daydreams take

control. Only there it seems to have some form of sanity. Even at this point, I continued to call out for my sister in my mind. But I never could tell if I was speaking out loud or not. Each day I felt as if Claire was disappearing, and Maggie had become more of a real person than I had been in the past.

A sudden burst of cold air and cold rain hit my face waking me temporarily into reality again. With the wind stinging my face, the weather was getting much worse outside as we were getting closer to winter. Sliding myself further away from the window to block the rain and wind not that there was anything to block the weather from coming in. Cutting my hand on a small piece of glass that had come loose from the window, most likely when snow fell from the roof it hit the window on the way down. Even with the bars on the windows ice and snow from previous winters or even bad storms still managed to break the window at times. Managing to leave a small trail of blood from where I had been laying on the floor, now leaning against the other wall just as cold, slowly slipping back onto the floor.

Trying again to walk along on the floor I hadn't been successful there either. With no shoes on I stepped on the glass also embedding some of it into my foot so that I no longer bled from just my left hand, I was leaving fingerprints of my blood along the wall as I walked, I also left bloody footprints. As I made it into another room, I could smell the old stench from the asylum that used to make me sick. The treatments the doctor would use would leave some so badly burned. The smell of rotting flesh, embalming fluid as well as other things he would mix still lingered in the air. Before it only came from one end of the building. Now with it crumbling and falling apart, it whisked through the whole place.

Before blacking out again for a short time I didn't know if I had imagined it or seen my sister in the blood that was pooling on the floor. She was with someone I only slightly recognized. I felt I must be losing it since it had been the hunter that separated us in the first place. Why would my sister choose to travel with a person like that? He would have killed her, not stayed with her. She wore a different outfit from what I had last seen her in, her navy-blue riding dress with her heeled boots. She traveled on foot with the stranger trying to keep up with her. Not seeing much more I slipped down on the floor and passed out again, my blackouts lasting longer each time. I wasn't sure if the last of the medicine was kicking in or if my body was finally fighting it off by forced sleep.

The feeling of being moved around started waking me from my deep sleep, leaning against the wall now looking down at myself I was aware of how little clothing I had. At one time I had the hospital gown on with only my underwear and the doctor's jacket I had taken. At some point, I lost the gown even though I vaguely remember not wanting to be recognized. I had taken it off. Already cold the air felt worse. Trying to remember I couldn't remember where I put my dressing gown. Damn doctors for leaving me in a gown and not my clothes. At first, they had taken my undergarments away from me saying I might strangle myself with them, protectively putting my hands over my belly rubbing it, the blood from my hand covering it as I rubbed it.

Standing up again sliding against the wall to the doorway, I was no longer in the same room and didn't remember how I had gotten here. So much was going through my mind that I couldn't keep straight the real from the unreal. Stepping out into the hallway. I slumped forward and fell to the floor.

"Soon all of this will be over" I whispered to my belly. Looking up at the end of the hallway I could see a curtain coming loose from the end window coming towards me. As it was getting closer. The curtain was black and flying violently towards me. I felt this must be my entrance into hell. The demons were coming for me. Stopping abruptly, it retreated. I wasn't sure why until I heard the voices. Their voices garbled so much that I could not understand a word it was saying to me. Then I realized it was asking me for my name.

"Do you know who you are? Miss, are you okay?" The young doctor placed a wool blanket around me trying to keep me from freezing anymore. He could see that I was covered with blood. Most of the blood had come from my hand and the few cuts on my feet. I felt so out of it that I didn't even know when he pt the soft shoes on my feet. Calling out loud to his partner for him to come in and assist him with me he had chosen not to move me in case I was injured. He waited for his partner to come in with the flat board he planned to place me on.

Still not in my right mind, thinking I was outwitting the demon. I said my name was Scarlett. I hadn't given it a thought if I could trust him or not. Thinking if he thought I was someone else I might buy more time before the baby was born. My eyes fluttered shut as I went back into my own created reality. The man who originally trapped me here made it clear he wanted my baby. The one I had been escaping from. He saw my baby as a tool he could use and control. I didn't want it used to kill. If hell existed, I wasn't sure if it would be where I would end up if I died at this moment, however, it no longer scared me compared to what I had already been through.

I wanted no connections to the doctor for my baby. He had gotten me pregnant along with several women when he was trying to create his army. He was rather disappointed when he found that not all were half breeds. Neither did he know how to stop the vampire part to stop killing the human half. When the human half became far too weak the vampire side would completely take over. They were uncontrollable which is what one of the doctors found out the hard way. They destroyed him. Very few lived. Many turned to dust quickly as soon as their human half was gone.

Slightly lost in my delusion I could have been anyone at this point. At least in my delusions, I started thinking about what I needed. I wanted to find the address and hoped to find it here, a way to find the doctor. He was still alive; no one had seen him only dealing with notes or messages passed on by others. I knew he was wounded, and I wanted to destroy him before he killed more innocent people. He fed off his patients, even the ones who he felt had been failures in his experiments. After laying here for a while. I remembered why I was here and fighting so hard.

The grey almost smoky black walls had been so depressing when I was forced to be here before as they still loomed out at me in a menacing way. Now there had been two men hovering over me, the one lifting me putting me on a flat board, the other placing another blanket over me to keep me warm. They looked at me as I made eye contact with them. I hadn't recognized either as the ones who worked for the old doctor. They must have worked for the hospital that he was supposed to collect me from earlier.

"Miss, my name is Grant, and I am doing what I can to help you. Unfortunately, you are ice cold and can die if we can't get you warmer; we are taking you to the hospital to get care. They will know if your baby is okay or not. We won't know until then, are you able to hear us or understand us?"

Barely above a whisper, I said, "please don't take me from here. I need to find some people. I can't leave without them. I don't have a cold of any kind, I'm always cold."

"I'm sorry we can't do that; we need to get you medical attention now. Not just for your baby but also for you, if you want to live. This isn't a home you're at. No one else is here. If you understand us, we know your name is Margaret Mallory Lynn. They are ready at the hospital to help you the best they can, but we need to get you there."

"My name is not Margaret that is not even my mother's name; it's the one they made up. My mother died years ago. My real name is Claire. I had been convinced it was Maggie for a while, but I at least know who I am." I had such a hard time holding back my frustration. As soon as I said that the ground began to shake violently. It felt like an earthquake hitting at that exact moment. The two men tried their best to steady the flat board. The old hospital had been in a state of such ill repair, parts of it had begun to crumble. Now with the violent tremors, the walls were also falling apart.

"The demon wants my baby; he doesn't care if I live or not. He doesn't care if you live either, therefore I must have it here don't you understand? The real reason this place was closed had been the curse put on it. He couldn't enter it anymore. A witch cursed the place against him to protect those who were stuck there. The protection won't work forever and I must get them out. If I have my baby outside, they will get it one way or another and will kill the others." I knew I must have sounded crazy, but the doctor truly had made himself into a demon and others not seeing the truth still viewed him as a respectable man.

As soon as I finished speaking the floor beneath the men crumbled and gave way causing them to lose grip on the flat board, I fell to the floor below them.

The two men barely held onto the floor they were on sticking to the small piece along the sides that had not separated from the wall. The tremors kept shaking for hours after but the major one stopped for now. The tremor lasted long enough to give me time to get away. Not sure where the tremors were coming from since earthquakes normally didn't hit this area and when they did it had been so rare.

One of the doctors who was genuinely concerned and never worked for the old doctor could do nothing but watch from a distance as I climbed off the gurney, as I barely slid myself along the hall below. Pulling at a door it led to a staircase to one of the many narrow passages that at one time linked several of the mental hospital buildings together. Some overtime caved in while others were still barely passable. My sight had still been impaired as I tried to get to the room I needed to. Unable to handle the stairs falling sideways I went plummeting down to the lower floor. The last view I could see had been the door closing behind me and a white figure came floating down behind me. As soon as Grant had seen me fall, he took a risk and jumped down.

Hoping he was not a fool for doing this or risking even falling through a third floor, he jumped down where I had originally fallen. Walking along the wall following the light bloodstain that I left, he followed it until it came to a handle. Opening the door, he could see where I had fallen to the bottom of the steps.

Something unexpected happened. From behind him, he felt the strongest gush of wind blow behind him and a large black shadow almost a mist flew right past him. It had been enough to give him chills, straight out of a nightmare. Following the stairs down it seemed like they came to a dead end. There was nothing more than a brick wall. Odd to have a set of stairs go straight to a dead-end at the bottom, why would she come in here unless she kne where she was going? The woman had been laying here a moment ago. She wasn't down here now so where could she have gone? He hadn't seen her come back up. Turning facing the way out now leaning against the wall he looked up at the stairs.

Odd how it seemed like so much fog was rolling around up top by the door.

After leaning on the wall for a moment the wall jerked back and Grant almost lost his footing. Stepping forward to turn around to see what happened to the wall. It had moved back enough that he could see there was another room and it had been perfectly intact. Pushing at the wall as hard as he could to make it move further, it had only moved a little more. Not as much as he would have liked but enough so that he could squeeze in. The blood trail hadn't ended before the stone wall continued after showing she did come in here.

This room looked nothing like the rest of the hospital; it looked perfect, almost brand new. No one would have ever assumed this was here, judging the outside of the place and the rest of the rooms on the other floors. This tunnel had not caved in like so many of the others. It looked like it had even been kept up. Walking along the path there was a door to his right with a bloodstain on it. Hesitating for a moment he took the handle and opened the door. Not sure what he would see he swung the door open quickly.

She must have wanted to escape even though it had been against his better judgment he wanted to find out what she searched for so desperately, that she was willing to risk her life as well as her child. Figuring if she wanted to be called Claire, he would call her that for now. Inside the room, it looked like a mini office that could investigate three patients' rooms. The patient rooms were nothing more than glass-enclosed rooms with one bed per room.

Just like Claire had said there were still three people in here. She was struggling with the clasps as Grant walked over and started to help her unhook them. The first and second person was still laying still, he thought they were already dead having no heartbeat. The third one had no heartbeat as well. Only continuing to help unhook them he hoped it might give her some peace of mind. Moving Claire over to the extra bed in the main room he had tried to get her to lay down, instead she sat down on the cold floor, trying to figure out how to get the others out. Looking up in astonishment the beds were now empty. Now he was beginning to wonder if he was losing it himself. Maybe it wasn't Claire who was crazy, but this place did it to you?

"I did what I promised I would. I didn't forget them. I came back. We weren't weak, we just couldn't get that metal off. It's mixed with something strange, it makes us weak." My head was spinning as I started going completely numb. I wondered if my human side had finally given up enough that I was finally dying. I hoped my baby would not disintegrate with me and would be safe.

Grant placed his hands on my shoulders, trying to get me to respond or wake up. I had been in a wonderful dream; I was home with my sister in front of the fireplace reading books. It was like a horrible jolt to reality. The whole scene of my being in the hospital took me for a moment from my dream, waking me back to the cold damp floor, remembering the look on the doctor's face. The image of my sister and the stranger with her disappeared, they were no longer there. Now the current pain I felt took over. Grant tried to get me to drink something. Not fully trusting it I hadn't wanted to drink it from memories of things being forced on me here. The pain was burning, and I started to feel numb again. I knew he was doing something but wasn't sure what since I could barely see him. Was he drugging me again? I was hoping to sober up at some point to feel normal again. I began to wonder if I would ever feel like myself again. The pain and burning I felt left me wanting to be anywhere but here.

The stone floor was no comfort to me either. Seeing the stairs again the vision of the doctor disappeared. The figure in the white coat got larger. He had moved my knees back. My stomach was seizing up in pain. I couldn't tell if he was doing this to me or if the baby was coming. I didn't know what to expect and I didn't know if my sister could handle the birth if she had known I was pregnant. I had been separated from my sister at least for four years. More than any other time I wished she were here with me.

"I'm here to help, the baby is coming, and right now you're having contractions. As soon as the baby is born, we are going to move you out of here. It's not safe and we are expecting another quake. We need to get you to safety." We could both hear from the man still upstairs. He was not only speaking about the urgency of the quakes but also how angry the doctor was getting, waiting for his patient to be brought out. Angry enough he was failing at holding back his real personality, willing to risk the life of a mother and child to bring them out now instead of waiting for the baby to be born safely first.

Grant spoke to me again trying to calm me hoping the doc upstairs wasn't upsetting me too much. The voice felt so soothing and comforting. Like it had come from one of the few I felt safe with. One of the very few I had confided with about the abuse I went through. However, I knew he was not one of them, would he end up dead also along with the others? The doctor who I trusted the most was going to get me out also. I had been told he died and they would not tell me how other than I supposedly snapped and killed him. Did I? I never knew if it were true, but then how would I be able to find the truth in this place? Then there were many times I came in and out and did not remember anything. When I had been over-drugged, I couldn't remember several days at a time. I could have done anything if I were unable to be alert enough to control my actions. Would I kill this doctor? My eyes fluttered again with the pain so intense I was in and out quite a bit.

Grant laid a large jacket on my stomach not sure why he was covering me up more until I realized there was a baby wrapped in his jacket. He placed my son on my stomach so I would know he was not trying to take the baby from me.

"What else are you trying to get in here? Maybe if you tell me I can help you find it; it would be safer for me to move around than have you move around with the baby." Grant sat down next to me helping me balance the baby on my stomach as I moved him up in my upper arm so I could get a better look.

"I am trying to find the address of the main doctor who practiced here. I know his new facility is basic but that's not where he does his testing, it's his own home. I know you won't fully understand why and might even find me a criminal for the reason that I need to find him. However, he can't get away with what he has done. Rumors all have some grain of truth to them; at least it is the way that I had been raised. Please help me find him. He needs to be exposed or he will keep testing on innocent people. Others will keep trusting him and bring those to him thinking he is helping them when he has no intent on helping. There's a woman who checks on him and he always leaves her a clue. We must find it. He keeps records of all those he goes through. He has a great memory but it's for those under him." I looked at him hoping he would not attempt to bring me back to the new hospital.

"It's just not safe to look through here for it. I know where the old doctor lived; a lot of people have talked about how fabulous his house was when he was alive. His son is outside right now. We can speak with him out there. If you will trust me, tell me what I can do to help you? I can bring you there. But I need to know what you plan on doing."

"I need proof for the humans; otherwise, they only see me as a crazy person going against someone they think they can trust. I can't tell you; you would never understand unless you saw the things that he did or what I went through. I won't be able to handle it on my own. I need my sister," holding the baby as close as I could, trying to stand up, Grant helped me, "if he knows your helping me, he will kill you. Just pretend you don't know anything. I could knock you out that way he won't assume you know anything other than trying to do your job. It's safer if you stay away from me. I don't want you to die." Starting to feel a little stronger and able to think a little clearer.

I held my son in one arm as I stood near the wall. I wanted to show Grant or perhaps to scare him off so that he would know what he was getting into. I smashed my hand through the stone wall smashing it to pieces.

"I'm not human, at least not anymore. I don't know what I am anymore. I'm having a hard enough time fighting this, but the doctor isn't human either. You're human and very vulnerable, you won't be able to stand against him. When I'm not as influenced by the drugs, he gave me I will be much stronger and faster. Once I find my sister, she will know how to handle it."

"I can't leave you; I need to make sure you're going to be okay. Strangely enough, I believe you, please don't fight me. I want to help but the first thing I need to do is to get you out of here. Dr. Denthre is getting so angry out there that he's not acting like someone safe I would want to hand you over to. From the way he's reacting and if what you're saying is true, then most likely he is going to kill me like he did the others who tried to help you. I can help you get the proof, but we need to get going to prove it. The only way out I know is straight up. This tunnel looks too dark; I don't know if we can even get out at this end."

Following behind me I walked down further down the tunnel until I stopped. There was a bright light with a flaming blaze shooting through it, and then it stopped rather quickly. There were a few more minor tremors but nothing that prevented us from standing.

"Do you see the flames coming from the hole in the ground?" Looking at Grant who was now standing next to me looking down the narrow hallway trying to figure out what he saw.

"Yeah, I saw it and am not sure where the fire came from, I'm not sure if we should get any closer." Grant placed his hand on my shoulder trying to hold me back without griping me, pulling me back tightly trying to protect me from the unknown source of the fire. Slowly a hole started to form right above us.

"I can see my sister. She's up there but she's with someone I don't know. It's safe we can go up to it, I just don't know where the fire came from?" Claire could sense her sister's smell and know beyond any doubt it was her and things would be okay.

Things had quieted down from the other side of the tunnel. I wasn't sure to assume Denthre left or if they were quietly coming down?

While I was talking, I continued to walk forward with Grant walking behind me nervous but still not wanting to let me out of his sight. As soon as I got ahead of him, he saw a man jump down in front of me. Handing the baby up to the arms waiting above, then he took me in his arms and helped me up, out through the hole. Then he came back down and looked at Grant. Grant was trying so hard to climb up the side and making no progress. He felt sick not being able to protect her and this person jumps in and moves her to where he couldn't see her anymore. The moment of panic on her face scared him more than anything even though she seemed to trust the hands that came down after.

"Do you need help getting up; it's quite a way up there." Andrew seemed surprised to see a human down here helping Claire out.

Andrew was wondering if the baby was his and how he got involved, did he know he was with a vampire? Most wouldn't be trying to follow one if they knew.

"Yeah, probably wouldn't hurt since I'm not a climber." Accepting his help, he pushed him up the side. He barely had to do anything he could tell how strong this guy was from just how fast he pushed him to the surface. Being curious himself he wondered more of what Claire was let alone this guy who came to save them. Then a second of panic wondering if it was safe being with them and wondering if he had still lost his mind.

Once up there, Grant saw a woman hugging Maggie or Claire, he wasn't sure what to call her. He had been curious about who they were and how they burrowed such a deep hole into the ground let alone knew this was the direction she chose to go. He also wanted to know where the fire had come and gone.

Chapter Nine
More Complications

It hadn't looked like Dr. Denthre stuck around, only the other medic who was back at the building, not that he was looking in our direction. The three of us went walking away with Grant in tow. Not sure if he should follow or just choose to walk away and pretend the past few hours never really happened. He knew he would get questioned by his workmate and he certainly didn't want to walk into Denthre trying to explain to him what happened or what he found out. He was sure by now that he had to know.

"Fill us in, why do you look like such hell and weak? And where the hell did this baby come from? Is it his?" Walking in the opposite direction away from the hospital, you could barely see it in the distance as they sat down next to the tree.

Charlotte pulled out a fresh pair of clothes and helped her

sister get dressed shielding her for as much privacy as she could give her out there. Right now, all she had on was a blanket and a jacket while the baby was wrapped in a jacket.

"First to start, the baby is mine. After we split, I went running south, except I ran into a group down there. They searched after me for a while until I lost them. As I was hiding, this doctor who seemed nice started talking to me while I was sitting in the park. I wasn't feeling well, and he offered to treat me, however, I told him it would be best not to since my situation was a little different, and that I would be fine soon. He pointed out that his hospital wasn't very far. We could see it from where we were sitting. I commented on the design of the place. I said it looked amazing and hadn't looked a thing like a hospital. It looked more like a large extended home. Then he told me something surprising at first. He said he knew what I was, and not to be afraid that he was also. It had been why he offered me help. He knew I would not normally take help from a human." I hadn't liked explaining how I had been caught in front of the one who chased us; Charlotte had yet to explain why he was here with her. Starting up again I knew Charlotte would want to know the rest.

"Next thing I knew I was out cold. When I woke up, I had a huge headache. He had knocked me out somehow and I passed out. According to the other doctors he closed off an entire wing and had me in there with no other patients. He knew from the first time he saw me that I was a half-breed and he became obsessed with trying to find out how to make himself the same or at least immortal with the human traits. He tested on so many others first. I saw so many of them in pain and die in front of my very eyes. When he figured it out, he went into an insane rage and took it out on anyone that got in his way. He was so enraged that he couldn't figure out how some of us still were human and others completely changed into full-fledged vampires. I didn't have an explanation to give him, I didn't understand it myself. It's just the way we are."

Taking a breather now that I was starting to feel a little clearer in my head, I looked affectionately at my baby son who still did not have a name yet.

"In one night, he went on a killing spree and killed at least thirty innocent people. That's when he tried blaming it on one of those who died. He got me pregnant. He was hoping testing on an infant might give him different results. I was shocked I didn't even think I could get pregnant let alone him impregnating anyone. He's experimented with so many other women. I tried to escape a few times because I didn't know if he would kill the baby once it was born. I was so drugged up that my human side slowed me down a lot, it was the main reason I didn't understand why he would want any human traits. I kept getting caught. The last time I finally got away. I was at an independent hospital. It was so easy getting away, but I only came back here because I made a promise I had to keep. Others were waiting for me. Besides, I knew you would find me, and I needed to stay put. Also, I need to find the doctor and stop him or he's going to kill more, not just to make his army, he wants to gain control, he can barely keep his insanity hidden, he wants to gain control. He wants to kill, the look in his eyes is terrifying, he looks excited when there's pain. And he must be stopped. Grant here helped deliver my baby and he knows where the doctor lives and is willing to show us where that is or at least I hope he will still."

All three of them were now looking at Grant who had also been listening. He finally figured out what was going on and the rumors he heard had been true. He could tell that even by looking at her she was clearing up and thinking very clearly on her own.

"Before I tell you where he lives, I want to go with you. I also would like to know Maggie's real name. Who are the rest of you and how do you know her, let alone find her? Also, one last thing. I want to know if you're going to let me live?"

I smiled at him responding. "Yes, you're going to live but it would be safer that you go home or stay here. The doctor could kill you. My real name is not Maggie, which had been a name the doctor invented for me. My real name is Claire, and this is my sister Charlotte. I don't know who this person is. He's sort of the reason we split in the first place and why I even ran down this way." Even I wasn't sure how to introduce him.

As I said in the last part, he had a wave of guilt cross his face feeling horrible that I went through this because of him. Not that I was blaming him.

Piping in with a brief response. "My name is Andrew; my old group is the reason the two of them were separated in the first place. I take complete responsibility for that. My old group that had been with me, well....they're not around anymore. I came with her to help protect and find Charlotte's sister. Then I have other obligations I need to keep my promise to."

"The doctor doesn't live far from here. Behind us, there is a lake. If you cross it and head straight ahead for a few miles you will come to a mountain and his house is somewhat hidden up at the top of the hill. Are you sure I can't come and help?"

"We are sure; we don't want you risking your life since what we are trying to do is save human lives. However, you can do us a favor. Do you live nearby? Maybe you could watch the baby until we get back? That way he is safe and out of the way." I was now standing on my own without any assistance ready to hand my son over to Grant.

I felt I could trust him from the way he took care of me and trusted me by following me into something very unusual.

Obscured Darkness

Grant reached out and took the little one in his arms. Held him close to his body hoping his warmth would warm him up. He felt so cold just like Claire had.

"Take him to your home, we can track you, but we need to get going, it's getting darker out and you need to stay out of the moonlight." I gave my little one a last hug goodbye even though Grant sort of got in the hug as well.

All three turned and took off in the direction Grant told us to go. They took off faster than anyone he had ever seen a person run before. Andrew was stunned as he had seen us take off running. Then a streak of lightning shot across the field catching up to us. At first, Grant thought it might have been lightning but since when does it come up from the ground? It looked like another person had joined them. Instead of standing there watching anymore, Grant took the baby home as they had asked him to. Hoping they were right and would be safe.

As the three made it to the water a fourth joined them. As promised Mathais did not go far and he was glad he hadn't, he wanted to help catch the doctor also. The second he heard the whisper from Charlotte she did not even have to finish calling his name before he shot off to join them.

The forest heading up the hill had been thick barely leaving space to move. No one used this direction since it was so dense. There were so many bushes and trees and then finally they saw it. Heading up the mountain they could see the house in view. Grant meant it when he said the house was built on top of the mountain, being careful to survey the area before they reached it to make sure there were no others nearby to pounce on them. Not sure what they might be running into, they had to take extra care.

Andrew even poked ahead with a stick in case of traps. Ones he had hunted before were very good at laying out traps for those that were unwanted in certain areas, or just wanted to be left alone. Oddly enough the doctor wasn't worried about anyone coming up from this angle which worried Andrew little more than actually finding one. At least if they had found one, they would know how often they turn their attention to this side of the mountain.

For some reason I felt uneasy on my feet, then realized the odd feeling. The very small spot below me shook a little. There was a reason for the earthquake. It was being generated somehow from the mountain even though the shaking seemed worse as it reached the higher part of the ground, moving up closer to the house. They were sure the doctor must have built tunnels under the ground. Getting up by the house no one had been standing outside. There had been a couple in the one-room talking to each other. As far as we could tell they had been human and not forced to be there. Looking for a window no one was nearby as we worked our way down to the other end of the house.

The window we used led to an empty room. Andrew climbed into the room on his own. He had figured since he can hide better, he blended in with the dark shadow. Slowly opening the door, he peeked around the corner and walked down the hallway. He heard people talking down the one direction, so he walked away from where they were. There had been one door that led down a flight of stairs. It had been pitch black with no light showing at all. Choosing this way to go down he closed the door quietly behind him. He had to have gone down quite a few feet, he counted one hundred and fifty steps. The odd thing hadn't been the fact he went down so many steps, it had been the slope of the steps branching outward to other floors. Once at the bottom there still hadn't been any light or any peeking through from a window. He was guessing this was sort of like what they walked over when coming up the side of the mountain.

Even without the light, Andrew could see well enough. In his morphed form, he could see exceptionally well in the dark. There were a few chairs in the corner along with a desk. Walking over to the desk there was a light coming from the other side, a door he hadn't checked yet. The person left the door wide open to the room he was currently standing in. Someone was coming up another set of steps from across the room. If he hadn't heard the set of footsteps, then he might have been caught.

The light started getting brighter as they came closer, the oil lamp lighting their way. Hoping they would not see him he hid by the desk and watched them as the person passed and went up the stairs to the upper half of the house. It looked like a young woman but nothing out of the ordinary about her. At this point, he was beginning to wonder if they were in the right place.

Once the person was out of sight and closed the upper door. Andrew started to rummage through the desk. Basic medical papers didn't make much sense to him since he never dealt with doctors or certain types of papers, the usually hard-to-decipher signatures on most of them. Then he found a few papers with some interesting names. Wanting to take a little longer to look them over, Andrew took them with him. Grabbing a huge stack and tucked them under his arm planning on looking at them in a safer location.

Scanning the room to make sure no one else was in the room since he didn't know who else could see well in the dark. Walking up the steps just as carefully as before, he opened and closed the door behind him, then went back down the same hallway and into the empty room. Working his way out of the window both Charlotte and I were still there waiting for him.

"Four people were leaving out the back, and we had to hide.

One of them spoke of the doctor and their needing to catch up with him up north. They mentioned there would be more in a few months joining them. There are too many for just us to take on if they happen to be special humans with gifts. I have a few friends to call in, but it would take a while. Maybe it would be better just to leave and hope one of his prodigies gets out of control and takes care of him for us? That is if it's an option" Charlotte waited for Andrew's response.

"I don't think that's an option. He has the name and locations of several vampires and a few other odd creatures. He has your family as well as a friend of mine on there. He even has my name on here. At some point, he must have come across me or someone else who did. I was with hunters myself and hid it well, they never let on that they had any idea I was different. He has been studying people for a while which is what helped him understand there are people out there that are not quite human. I think he's planning on exposing those who refuse to follow him. If he does do this eventually, he could find you again, and then you might not be able to defend yourself if he makes a surprise attack.

What makes this even more difficult is the fact that I know who he is. I know him under another name. This even makes things difficult for humans when he's doing tests on the venom to see how they react. When he decides to go and experiment on others with other powers to gain more control. At this point, we don't have much in the way of options. We need to get up there before they do and finish this. I don't know exactly how he came across the others, but I will get answers when I see a friend of mine and ask her. We need to strike him while the group is still small and we don't have to corral them ourselves."

"Then what do we do now? What's our next move?" I asked as I looked at Charlotte and Andrew who already seemed like they knew.

"Charlotte and I will gather some of our friends and meet up north. My friends are already close to that area and they will want to know regardless if they choose to join us or not. We will need all the help we can get since we won't know how many there are going to be. I'm sure the group is still rather small in its infancy however if we don't take care of it, then it can get much larger and who knows how soon. Since it's involving a person, I know he's been around for a while, the group could be larger than we are aware of. Claire, you need to find out if Grant will watch the little one nearby or we can leave him here with him. It would be safer to take him with us, that way we know where he is while he cares for the baby."

Andrew gave me directions that he wanted me to follow once I collected Grant and the baby. Not wanting to waste too much time Andrew mainly wanted to make sure that Claire would be safe enough to join them, feeling having a human with her would help her pass for one if they ran into trouble. Grant could cover for her. They most likely would not dare go past the man in the group or at least he hoped they would not. Before leaving and risking my traveling again without the protection of my sister, Andrew walked over to me.

"I promise you will never have to go through this again. I won't quit until you, your son and your sister are safe. I intend on making up for my horrible mistake that put you in this position in the first place. I just wished I had known what I was doing early and spared you from all of this. I should have taken responsibility and taken care of this long ago. I wish there were more to the words I'm sorry because I don't feel they will ever make it right." Andrew let out a sigh and I knew he meant what he had said.

It would have been hard staying mad at him after that with

his expression if I had been mad.

"What's your middle name? I don't care for the first name." Not sure why I had asked it in that way Andrew gave me a strange smile with his eyebrow tipped a bit. He wasn't even sure how to take it.

"At least my mother liked it; I guess that's all that matters. My middle name is Jacob; I had been named after my father and his before him." Not sure why he was asked this, he looked at me curiously as Charlotte worked her way over to me.

Charlotte hugged me goodbye and had been preparing herself mentally for who she would be contacting and timing to make it back as the others would be meeting up where Andrew was sending Claire. Before they left, I had finally decided what to name my son. I was never good at coming up with names for things and I wanted my son to have a good name. He may not have been perfect but I'm sure he would have given me a chance to escape if he had followed me instead of my sister. He had no clue any of this was going to happen but then none of us did. As easy as it would be to blame him for all of this, I chose to be angry with the right one, Dr. Denthre. Besides after he rambled on about his father trying to figure out what he would do in our situation, I liked the way his father sounded.

"Andrew before you go, I wanted to tell you the name of my son. I finally found a proper and well-deserving name for him. Your middle name and your father's first name, both of you could be considered rather valiant men in your own right. And it happens to be the middle name of Grant as well who is also a wonderful man. It also happens to be my favorite number, my personal feeling that things come in threes. It suits him well. I have decided to name him Jacob."

Andrew listened with constant interest, looking shocked when I compared him to a valiant man. Andrew couldn't help but chuckle when he heard that, even the concept sounded funny to him. However, he felt proud I chose such a name. Mainly since it had been his father's name a person people and he could be proud of.

"You don't have to name him that. Don't get me wrong it's a very sweet and generous gesture on your part but make sure it's a name you wish. I'm sure someone in your own family could be more suitable for him."

"I don't know my birth family or at least if I did, I've forgotten. This is the name I want and I do not regret it one bit. I want him named after strong ones that he can be influenced hopefully by in some way. Besides, I like the way it sounds."

Andrew nodded his head showing he understood and accepted it.

I watched the two of them streak off in separate directions.

I didn't want to stay here too long in case I ran into someone else or even the Doctor again. Now all I had to do was pick up on the trail of my son. Standing still closing my eyes I tried to sense him. Even with the wind that slightly picked up. There were many scents around. Then that familiar aroma hit, and I took off almost as fast as lightning in the direction that it wafted from. My son's scent was rather faint but the main scent I followed had been Grant's.

Following it as far as it had led me. When I stopped at the stream only temporarily had I lost the scent until I crossed, picking it up once again on the other side. I could tell that Grant originally traveled around the stream however his scent collected again directly on the other side. Coming even closer I could smell my son's scent. It had not been blood that led me here but the scent of his skin.

Closing in on a rather small but humble-looking little house, I slowed down just in front of the door. I never asked Grant if he was living with anyone. I couldn't pick up on any other scents except his and my son's. Opening the door without even knocking I entered expecting to see Grant there with the baby but not quite in the way I found them. He had caught a glimpse of a flash streaking across the field toward his house and past the window. Grabbing a knife as quick as he could that had been on the kitchen counter. He tried to defend the baby the best he could. Not that he felt he could have defeated a vampire with only a hand knife if he had wanted to. He had to at least try. Then relief came rather quickly once he saw it had only been me standing there in the doorway, even though it still took a while for his heart to slow down after being hurried from the panic.

I crossed the room taking Jacob from Grant. Smiling and cooing at the baby happy to see he was safe. The feeling I felt knowing that Grant would have given his life to protect him even though I knew there would not have been very much he could have done. I still felt very proud of him for trying.

"I don't know how you feel about this. Denthre wasn't up there, and we were hoping to catch him off guard unfortunately it's been put on hold. There are others and we need to find out how many, but mainly to take care of the doctor. He's already up north and we need to catch him up there. He can't be very far since he was last at the asylum when we were there. At some point, he left and headed up north if the ones we listened to were correct. Charlotte and Andrew are getting a few friends together and I will be meeting them up north. We are trying to do this rather quickly but there are complications. They might need my help, but I can't leave my son, it would be safer if he is out of the way or at least nearby. I worry if I leave him back here even if he were safe with you, if it turns out to be a trap the Doc could come after him and neither of you would be safe. According to Andrew a friend of his, her family has two little ones also and they will need help if they do decide to help us."

Before I could get another word out Grant had already made up his mind and what he wanted to do. I barely had to ask him. I could have asked him anything at this moment, even from the moment he first laid eyes on me he knew he wanted to keep me safe. Not being drawn to me for some inhuman draw except for the intense urge to protect me. I seemed so childlike to him. He was already addicted to my son. For being so small he could wrap you around his finger just with the way he looked so intently at you.

All he had said was "tell me what you need me to do, and I will be more than happy to do it."

"I know you already agreed. I want you to know that you have the option of saying no. I would love to have you come with me, I don't want you to feel you're trapped into coming and I want to make sure you're comfortable with this. You will never be near the fight. I'll make sure both of you are far enough away. I just want to make sure this is really what you want."

"I don't have anything holding me here. I have no family to speak of anymore. I live alone and pretty much live to work. Not much of an existence. At least coming with you I get to protect both you and your baby. Looking at him I can't help but love him. It's probably the closest I will ever come to having a son of my own. Even if it is temporary, it's well worth it for me. Besides, it will get me out of the house." Smiling he seemed more like he was trying to convince me even though I couldn't help but love the way Grant spoke of my son.

"My family always has room for one more." Not saying much since I didn't want him to feel any other way than the way he did. I could hope.

"You don't need to say anything further, I would love to be part of your family. I know because I am human it will take time for me to get wherever you expect or need me. If there is any faster way let me know, otherwise, we should probably start heading out now. I have a carriage that should make it faster; at least that travel would be faster for me."

Grant packed light, only grabbing a small bag and packing it with what he felt necessary. Watching him get ready I broke his concentration when I commented about the transportation.

"There are areas that you won't be able to take the carriage. The brush and forest are far too thick for a carriage to make it through. There are also thick swampy areas that are not good for the horses to go through. I would hate to leave the horse off on its own."

"Then I will release him up here, at least one of my neighbors will find him here. He won't starve in the barn. I have a neighbor who usually trades eggs for hay. I want to leave a note for my neighbor so that he knows he can take the horse and all the bales of hay I have on the side of the barn. That I won't be back home. I'll leave the note on his house door. Then how will we travel? Depending on how far it is we couldn't possibly travel that far by walking. At least I won't be able to? Is it not too far up north then?"

"After you handle the note for your neighbor, I will handle the travel. You're going to have to trust me. It's the only way that I know. It's about four days' travel from here, perhaps farther for you. We must travel across a rather large distance to get to where we need to meet up. I'll be right here. I need to find something that will secure the baby. Since this will be the first time, I have ever done this with two."

Glancing at Claire not sure if he wanted to find out how they would be traveling. Heading off to the neighbors' farm Grant rode the horse trying to cut down on some time. At least he was home so there was no note needed. Leaving the horse in his care,

Obscured Darkness

Grant wasn't asked why he was leaving, his neighbor trusted he had his reasons. Planning on picking up the rest of the hay the next day at least everything was taken care of. Trying not to think about it yet Grant came back around to the front of the house to see the baby wrapped in a sling of sorts made from his bedsheets. I was smiling, not a wicked smile but sort of like you're not going to like this but it's going to be interesting.

"So, what do you need me to do?" Standing there in front of me while I smirked.

"Don't worry, it won't be as bad as it looks at first. You might even find it fun. Last human, a good friend of mine I had done this with loved it."

"What happened to that human?" Grant stood there curious and a little nervous.

"Dead, but don't worry not from traveling with me." Not elaborating on what happened I stood in front of Grant.

"This is going to be a bit awkward. I'm not sure if it's going to work too well since your feet might drag. I've never done this with someone taller than myself. And I don't want to risk having your legs or arms getting ripped off because we get too close to a tree." Placing my hand on my chin concentrating, trying to figure out a better way of moving him.

I didn't think carrying him might work, it would have been easier to carry him if he had been shorter. One of the few times it doesn't help that I'm short. Charlotte had always been taller at five foot seven while I was five foot one.

"I would prefer to keep my body parts if possible. I'm definitely in favor of anything that would promote that." Smiling at me Grant looked so trusting assuming I knew what I was doing.

Then it hit me. I went into the barn and made a few alterations to his wagon. First chopping it in half and tearing off the top, stripping down the sides leaving a flat board with the smallest seat in the center with two wheels on either side and a small section to hold onto. Sort of like a bench with large wheels on both sides. Pulling it around to the front where Grant and Jacob were waiting. Grant looked like he was trying to figure out what I was pulling.

"I hope you don't mind I made some alterations to your wagon. Wheels might get stuck from time to time but it's the only thing I could figure out. If we go fast enough, they won't sink, hopefully, that will help. The last person I carried was much shorter than you, I just don't think that will work for most of the areas we are going to get through. It would work, I can carry you with no problem, but you would need to keep your knees and arms in. At some point we will have to deal with it when that comes, we will have to go slower." Standing in front of the wagon now having Grant climb into it holding Jacob and getting as comfortable as they could for now.

With only two wheels but a very small lightbox frame that would make travel a little easier for now.

So far until we reached the water, I could use this, then I would have to find a way to carry Grant and Jacob.

With the two poles sticking out I used those to hold onto. Grant secured it with his legs safely inside with no risk of hitting anything. He sat in it and held onto the sides ready for the fast speed he had seen me run at, even though I tried to keep it slower than that to keep from tripping the cart. First testing how well he could hold on; I only ran at a medium speed but still faster than a horse. The barrow bounced not as much as I thought it would but then it almost seemed like it was floating in the air from the speed we were going at. The air rushing under also helped keep it up. Grant seemed to be enjoying it, so I picked up the speed until I was slightly under a full run. Grant was still handling it holding on, his knuckles turned white from gripping so hard. Even though he could handle it I didn't want to wear him out too much, so I slowed down.

This way made it so much easier to cover more ground, lifting the handle to get slightly more airborne when we passed bumps or roots in the road. What would have taken us three to four days to cover if we had taken a carriage or moved at human speed, we covered in a matter of half a day. I had chosen not to take any of the roads. The fields and other terrains would have been easier to cover than the cobblestone and dirt roads. The wagon shook far less making it safer to travel at these speeds. We also didn't have to worry about anyone seeing us and wondering how I could pull the wagon like this let alone go at the speed we were traveling.

The benefits of this century had been the simple fact that not much settlement occurred in the center of the country. Most stayed along the outer rim near the waterways, oceans, and lakes. Very few settlements were spread in other regions. Mostly native groups lived further in. Eventually, it became inevitable that the makeshift wagon had outlived its usefulness. Traveling as far as we could even where there had been a slight path to follow or moss to go over, we reached the great forest that had been too thick to pull anything no matter how thin it had been. This had been the part I dreaded. Thankfully, Grant had not noticed until I came to a stop.

"Are we there? This wasn't too far, not that I could see very much it was all pretty much a blur at one point." Grant seemed surprised we stopped already.

"No, we're not there yet, but we have a lot of forests to travel through before we break into an opening and it's a lot further if we were to go around it. We might have flat enough land. It would be easier if you were the one to do this but then you're not the vampire. I'm going to have to carry you on my back; we can make it almost the rest of the way there."

"Carry me? Are you sure?" I didn't think Grant believed I could carry him all the way there.

He may have started to see me when I was strong, but it was hard for him to get it out of his head when I was so weak and had depended on him.

"What are you worried about? Is it the losing the arm or leg thing I was talking about earlier? I promise I'll be very careful. I'm not just fast I'm a lot stronger than you will ever be." Smiling at him as he tried to figure out how this would work.

It was fun watching humans try and figure out what they're not used to. I had always been fascinated with mortals and their simple moves, reactions and imperfections, and most of all accomplishments. I used to call them meat bags or fleshies at one time, except the concept and wording had made Charlotte sick so I stopped referring to them this way.

Standing behind me, he felt strange for a second not sure how this was going to work. Guessing I must know what I was doing trusting me he stood there for a second and only for a split second shut his eyes as I stood in front of him, with the baby now in the harness that I had made in the front tightly hooked made from the bedsheets. Leaning forward putting his full weight on me, Grant had never been carried by a woman let alone been in a situation where it would have been needed. Most women would not have been able to even pick him up.

Trying to keep his legs as close to my waist as much as possible since he was taller than I was, Grant was almost in a kneeling position with his knees at either hip with his feet outback and only his knees facing forward. With his arms wrapped around my shoulders and chest, if there had been a more dignified way to carry him, I would have, except since I was short and he was tall. I only had so many options. I may have been strong, but it was hard to maneuver him without the risk of him getting hurt when we traveled at such fast speeds. At least it wasn't as if others would see him. I held onto his hands so I would not risk dropping him. The movement had been so fluid that it barely felt like my hips were moving. Grant only knew they were moving because of the sudden rush of air flying past and flowing through his short hair. I could tell Jacob liked the fast movement.

During the entire travel, Jacob never made a single sound. Otherwise, the motion could have put him to sleep. Occasionally opening his eyes, he would see the trees whizzing past, at times going through a narrow opening, they would speed through when it didn't even look as if there had been space for them to pass through, however, they made it through. Only a few times had he felt the brush of a branch or leaves touch his arm or leg. Even though I was holding him and running, doing the entire work, he had the uneasy job of holding on. Grant felt very tired trying to hold on, his legs feeling shaky at times. The shakier he became, I held on tighter to his hands and with one arm I leveraged it behind trying to add support to his back to make sure I would not drop him if he were to let go. Looking for a place to stop. I could see it in the far distance. Not wanting to stop, he held on for as long as he could. When we came to our first open wide space that did not look like the ground was covered with moss, we stopped so he could lay on the ground.

While we stopped, I took the opportunity to feed Jacob, his eyes wide taking in his surroundings. He looked very interested in everything. Then Grant realized he might have been captivated by the running since I had him facing forward, so he could see some things. The second we stopped it had almost been as if he was trying to figure out why we stopped? Jacob hadn't known how to voice his opinion; which might have been why he was so quiet. Jacob was a cute baby. Head full of black curly hair, his skin light Carmel shade. His tiny fingers wrapped around my one finger. Smiling he seemed so happy. Then it almost seemed like he reached out for Grant.

Sitting a little closer Grant reached out and held Jacob for a while. Then as the sun started to set there was less light in the forest. The mosquitoes began to come out more. Not that they bothered Jacob or me. Any that landed on us to taste us fell to the ground soon after making a poke. Grant tossed Jacob up in the air playing with him which he seemed to like a lot. Being careful not to take too much more time. I was ready to take off again. I wrapped Jacob again close to me making sure he was secure. Getting ready to take off. Grant got back into position and held on tight. Finding he could hold on much tighter around my chest now that he knew he couldn't possibly hold too tight or choke me. Grant didn't feel like he was going to fall as much as he had earlier.

After a while of the tree's passing there had been another clear opening. Stopping briefly to let Grant get feeling in his legs and arms we didn't stay long before we were up and running again. Still running at a rather fast pace we continued straight ahead. Not once did we have to stop for anyone, there had been nowhere anyone would have settled with the wilderness being so close in, never running into any small towns. There had been one on the outside of the forest, but we kept to the thickest part trying to avoid anyone seeing how fast or just in general how we were traveling.

Far in the distance, Grant could make out something that looked like a long strip of blue. As he tried to decipher it, the image came even closer until he realized what it was as it approached, and I was not stopping at all. Then a moment of panic hit. Grant realized I didn't intend on stopping at all. I intended on hitting the water. He wasn't sure if he could hold on or not. Just before we did get to the water, I did stop but only to alter our traveling situation. Instead of Jacob being strapped to my front. I securely strapped him onto the back of Grant. Then with Grant and his long legs wrapped completely around my waist and still holding as tight as he had before I ran for the water's edge, we went straight in with both on my back. Jacob never once touched the water except for the occasional wave that went a little high that splashed him. When he felt the cold-water splash, he seemed to get excited by it. A small sound almost like a laugh would escape him. At least he was enjoying it. Grant tried to fight the panic as he saw the land behind us disappear and then no land had been in sight after that. He was more curious about how long we would be in the cold water. I tried not to leave him in too long since I didn't want to risk Grant getting sick or suffering hypothermia.

Most of the time I had been under the water or covered by the waves, even after getting tired of holding on Grant couldn't afford to let go. He knew if he had it wouldn't just be himself that would suffer. There had been no meadows or any other area to stop and rest. The water rushing past helped a little with cooling his muscles from holding on, however, it also made it tiring holding on, now he was shaking not from being tired but from being so cold. We didn't stay in the water for too much longer. I mainly swam in the ocean to get up to the furthest north I could before the water froze too much for Grant. There had only been a small separation between the two landmasses.

Usually, humans would have needed a boat. However, I was used to swimming long distances. There had been a few areas I knew of along the coast that had small mining towns that I wanted to avoid. Following along a rocky ledge side there had been an area that I came up and stopped as soon as I reached land. Grant with his legs and arms cramped from holding on for so long, so tight and from the water stiffening his joints.

Pulling out a large glass bottle from a wet bag, then taking the cork off, there was a dry clothes never touched by water. Changing from his wet soggy clothing to dry clothes he felt so much better. I had even changed Jacob even though it was mostly the front of the bed sheet that was wet. Grant was rather happy he had used his large medical glass bottles, or the rest of his clothing would have been wet also. Lying down on his stomach happy to be on solid ground again, not realizing how tired he was he fell asleep while I sat next to him watching the expressions change on his face. I could only guess the trip was influencing them. At times I had to keep myself from laughing when he mumbled incoherent words. Jacob had been worn out from all the sightseeing he had done and slept also, even though most babies would sleep more than he had. He only slept when we stopped and hadn't been anything to watch anymore. For once I wasn't tired enough to sleep so I stayed awake. I was hoping we were not too far; I was getting tired of traveling. While Grant and Jacob slept, I gathered berries and anything I thought Grant might eat. There was a small town not far. I picked up a loaf of bread for him. By the time I got back, both were wide awake and wondering where I had gone to. Grant wasn't too worried since he knew I would always come back for Jacob. I tried to reassure him I would still come back for him also.

It had only taken one full day and a half to get up north. Now, all we had to do was find the cabin that Andrew gave me directions to. Not wanting to get there before Charlotte and Andrew. I didn't mind waiting. Sitting in the tall grass not that I felt I needed to, except this had been the perfect angle to watch my son and Grant. Both evenly breathing at the same time, and both were very sweet. I loved the fact that I found someone after all these years. I never thought I would have fallen for a human let alone because of the circumstances that it happened in. But then love blooms from the strangest situations and adversities as well as the most innocent moments. As Charlotte always tells me you never know when it will finally find you.

While I was sitting watching Grant and Jacob play now that they were awake, I was not sure why, but I picked up on so many different scents. Both animal and human, if I hadn't known better, I would have assumed a circus had come traveling through, except these scents were still very different.

Seemed like such an odd mix to have so many strong scents in such a small area. After Grant and Jacob played and ate, they were even ready to get the rest of the trip over. I decided it was time we started making our way there again. This time instead of carrying them both we walked. The scents I noticed seemed to collide. Looking off into the distance much further than what Grant would have picked up, there had been a party going on in the distance. Didn't seem like much of a party. No decorations or traditional party attractions, perhaps a family reunion? There had been quite a few people standing outside. If Andrew hadn't called them friends, I would have been afraid of Grant being near other vampires. Andrew had made it clear before he left that we would be safe with them.

Some had been sitting outside on a bench reading while others lounged lazily against each other. Close to six thoughsand steps footsteps, which was roughly three miles away and we would be there. I had already been aware of them watching us. Not a constant stare but they knew we were there. Since they seemed aware early on this must have been the place I was looking for. Only other creatures, people with special gifts, or vampires would have seen us coming from that far away. Coming up with Grant's hand in mine while he held Jacob nestled comfortably in his arm. I could see Nichole's twin's as they were on the bench with her. This must have been the mother that Andrew was telling me about.

Waving to them trying to let them know we were friendly, especially since they would not be expecting us. Pulling a note out of my pocket that Andrew had written before we separated.

"I'm supposed to give this note to Andrews's friend Evangeline. Is she here?" I felt nervous asking.

One lady had gone inside the house as we approached. Not sure which one it had been however I didn't think she had a child.

"Evangeline's inside. I'll get her for you." The slender lady sitting on the other bench stood.

Her voice sounded so light and airy and very friendly. Dark curly hair, loose cascading down to her waist, for sitting out in the middle of nowhere, the clothes she wore she looked like she was ready for a wedding. She looked so strikingly perfect. Even the young man she seemed to be with was impressive looking. Not a muscular build, a little smaller but his skin is flawless. The smile on his face would make the grumpiest person smile. He seemed so warm and inviting. I could tell they were wondering how we found Evangeline up here. None of them recognized us. Even though they whispered. I could hear them inside. A human never would have caught their whisper and even for vampires, it was rather low still.

Evangeline came out with a questioning look on her face. Lorah came out behind Evangeline with Charlie in tow who also looked just as curious at what the guest was here asking for let alone how I knew Andrew or why I came looking for Evangeline. They had been very curious about what my connection to Andrew had been. If it had been because of his old demon hunting or his promise he mentioned that he needed to keep. It didn't take long to see who was protective of Evangeline. Not that we were much of a threat.

"I'm Evangeline; you said you had a note from Andrew?" Evangeline wondered what this had been about.

The last time she saw him had been a few months ago when he said he had a promise to keep.

"I'm supposed to meet Andrew up here, but he wanted you to read this in case we made it here before he did. I'm not surprised he's a little late, but he had to collect something. I'm guessing his note will explain it."

Handing the note over Evangeline read it, and then concern spread over her face causing Charlie to come closer to her. Handing the note, it went from family member to family member, and each wound up with the same concerned look on their face. I had almost wished I read his note so I would know why they had the shocked expression on their faces.

"You're certainly welcome here to wait for him. If you like you can use the guest room. Anything you need just let us know." Charlie tried as well as he could to welcome us and help their new guests feel comfortable.

All still with concern on their faces I could only assume they were worried about what was going to happen very soon. Charlie seemed to be talking to an owl that squeaked at him and then flew off in a rush. Smiling at me he walked back into the house.

Evangeline sat down on her bed with Lewis handing him the note. "What do you think Charlie said to your sister?"

"I would only assume that because of the note he is calling in friends now to help out, from the sounds of this letter it seems a rather urgent matter and quite frankly a bit dangerous doesn't hurt to have help. Perhaps it won't be as bad as I am thinking but hard not to think that way. Andrew's letter is rather urgent-sounding. If it's only one rogue vampire who is posing this threat, we should be able to handle it, but if he has others like himself then there could be a problem.

Looking over the letter she realized Andrew would only have sent her this letter if it had been urgent otherwise, he would have stayed the first time. Then she wondered would she have met Lewis if he stayed? Not that she was interested in him that way, she might have stuck with him because of their new friendship. Lewis might not have felt comfortable enough to come to speak with her the way he had. Not wanting to think about that she knew she made the right choice. She didn't feel this way for Andrew, but she didn't want to see him, or her family gets hurt. Wishing they could finally just blend in, always fighting to be safe or to keep secrets. It gets so tiring after a while never being able to settle down and be content. There was always something, holding the note in her hands. Knowing there was a lot of activity now. Charlie had taken control over the informing, leaning against Lewis and reading the words yet again.

Dearest Evangeline.

I wish this letter would have met you under better circumstances. However, there is a problem. It is because of this danger I need the help of you and your family. I know you don't owe me this, but I do ask please for your help. Your family is implicated in this problem as well.

A doctor that I used to deal with at an asylum had been turned into a vampire years ago. Normally this would be nothing for us to get involved with however there is much more to it. It turns out that I know this one.

From the time that I used to be with the demon

hunters, I had known him well. He used to take in patients we checked into the asylum. He had always been much more obsessed over certain creatures than others, particularly vampires. We assumed he had a personal hatred towards them that none of us knew, assuming it must have affected him personally. It was something he never discussed with anyone. He has been experimenting on many innocent people and killing both mortals and creatures. On the papers, he did include a few names and has several crossed off. He's kept track of the ones that are dead.

Others he plans on killing himself. Even though he is a vampire now. I am unsure what he plans on doing about his condition. It almost looks like he is trying to find a cure that for him it would be fine however he's not searching for it to use on himself. It might be to control those who he changes. He keeps experimenting on humans and torturing many. I can't help but wonder if he is trying to find an easier way of killing our kind and those of other creatures also?

According to the papers, we found it lists a few of your relatives, particularly the half-breeds. He had been the one to diagnose your family with their illnesses. I am assuming he did this before the change, which shows he has been around longer than I had realized. He used his power to kill special humans and creatures. Sadly, enough he had been the one who put my group together.

The main reason for needing to stop him is that he is searching for those known to him and he is trying to either control them or kill them. Claire had been one of the lucky ones to escape him. She has a power he didn't understand, or he would have killed her. I can only assume that is why she was not dead. Right now, he is obsessed with half-breeds. He does not wish to expose us, or he would have done so by now. As far as I can tell he only has ten working for him. They seem oblivious to even *what is about to happen to themselves at this point.*

My friend and your family are still on his list, he has several experiments he intends on handling on your family. He knows where your family is located, for whatever reason he has gone up north near you. Just how close I am uncertain. However, he intends on finishing his plans and we are not sure just how far he plans on going with it. Sadly, this problem does not intend on going away on its own. I fear for your safety and those of others as well as my own.

He is not far from your area right now. After reading some of the papers. I had put the connection together. He is the one who killed Charlie's father. We would have simply killed him where we were at, however, he had already left. Right now, I have a friend who is going to help me track exactly where he is so we can take care of this problem. It was bad enough that I used to be a demon hunter, but this does not need to keep going on. Claire is the one giving you this note. Her sister Charlotte will be showing up soon with a few friends as well. I also will see you soon myself.

For now, I hope all is well,
your dear friend Andrew.

Leaning against Lewis putting her arms around him enjoying as much as she could while she had him with her, not wanting to lose this world she was finally now introduced to. Holding onto him a little tighter not wanting to let go she set her head on his chest listening to his breathing.

Lewis must have sensed her concern as he held her closer. Thinking to herself about how her foster mother used to call her an angel of love. As much as she wanted this killer to die, when had it become acceptable for an angel to desire something demonic enough to want to kill something even though it was for the right reasons? An angel of love turning into an angel of death, even with Lewis holding me close. I wasn't looking forward to the impending confrontation.

Chapter Ten
Charlotte

Only looking back for a brief second till Claire was no longer in view, racing far out west. Andrew had taken off to the east. There had been many friends who were out west who would be surprised to see her again. Mathais had already left for up north. He already made it clear it would not take him long to get there. He decided to stay back and would show just after Claire made her appearance.

Mathais had been more of a loner living alone as many vampires had. At one time he traveled with his mate Lily until he lost her. Not to death but just simply forgetting where she went. He always figured someday he would find her. At least he kept hoping. They had been together for many centuries; this hadn't been the first time they lost each other. Both had been very forgetful in their human lives and certainly didn't change for them after the physical change. Lily was never a vampire as Mathais had become. For some reason when she was bit, it never took effect until they found out that she already had her change thanks to an old distant relative that had passed it on without knowing about it. She had shade qualities that continuously healed her as the venom tried spreading until the venom dissipated.

Charlotte wanted the aid of an old friend when she was in trouble in the past had been a huge help. Edmund and Grace were sort of like family to her and Claire. Grace had been the one who saved her life. Originally when she was fully human, she grew up as Jeannette in a rather rich family. Later so there would be no connection to my old life. I took Grace's middle name as my first. It had also been a way of my saying thank you.

From the point I was born, my future mate had been chosen for me. Every move and choice had been dictated to me. From Charm school to my private education at home. Even my friends were chosen for me based on their family lines and family fortune. My father was not happy when he heard his only daughter was to move across the ocean and away from their homeland. He had hoped to create a stronghold with the family. Instead of gaining a son, he lost his daughter.

Even I did not know where we were going. To my new husband this was his business and for me as his wife to follow his lead. Hugging my friends and family as we left everything I had known growing up. Sadly, I had not even known what my new name would be until the day of the wedding. At the time it had been such a surprise but sadly meant nothing to me as the years went by, I could no longer remember the last name if I had wanted to.

I had been sleeping on the fainting couch in the study even though I could not sleep through the swaying of the ship. We had been married already for a week before we had left on the ship. So far, a few days had been enough for me, I would get seasick, and my husband was no help either adding bruises or insults to an already upset stomach.

My husband still laying in the same position as I had left him with the covers off and laying on his stomach he had not moved. He didn't even look like he appeared to breathe. I knew he hadn't been feeling well and the day before coughing extremely hard and now throwing up himself this morning. Since our very short marriage, he had been physically and verbally abusive toward me. When he had been sick, it was a welcomed relief from him. He had only married me for the needed money to finance his venture.

I did not want to find a dead body and felt horrible if he had died even though he had been such an angry person. Then I felt slight rage knowing he did this because he was with another woman when we had just been married. This would be a fitting end for him. Sadly, I felt worse for the woman he was with wondering who she, unfortunately, caught the sickness from. I was more interested in the woman he was with. Was she a prostitute or an innocent girl? Was she still sick or possibly dead now like he was?

Leaving our port room, I went out and spoke to one of the shipmen that my husband seemed to like talking with. Without hesitating, he walked down to our room. The look on his face was neither shock or surprise.

"I think it is best Ma'am if you let us handle this." Waving me around him, he called out to a few of the others who were within hearing distance.

Three other men passed by me in the hallway and rushed into the room. Another gentleman who had been traveling alone came up to me.

Obscured Darkness

"I think it's best if you come with me, you won't want to see what is about to happen," taking me by the arm he led me back to his room. Setting me down and offering me a cup of tea, "do you have transportation once you're off the boat?"

"Yes, there is a carriage that will be waiting for us." Sitting with my hands on my lap fidgeting with my fingers, feeling very nervous now.

"Is he going to be, okay?" Still looking down at my hands almost too nervous to hear the truth.

"I doubt your husband made it. Just like the other men earlier that were thrown over, that's what I assume they are going to do the same with him, as they have with the others. You will need to decide if you're going to get a ride back home or set up work here at your new home. Do you have any friends or family waiting for you there?" Kneeling beside me with a look of concern on his face, taking another breath he started talking again.

"It's not safe for a woman like you to travel alone." Sadly, he had been correct.

This kind gentleman had offered to walk me to my carriage when we docked. He had let me know if anyone asked to make it clear that family had been waiting for me. Hoping this might deter any dangerous interest.

Thanking him for his offer. I had him walk me to my stateroom for that night. It was nice knowing I had someone looking out for me even though I didn't know what I was going to do when we docked. Sitting down looking at where my husband once lay. Even though I was alone. I felt relieved not to be with him. The handle to my room shook a little and then opened. One of the crew had made his way in more than half drunk. Looking at me the expression on his face was scary. Grabbing the little sitting chair next to me I threw it at him slightly pushing him off balance. Running past him, I saw another man waiting down at the other end. I couldn't make it back to the gentleman's quarters who offered me help earlier.

Turning and running the other way up to the side of the ship. There was nowhere to go. Leaning backward, I could see them coming for me. The waters had been choppy as the ship shifted; I fell overboard with three men watching. I could barely see the ship anymore as it continued to sail away. My heart still beats but I thought I had taken my last breath. All I could remember, I had been in almost unbearable pain. Thinking this must be the end, my final death. I thought I had seen an angel in the water. The venom slowly spread through my body. The cold water had numbed my body so much I had already lost so much feeling, then the change finally started taking over gradually. Eventually not even needing to breathe however out of habit I started taking breaths.

Feeling overwhelmed when I realized I was doing this underwater. I was breathing. Grace raced me to a small island, staying with me while the rest of the transformation occurred. Grace had cleared the water from my lungs. She had stopped my heart right away with the venom so that the water would not take a victim while she was there.

At this moment from the way I felt. I would have gladly welcomed death to this. Not knowing what was happening only made it worse on top of the fact that I thought I was hallucinating when I had seen grace. I felt like I was lit on fire from the inside almost about to burst into a million little pieces.

Grace had been out traveling with Edmund when they heard the shouts coming from the nearby ship. She already had known she needed to be here. In a vision, she saw this would be where she would inherit her daughter. Not knowing exactly how but that I would be here and need her. Grace had the power of premonition. In her human life, she lived as a natural witch. Not wanting the others to see them they did their best to save me but also conceal themselves as well. Because I lived, I never once thought about my ex-husband after that.

Claire had been my sister. We had become sisters in a very sad way. I found a pregnant woman who died in the woods. She had been drained of all her blood; another vampire had gotten to her before I did. Somehow it did not fully affect the baby. Only being offset somehow and the blood did not drain fully from the womb. In a way, it made it so that the baby forming somehow developed immunity to it. Since the woman already been dead, I tore into her stomach taking the baby out. It seemed like Claire had made it far enough in the term. Then she might also have been why her mother died. Her mother had been dead for at least three days. The bite mark could have been extremely old. There were bite marks inside, all over her body. I had never seen anything like this before. Neither did I know what could have been inside to do this except for the baby. The woman had a card with the name Claire. I didn't know if it had been the mother's name or what she intended on calling the baby. On the other hand, perhaps it was someone she was meeting with. Either way, it was how I decided to name her. When she grew older, I tried to make the change full however her body never fully took the change keeping her human side alive still.

I hadn't visited Grace and Edmund in a while. I was looking forward to seeing them again. Trying to avoid any towns that might have strayed from the waterways or the usual railroads, passing a few tribal groups, none of which seemed surprised to see me, they were used to seeing vampires and other creatures pass as we always left them alone. One of the very few groups vampires never had to hide from, an unspoken trust between the two groups.

Racing across prairie plains and mountain passes. Not until I came to a large carved-out mountain did I finally stop for a moment. Trying to sense the area I could pick up a familiar scent. I could tell my old family had guests. There was the scent of fox in the air. It followed the same path as my family. One of the things I couldn't get over had been the fact that my family got along with wildlife. They learned which animals were and which were formations of another kind.

Grace only would consume the blood of animals. However, Edmund would hunt out the already dying, mostly criminals or killers occasionally disease inflicted or terminally sick inflicted humans. Not to change them but to drain them of their blood. Trying to respect life as he could with his own reasoning. At least it had been what he convinced himself that he still respected life. This was the way he had been raised. It never seemed to be difficult for the two of them even though they had different views towards humans and animals. Regardless of the reason, Grace refused to touch a human in that way unless she knew they were near death she would try to save them, most of the time she allowed them to die. Knowing this life isn't for everyone, that death was the natural way of life.

The scent had become stronger as I followed it to a mountain cliff. Down lower, there was a small hole in the side of the cave. Climbing down and slipping into the opening, there was a door built into the rock. Before I ever had to announce myself or knock to let them know I was there the door opened.

"We knew you were coming. Grace saw you. You have our support, you always have. We would be happy and honored to help you and Claire out; we tried to find Claire earlier, but we couldn't find her. The surroundings were not of a place we were familiar with. Grace saw you find her. You were always a natural tracker." Always straight to the point, Edmund spoke his mind.

Grace standing behind him was looking so happy to see me again. I hadn't been home in quite some time. Coming in and hugging Grace and Edmund, they showed me to their living room. They made their home inside of the mountain. Besides being dark it looked like an underground palace.

Unlike my own home where it all had been built above the ground with large windows inviting the sunlight in. Over the years I found other creatures were extremely different when it came to their taste in homes. They were either large or wide open, or extremely small and private. Many were built into stone either burrowing homes into the ground or cave walls. My favorite had been a friend's home, she built hers inside of a cave with a natural hot spring to shower in. Then there were the few who liked to be wide open with windows all around one side to allow the sun in favoring the natural scenery around them.

"We don't have very much time; we want to get this taken care of before it gets too far out of hand. I know Edmund has dealt with this sort of situation before and was hoping he might be able to lead up some of it. Andrew the one that is helping me used to be a demon hunter, he knows the person we are going after."

"Are you sure we can trust this Andrew? Generally, a person who is a demon hunter never goes against what they have been taught. Why the change for him? I want to make sure you are not walking into a trap. You have our full support. I want to know what his defection is based on. Grace has already told me she sees us in a great war, I just want to be prepared for who might turn against us." Edmund grew up around many wars, even dealing with them himself, both human wars and vampire wars.

Regardless, if his side of the war won, it always left him

feeling defeated since the wars seemed so senseless. If there had been more meaning behind them other than fighting for territory or how the humans were to be owned by vampires.

"As far as we understand the man who we are going after had run an asylum for a while. Not a regular one. It was his private practice. Ones would get checked in and never leave. Not that he left them to live. Many who were considered mythical creatures or possessed special gifts or powers were placed under his care. He didn't try and cure them, he killed them. He has been around for a long-time killing others, except now he is stronger than before. At first, we thought he was able to make the change when he came into possession of Claire. However, Andrew and I believe he was already a vampire. Claire was stuck at his asylum for a while, he kept her alive only for one reason, so he could experiment on her. He never knew there were half-breed vampires until he started noticing strange things in certain people, especially those he experimented on. He realized this with Claire and tested on her, realizing the human side made her weak physically and easier to control. We think he was trying to cure himself or to find a way of controlling the venom that infects. It's hard to know what exactly he is trying to get at, other than all the people he's killing to get it. He's also testing humans looking for something. Claire heard him make a mention of a stone. How something would be much easier if he just had the stone. Claire escaped a few times, but her human side held her back because of the chemicals in her. The last time she got lucky and did get away with our help and the help of a human. Right now, she's okay."

Winking at me Grace was smiling. "We know and speaking for myself I can't wait to meet the baby. In my vision, he looks beautiful. But was it necessary to bring the human?" Still, with her sweet smile, Grace had a look of concern on her face.

Obscured Darkness

"He's one of the reasons Claire is okay. He's protecting Jacob while we are in the fight. I'm assuming he will be watching the other infants as well. He won't have to contend with the fight at all, he will be back at their house with the kids far enough away. Even though they have grown since Andrew last saw them. The doctor is going to be rather difficult to kill. Dr. Denthre has been a demon hunter for a long time now and has memorized some of our fighting skills. He was the one who started Andrews's group. Because of Andrews's experience from his childhood, he wanted to make up for mistakes, mainly giving some of those a fighting chance or a chance to get away. His group had been hot on my heels until he came back for me. He allowed exceptions where the others did not. He also found himself with a unique power. If he wanted to kill me, he could have done it long ago and I doubt he would have needed my help finding others. I believe one hundred percent that we can trust him."

Taking an un-needed, breath more to sort out what I wanted to say not that I needed a breather. After so many centuries it came more out of habit than a real need. Sort of how some stammer with their words or have certain habits when they are speaking. This had been my habit even after death.

"The doctor is going to hunt us down till he kills us all. Normally we stay out of sight and just don't get caught but he has learned a lot of our habits, he will continue destroying for more than what would be normal for a human, since he has the immortality side now. He plans on hunting down many of our families. His path is either to control us or destroy us. And after what he put Claire through, I want revenge. Not for bloodlust but to stop him from killing more of our kind and the special gifts of others. He's not just a threat to us but if humans get in the way he eliminates them as if they were nothing more than a dust spec on his clothing."

I know Grace and Edmund had given me their word they would come. I wanted to make sure they understood why we were doing this and that it was something they chose to do. Not just because it had been for Claire and me. Hoping they accepted my brief explanation I waited to see if they had further questions or words for me. My parent's guests were rather silent listening to me the whole time I spoke. Edmund was pondering over what I told him. Grace stood still next to him.

"We will take only what is needed since we travel light anyway. We can be on our way in a few minutes. The Emerson clan is joining. They were here visiting us a few days ago and happened to be here when grace had the vision of you coming to us. They wanted to help us. They are already heading north. They don't know where to meet but will hear us calling them once we get in range. So, we should leave rather quickly." Not taking too much time after explaining, Edmund rushed from the room, in a matter of minutes both Edmund and Grace both had a small leather bag in their hands. Both were ready to take off. The two that had been sitting opted out. As we left, they took off in their own direction.

With Edmund in the lead both Charlotte and Grace followed behind. Heading straight up north and cutting across east now to catch up to the others.

There were six members in the Emerson clan, Lauren their mother with her two sons and two daughters. They also traveled with their uncle. They were originally family until one of their untimely deaths. They assumed the mother was the first one who had been attacked. She had been left for dead, with the venom leaking through her system. At first, she had been blinded from the venom spreading and the extreme fire that burned through her. She couldn't think rationally for a while and didn't want to risk going home; she was filled with desires that scared her. She panicked that she would kill her family. She had been assumed missing and dead until she showed up at her home three years later wearing the same outfit, she went missing in. Their father had passed away from an illness while she had been gone.

Walking in the front door shocked the rest of the family. She wanted to see that they were okay. Still worried about what she would do if she were ever near them, even though two of her family members were still in shock when their mother came home. Her oldest daughter came straight over to her without hesitating. Trying to warn her she realized she didn't want to harm her. The desire wasn't there. It never hit her, the fact of the situation until that very moment.

Her daughter Lacey explained how she stayed at a friend's house for a few months when she had been bitten. Lacey and her friend had gone for a walk together as they spoke, they were overheard. She admitted she wasn't sure what she was getting into. The stranger said he could make their friendship permanent. Being shocked by what he did by biting Lacey, her friend went running leaving her there. Later they came with a wagon expecting her to be dead. Only her friend and her brother knew what happened to her. After her change, she was extremely careful not to get too close to the family or other humans until she knew she could control herself. This happened long before their mother went missing. Lacey assumed she was fortunate to have control.

Knowing she had to hide it kept it in her constant thoughts, always working on control. No one paid attention to the lack of growth since she was already older than her younger siblings, she blended in with them easier now. Later as the youngest children were finally older, they chose to lose their humanity. Not every family would change their own. Many even watched their family members die and lived centuries past them, while others insisted on not leaving anyone behind. Some even tried destroying themselves not wanting to be a creature or vampire feeling they committed the worst crime against nature. Unfortunately, what most families were worried about has also happened. Three families they knew of, wiped each other out when they found they had no control. Not everyone was able to control their cravings.

As the scenery flashed past them, I could only think about how often this sort of thing would happen. At one time there had been a lot of demon hunters. Some were much more ferocious than others who were not even worthy of any kind of fear.

This doctor had been around for a very long time. Not many heard of him other than what words came from humans. Any other creature didn't seem to escape from his grasp. But then that's what worried me about him. He has had time to stock up and prepare for any kind of major attack. He had to know not all vampires were loners, that they would make friends with other species.

Racing along fast as we could. I was rather eager to catch up with Claire and Grant. Following directly behind Edmund and Grace, we shot through the least occupied areas we could find, even if it meant going through some more difficult terrain. Then without any warning Grace came to a dead stop with Edmund, stopping seconds after looking back at her to find out why she stopped.

"There are two demon hunters ahead and one directly behind us. I think we picked them up from the town behind us. They smell like mortals, so we won't have a problem." Pointing out the direction and exact spot of each, Edmund decided to take the one from behind. Grace took the one on the right, while I occupied the one to the left.

We each led them in a different direction. Edmund hadn't wasted time with the one following him. Draining him rather quickly, he dropped his body to the ground and ran straight ahead knowing as soon as we were done, we would meet again soon. Grace anticipated the moves of her follower trying to frustrate him. Using the Hun Bow, he tried several times to catch Grace while they ran. Running closer to each other. Grace angled herself just right and shot behind the one I was occupying. The one following Grace wound up shooting the arrow and killed his fellow hunter. Standing still, he was shocked. He never saw him there; he had only seen the two of us moving in a blur. As soon as the blur was gone, he saw the other man drop to his feet with the arrow in him. Not even needing to handle him. He stood there in disbelief as we ran off to catch up with Edmund. It hadn't taken long. Still trying to avoid as much as possible and keep our eyes open for any more hunters in case there were more of them heading up to meet near the doc.

I couldn't help but worry about Claire and hope she was already at the meeting place by now. It would already have been a little traveling with a baby. They've never had one around before. I didn't even know if she would naturally know how to care for him or not. Perhaps the others she joins might be willing to help her or she might be fine on her own.

Vampires just didn't have children other than those they rather self-created themselves, which never ended well. For full vampires, it was too frustrating creating one of their own. It never grew past the point they changed it. For some reason, they would simply die on their own or be left behind and destroyed by humans or hunters. There had been rules to live by even for vampires. They lived as they wished if they kept their secret at all costs. Children could simply not be trusted with secrets like this, children did not discriminate against who they killed. Half-breed children might have been allowed but still faced many of the same problems.

Rarely do they raise a human who would die in so many years. Claire had been the first half breed that I was familiar with, even though lately because of Andrew, we were being introduced to others that were out there. I hadn't been aware of other special creatures until Grace and Edmund introduced me to a world I had never known about. Until I knew them, I didn't even know vampires existed. There are more of us out there, at times it feels like there are more of us than mortals. Except there are not, once you know what you are looking for, they are easier to identify.

Edmund was the one who taught me his believe as to why vampires existed. He believes the fact that we exist, that we had an original purpose and somehow that was lost, so we simply exist now. That normally for a normal human when the soul departs the body, the body decays and soul moves on. However for vampires, there is something within us that at death, traps the soul inside and that soul keeps the body from decaying and moving on. He believes that some were meant to be vampires and felt we did not belong where we lived, from where exactly he didn't know. That information was lost also over time. Gracie believed it was the venom that trapped the soul in the first place, she agreed with some of Edmunds logic.

Chapter Eleven
Andrew

Being the first to take off, Andrew stopped for a moment as he saw charlotte take off west. More curious how Grant was going to take this situation since he was rather thrown into something he never saw coming. However, for a human, he seemed rather noble for his actions. At this point, even Andrew wished he had been more accepting like Grant is now, even if it might mean his death. At least with my viewpoint on it, I was going to try and keep Grant furthest from any fighting if I could help it, especially since he's going to be left with Jacob.

No longer taking the time to look behind, trying to rush through now that I would be passing around a few towns. I wasn't as fast as Charlotte and Claire. I may have had some gifts however they were not speeding. I could run faster than most humans. However, my gift was more confusing than simply getting stronger and faster. Mathais had taken off in such a flash no one would ever have a chance to see him unless you knew what you were looking for. It may have been great to control wind and fire, but I still wished I could have run a lot faster. At least that gift I could get a lot more use out of. I knew the others would be able to meet up rather quickly, I was more worried about myself and if I would be able to join them in time.

My main goal had been to gather enough to fight that hopefully they would appear more intimidating that the docs followers would be scared off and hopefully no need to harm or kill them, they could keep their causalities low. Our priority and main concern had been the one person and not the others. It wasn't going to be easy going against the doc since he knew my fighting style. After all, he was the one who taught me. Not that he knew about my gifts. The doc himself was no mere measly human. Even when he had been human, he was rather impressive. He was tall with a rather large muscular build. A man even after the change was good at deception. In appearance, he seemed large but very gentle until he found out you were not all human. Then the evil side came out.

Judging who he felt had the right to life and who did not. Using his private asylum to dissect creatures and use them for experiments. As difficult as it had been to kill vampires, he had his style for this. He wielded a rather large ax to sever limbs and organs from their bodies. He always had his arsenal of sorts to pick from depending on what creature he was killing. Down through the centuries, he collected different weapons as they became available adding them to his collection. His favorites included the Francesca axe, Gladius, and the Celtic sword and Hun bow. So, depending on how well equipped he was at his new location. I wasn't one hundred percent sure what to expect when we ambushed him. Especially not knowing how many would be helping him. He had a few of his recruits that he created which he would no doubt in the end eliminate them as well.

Then along with those he had humans who were convinced as he was that mystical gifts were those of the devil and could not possibly come from anything good and needed to be killed, that these creatures were far too dangerous to allow walking the earth. He did not need a group to begin with to fight since he had gone on his own many times. The groups were to kill in areas that he wasn't in yet. To flush out what he hadn't found himself.

Not sure how to prepare the others for how difficult this was going to be. At this point, I wasn't sure. Reflecting on a situation I had been in when I was being trained by the doctor. They had been tracking a wolf across the snow until its prints came to a stop with no warning. There was no sign of the wolf. It was as if it disappeared from the face of the earth. Then they found it had suddenly run at such a speed that it no longer left prints in the snow for them to follow.

At the time Andrew guessed the doctor was good at guessing where their prey would run. Now it makes sense that he probably started tracking them by scent or sound. They caught up to the wolf which transformed into a person. Standing face to face with a killer, the wolf-man shot out from him a blast of heat along with a strong burst of wind that almost knocked them off their feet. He looked rather young so he might not have had full strength of his gift yet. The doctor even though the rest of us were unable to move with the constant wind barreling down on us, walked through it as if nothing was being forced against him. We could only watch from where our feet rooted themselves into the ground. Two swords were in sheaths on his back as he pulled out his favorite weapon of choice. The double-sided battle-ax.

I knew I could not even lift it, yet he lifted it as if it weighed nothing at all. Not being able to outrun him, he sliced the wolf-man in half. Barely any effort on his part, he had been so strong. No expression of pain, remorse, or a general feeling of loss that a life of a human even though it was also partly wolf had to die. He never showed emotion. No one ever knew if he was happy or sad. Always monotone and spoke only of his mission to eradicate the errors in the world.

Another time they came across a creature and weren't sure how to view it. It had almost been rather comical to me. The doctor had gone further ahead to the next town to check on a sighting. As we sat in one of the pubs, I was watching this barmaid, which seemed simple enough that she served her customers, always smiling. Even when she came over to our group, she was friendly and quick with our food and drinks. Then when she was standing near a wall, she was holding a tray she had been carrying food and drinks. It looked like she was about to sneeze. She even seemed alarmed by what happened. The tray she was holding dropped to the floor. It had been emptied so only the tray made noise. No longer able to hold back the sneeze, she jerked back from the force of it and went through the wall. Where she went through, there was no hole or door. She ran up the stairs as quickly as she could since the rest of my group had seen this happen. They took after her thinking they would corner her from up top. Then as it happened again, she dropped right through the floor. She sneezed again. I hadn't followed my group and stayed down below. The look on her face looked like she was astonished she went through the floor.

"Please I'm not a demon, this is all new to me, I don't know how it happens, it just does." She looked at me pleading for her life.

Obscured Darkness

As the others came down, I pushed her through the wall again as fast as I could, only hoping it would still work and not backfire.

"She went through the floor here, keep a watch on it here. I'm going back outside to check out the wall she first went through." Not questioning me at all, I went back through the door and went straight outside where she should have been waiting for me.

"My advice is to hide for a while till we are gone. We are leaving later today. They're dumb enough to think you're stuck in the ground. Hide your gift and don't let anyone know how you do it, even if you don't understand yet yourself. If you have to hide and live off berries and roots then do it till you get it under control, otherwise, there are more like us and they won't let you live." Making sure she went through the connecting door to the building she borrowed a jacket from the lady working there. Then discreetly left the bar without even glancing back she took off as I told her to do until it would be safe.

From the look on her face and seeing her fall through the wall and the floor amused me. Curious what kind of gift it was. I didn't want to interfere in case she could turn it into something wonderful. Besides, letting a few go and the others not knowing about them wouldn't hurt them. Sadly, any nice memories had been when the doctor had been absent. Watching him torture creatures in the asylum left me with permanent nightmares. Wishing I didn't need to sleep like vampires. I would have traded my mortality simply to get rid of the nightmares. Always hear patients screaming, begging for death for what they were put through.

Trying to shake these memories off racing through the terrain and trying to get up north would take almost all my concentration. However, I wanted to make a stopover quick.

Hoping beyond hope they would be there. I would be able to catch up to the others rather quickly with the help of my friends.

Daniel and Marcheline had been rather interesting friends I met a long time ago. After my training with the doctor, I would take time off. While others went to visit family, I went on vacations or just explored. At that time, I didn't have any family to speak of. I would stay with or Daniel and Marcheline or send off special creatures that I would try to hide with them. They understood what I did and why I did it.

It was a little unusual how I met them. I was out exploring looking around the countryside. I liked climbing mountains. It had been the adrenaline rush I looked for. I had seen these two people standing out in the middle of a field and rather quickly without warning, they vanished. It piqued my curiosity. I went up to search for them and kept finding nothing. Then I noticed the tiniest hole in the ground. Jumping down. I hadn't expected all the water below. However, I found out the hard way. I was thankful that I could swim. It was so dark I couldn't see until I made it to the end. I kept feeling along the wall and swimming hoping I wasn't going to run into something dangerous.

Following the long tunnel, there was a huge opening with a long shelf. There they were sitting having a picnic in the dark. They seemed more surprised to see me down there than I had been of them. They had been fascinated with caverns and underground tunnels and anything else hidden. I had known them for several years before I found out they had special gifts. They hid them quite well until they felt they could trust me with their secrets. I couldn't exactly blame them since I was known as a demon hunter.

I hadn't been aware the doc had still been alive; after we split from him, we hadn't heard from him for several years. No one seemed to know where to find him. Our old group had rather navigated itself following the old training not that we had any orders from the main teacher anymore. But then he could have assumed by now we understood what our assignments were. On the other hand, it could have been that we had not been successful enough. That the very few we did flush out, didn't seem worthy of stopping us but then neither had it been worth his time keeping in touch with us.

Without having to ask. I knew Daniel and Marcheline would be eager to help. Their gifts would help in a rather unique way. I wished I knew how many people we were going to need for this confrontation or if Charlie would allow his family to put themselves in danger helping deal with it. Even if he didn't, I couldn't exactly complain.

It was rare to meet a couple who shared the same gift, especially one like theirs. Usually when others dealt with Daniel and Marcheline they never quite knew what they were getting themselves into. Even though it was only the two of them, it was like having eight helping. Both shared a very similar gift. Standing still in a trance, a cloudy smoke would form from head to toe and then slowly shift outward from Marcheline. As each smoke started to form it would make an identical replica of her. Daniel had been slightly different. Smoke would rise from the ground from where he stood and slightly swirl around him. His would go out like Marcheline's would except it would take a couple of seconds to solidify in front of you as a double of him.

When duplicated you could still see them through these forms, each having three copies of themselves. The copies could not duplicate themselves. They were almost physically equal in strength, intelligence, and fighting skill. The only downfall is that if one of the copies gets injured then the main person receives the same injury. If a clone died, then the main would die also. They used to have Marisa however her clone died and ended in her death many years ago. If the main gets injured, then only the main is injured. But when it comes to just one person against three it helps.

With their swordplay, fast movements, and quick wit, they were quite a challenge for anyone who made the mistake of opposing them, tired of trying to run now that I was feeling tired. Sadly, endurance wasn't something I possessed enough of either. Getting close to a town now, I walked more normally not to attract any attention to me, but then just the way I was dressed caught attention. Checking out which stores were open and then inspecting how many people were around and watching. Seemed like none of them were even interested in the fact a new person was there.

Spotting a sign for a livery stable nearby, I walked straight for it. No one was at the entrance of the door. Even though this seemed far too easy. I slipped inside waiting to see if anyone would even pay attention. Not that I wanted to steal a horse. I didn't want to have to stop in every other town to take a break. It would take me seven to nine days to get there. I know I was trying to convince myself that what I was about to do was acceptable, but I had to stop and admit it to myself. I'm outright stealing a horse. Only one person peeked in out of curiosity as they walked by but still did not stop. Heading back for the spotted horse in the back, it was rather impressive looking, and looked eager to get out of this place as much as I did. Unwinding the ropes from its hooves and taking the rope that had been tied around the neck, it seemed excessive for a horse. The owners wanted to make sure he didn't take off.

Skipping the saddle since it wasn't needed. Swinging myself up and taking the horse out, riding the horse slowly until I was almost out of town. Not until then did we break into a full run. The wind rushing through my hair speeding along. The time would go much faster now and the length that needed to be traveled would be quicker with the horse. The horse seemed even more eager than it had when we first took off.

Curious if I would have to convince the horse to run through the forest that now formed in front of us. I didn't have to coax it at all, it shot off through the trees even careful not to knock me off as we whizzed through the forest. Not until we had the trees to judge speed, did I realize how fast we were traveling. A lot faster than a horse should go. I began to wonder if I had found the devil's horse or was riding on top of a shapeshifter or some other unfortunate creature. If so, his gift was much better than mine. At least he had speed.

I hadn't taken the time to notice which breed of horse I had taken. There had been a couple of others in the stables I assumed this one would catch less attention than the pure black horse would, as impressive as it was with a slight rust-red sheen to its coat and dark black eyes. I couldn't shake the feeling this horse would be better suited. At least looking at it I figured if the Appaloosa were good enough for the Nez Pierce Tribe then the Appaloosa would be perfect for me. Before I ever had to give it instructions, or give it a nudge in the direction that I needed to take off in, it already turned those directions. It's as if he was waiting for me and knew the way that I was heading. Part of me panicked thinking I was about to get ambushed, and I was just sitting there along for the ride. Then it could have been a lucky chance it wanted to go where I did.

Coming to the stream that I had seen many times from memory, we followed it till we came to a little quiet house. Out in the middle of nowhere next to the stream, there was a little house nestled between the rock hill and the water. Getting down from the horse. I walked to the house and the horse followed. Only to stop a few steps away. It didn't transform but whinnied quite a bit, then stopped as I knocked on the door.

"Go away, only lazy people live here." Came a shout from inside. It sounded rather gruff and determined not to have guests.

"Are you sure you want me to go away?" Standing there waiting for a reply.

"Ugly vampires are not welcome. There's a pine stick out front standing straight up, do me a favor and fall on it." The voice started to sound strange, I couldn't help but find it amusing.

"I'm sure if I were a vampire, they would find me ugly also. Now get out here before I burn your house down, you know I'll do it." I knew this would bring him to the door.

A few footsteps could be heard. Then the door opened wide to show Daniel at the door with a wide smile.

"Sorry, I thought you were someone else here to bother converting me to Christianity or how my life was worthless. It might be worthless for other reasons, but I don't have to admit to it. I've been getting a lot of that lately. Stupid humans don't know what they're doing anymore." Daniel gave an exasperated look on his face.

Opening the door to let me in. I followed as Daniel walked into the living room, a very simply decorated house. There were pictures of family members looking proud painted on the wall. Not even on a canvas just painted on the wall like one large mural that linked each family member to each other. A few chairs are centered around a piano. Marcheline had been sitting at the piano with two of her duplicates playing a rather intricate piece. They stopped as soon as they realized who walked in the door. In the chairs next to the piano, they had visitors, a young woman in a formal dress and a young man in a black suit.

"Let me introduce you to some guests of ours. They stopped

by to invite us to something rather interesting. If you're not planning anything you're certainly welcome to join us. Not much happens when your life is immortal. At least nothing too interesting that you haven't heard of several times that you quit keeping track."

The young man was of a muscular build which made the young lady look even tinier with her little frame and short height, both dark hair and dark complexions. Black eyes just like the horse from the stables. Even the one I rode had dark black eyes.

"The horse outside wouldn't by any chance belong to either of you?" Not sure if it would be an insult but I would feel bad if I had just stolen their horse.

"No, we don't travel by horse but from the looks of him, he is rather happy to you for freeing him from his last place of captivity. He's not anything other than a horse but he is an unusual one. His thoughts speak rather loudly."

"Good, I would hate to start on the wrong foot. I'm Andrew; I was just stopping to ask a favor. What type of event are you planning?" Curious about what they were working on.

"My name is Forrest, and this is my wife Ivy. We were recently contacted by a mutual friend. Not sure if you have heard of him but his name is Charlie McAllister. We were heading up north to help friends. We have done favors for each other in the past and have known each other for a very long time. My father when he was human used to know Charlie's father when he was human also."

"Then you don't need to invite me, happens to be why I am stopping here also. I was going to ask Daniel and Marcheline to help me out. I know Evangeline and she is Charlie's youngest sister. We sent Claire ahead of us to warn them of the problem going on."

"So, you would be the old demon hunter who's helping us out? Charlie told us about the papers you found and what the old doc was up to. Figured we happen to be on his list, can't hurt to help. We have a few of our friends that should be there shortly also. They have the same gifts we do. Not that we are impressive unless there is someone else there with an impressive gift. We replicate and use the power and energy from others to recreate their gifts. Then we can do the same as others. So far with practice, we have replicated up to four gifts at a time. Someday we hope to do more. Not too often do you get several different types in one area to learn and pick up from. It also sucks when there are no others around with gifts. Then we have nothing to copy and rely on our only gift at that point. Speed, At least we can usually outrun things when we need to."

The young man already seemed comfortable with talking to a former demon hunter. He even seemed to be impressed that I was no longer hunting but helping. Let alone the fact that the one we were going to stop had been my former teacher and hunting partner. Charlie had already told them about my confrontation with my old group, how I stood up for his family and protected them, especially Evangeline.

"Figures one more group that can outrun me, mind if I ask what kind of creature you are? I know I will never get to know all gifts that are out there, but I am curious." I had been curious if they were human their skin had appeared to be smooth almost very much like the vampires, their skin had the most beautiful golden hue. Their voices seemed so regular, nothing like Evangeline's angelic-like sound. Were they vamps also? Could they read my mind and know what I was thinking about them?

"We are human for the most part, but as for our gifts, we prefer not to classify ourselves. We are not vampires, wolves, or shades, we sort of blend in the middle of many groups. Our kind has been around for a long time; once we have found our partner, we are incapable of having children with another. If our partner dies, then our childbearing years are over. Our gifts are passed down genetically. Our daughter Luna is outside right now somewhere, we were boring her. She is the same as us, but we are still undecided if she will join us in the fight or not. She's only fifteen but don't let her age underestimate her. She could outdo me if she wished. We were leaving this evening if you needed help going up north since I notice you do not have the gift of speed."

"Normally I would take you up on the offer and I had hoped that I would catch a ride with Daniel and Marcheline. I think I'll stick to my horse. He seems to travel just as fast and I'm more comfortable traveling with him already. We'll still be slower than all of you so I'm going to head out now and take off. Besides before the fight, I would like to see Evangeline before things pick up. I still need to talk to Charlie since I have only conveyed the message through writing, I haven't talked to him since the day I left to get Charlotte. Before I go, I wanted to say thank you for helping. I don't know how many we will need. We can't underestimate the doc. He's tricky and very strong. He has absolutely no fear, not just physically but with weapons as well."

After shaking their hands and saying goodbye to Daniel and Marcheline. I left the little house. Down the stream, I could see Luna. She was rather young-looking. She looked younger than fifteen. More like ten or twelve. She had a tiny frame like her mother which made her age deceptive. However, she had a darker skin tone than her parents and in the light, her hair looked almost chocolate red rather than just a dark chocolate brown. The young girl had taken a glance at me but wasn't interested. She seemed more curious and fascinated with whatever she had been watching in the water. There was a reason she was more interested in watching the water than to look at me. She was watching in the water had been the next few days playing out in the picture to her.

Amazing how creatures of closely similar behavior get to know each other. Rarely did I keep company with those who chose to eat humans either their blood or carcass. It had been harder on the blood drinkers, even if they abstained from consuming humans or certain animals who were shifters. You know there had to be mistakes somewhere. Even for those who were somewhat borderline. Like the ones who liked to consume killers and other types of criminals. Feeling this justified their killings to themselves. Some made special cocktails that were neither blood nor carcass. Almost eating like hummingbirds but adding nutrients to get the iron they craved. You could tell the difference in their eyes, skin, and mannerism.

As for the gifts of the others that I have met over the years. I am always amazed at what others can do. Most I met were humans possessing powers, a few of them had immortality. They mainly passed their gifts along their family line. A very small few could pass their gifts on to others without being genetically related. Then when I met Evangeline, she had been the first vampire that I knew that came from a large family, not that she knew them until much later. Charlotte, I hadn't gotten to know her for too long let alone never met her family. This should be interesting.

Now standing next to the horse. "Marcheline said you prefer to be called Lapwai. I find it rather interesting that their last name is Lapwai also. We have quite a distance to go tonight. Hope you don't mind traveling with me further. You've been a good companion." When I paid the compliment to the horse he almost seemed as though he understood what I meant.

Standing on the left side I hoisted myself back up on his

back again. Without any delay, we took off. In what felt like several hours we were not alone for very long? Not too far off from where we needed to go, I could feel the electric presence of others catching up to us. The sun had finally started to go down so I limited my guesses to who it could be. I recognized the one presence of Marcheline first. I knew it wouldn't take long for them to get there, so it wasn't too surprising that they had already caught up to us. Even Daniel waved and smiled at me while he passed me as if I were standing still, even Forrest, Ivy, and Luna passed us in their dust. I was getting tired of being the only one who was so slow. I swear if I found someone with a gift of speed that can be passed to another then I was going to find a way they could either bite or infect me with it.

I wasn't even able to watch them for long, before we had gone very far, they were already out of sight. I guessed I would still get there by tonight. The others would be waiting for me as soon as I did get there. Besides Lapwai was already fast enough for what I preferred. My stomach always felt upset from the fast motion when Daniel or Marcheline insisted that they give me a quick ride wherever it had been that we were going to.

As the sun hid behind the clouds and night came. There had been in the distance a glow of light that grew even brighter as we were getting closer. Next to a house, there had been a bonfire with several people standing around it, either conversing or sitting looking anxious. As I arrived stopping just a few feet from them. I hopped off Lapwai. He must not have felt too comfortable being around so many vampires. As soon as I was off, he turned and ran away, back in the direction that we came from. Watching him take off I turned to look at the many faces already watching me. Some of those I already knew and many that I had never seen before. One I was surprised to see. I had known him before I just never knew he was gifted, a basic nod of the head in my direction as we both acknowledged each other.

Both Charlotte and Claire were already there blending in with the others. Funny how people seemed to know how to relate to each other. For so long I have learned never to trust anyone or be close to anyone that I felt I stood out more like an outhouse in the center of town.

From the looks of it, we should be okay. Even if the doctor had a large group, we in sheer number and power should be able to handle it. Not guaranteeing any casualties but we should be able to take him out. Hopefully, we won't lose anyone. That so far is my fear. These great people trying to correct an injustice and one of them may pay for it, even though it would be sacrificing themselves for not just their family and friends but that of others. No matter how noble I still don't wish to lose anyone.

They must have been waiting for the moment of my arrival as each group stood with each other. From the looks on their faces, I could see many had unanswered questions or had been curious about what our next move would be and how to handle the situation. Charlie had already gone over some ideas however he was waiting for my arrival to find the best form of attack would be drawing from my experience.

Standing there I took it all in. A sight I at one time never thought that I would ever witness. Such a large group of compassionate people who were so gifted, whether they were viewed as demons, angels, or simply a messenger. They all had the same goal in mind. At one time I would have hunted some even though as I could see all of these I would have personally let go. Not that the doctor would have seen it that way.

All eyes rested on me as I walked my way over to who I could only assume had been Charlie. Even without having him pointed out the presence he exuded showed him as a leader. The one who took care of things and was quite distinguished, standing a few feet in front of me still taking in my surroundings.

Just behind Charlie stood his family, Ava, Aiden, Mark, Lorah, Dinah, Bethany, and Aidelle. Not all his family lived with him however most of them made it a point to show up for this. On the side stood Nichole and Anthony both holding one of their little ones who appeared to be a year old now. Charlie's family seemed to share the same gifts, mainly strength, speed, and the ability to communicate with each other through telekinesis. The only problem they seemed to have as Charlie pointed out had been that they could not read the minds of others outside of their family. He admitted he could read one person's mind which was why he was drawn to her. Beyond that, he didn't describe any more of her to me.

Evangeline was rather new, and I hadn't learned her gift. However, I assumed she might have the same from her family. Evangeline now stood near her family along with Lewis, who happened to be of white arctic wolf descent. He also possessed the gift of speed but also the ability to freeze with a simple touch. In tropical climates, it was extremely hard for him to do this as he drew his gift from the colder elements around him.

Then there were my friends, Charlotte with her parents, and Edmund who had dealt with past wars, strength, and amazing agility. Then there was his wife Grace, who had the gift of seeing the future however very limited. She could see things as they happened from any distance or at least within four hours of when it was going to happen. Then Claire stood beside them with Grant still holding Jacob firmly in his arms. I knew that Charlotte had only the traditional vampire traits which are what most of Charlie's family possessed. Then of course I didn't know what gifts Claire had if any. If she had any, she certainly didn't feel any need to announce it or use it yet.

Then a clan I was not familiar with however had traveled with Charlotte. The Emerson clan, Jackson and Lauren, the adults stood with the kids standing slightly to their side. Their daughters Lacey and Crystal, then the sons Chales and Markus, no one in the family had special gifts outside of the basic vampire strength and speed.

Then the last of the group was Daniel and Marcheline with their friends Forrest and Ivy, the last two had brought their daughter Luna along. I had known Daniel and Marcheline; they had a gift of duplication in physical form. Just a bit different in the way that the gift was always there, whereas Forrest and Ivy duplicated the gifts of others that were around them. So, if there wasn't anything around them, they had nothing to duplicate other than their gift of speed. Their daughter's gift hadn't been known. She could see images whether they were in the past, present, or future. At times, she could be watching a person and it would look as though she was standing right behind them when she was nowhere near them. She could watch someone many miles away. She used water or anything liquid she could to watch her scenes. Luna had never been in a situation to test out if she inherited her parent's gifts. However, gifts like these seemed to be less common by the decade and no one understood why. There were many theories, either environment or the human body breaking down or others not reproducing since the carriers were human. At some point Forrest and Ivy, even Luna would pass away. Immortality was not something that came along with their gift.

There were several filling in the empty spaces that I had no idea who they were or even what they had been. Some you could guess from the way they were dressed, others were much less obvious, a rather diverse group. There were Vampires, extremely diverse shapeshifters, lycanthropes, Witches, druids, and Shades. I had never fought alongside many of these creatures, so I didn't know what their strong suits and weaknesses were. Neither had I ever worked with witches before so this should be interesting.

"Hi Charlie, I am Andrew. Sorry to have met you under these circumstances. I assume you will want to get right to it. That way the less time we waste the better." Trying not to be too nervous wasn't easy.

I had never been around this large of a group let alone so many special creatures. Next to everyone else, I didn't feel lesser I just felt in awe.

Chapter Twelve
Preparing for the Fight

Following Charlie into the house, everyone else had waited patiently outside. Closing the door behind us, we began to discuss the situation and how we would explain it to the others.

"It would help if we knew how many were with him. We know he has three vampires he made himself work for him. But we don't know how many humans are working with him now. It doesn't seem like he would want too many vampires around since it's the very thing he is trying to eliminate. The owls could search above since he would never suspect them. But they would have to be careful not to be caught since he would hunt them for food. This would give us an exact location and give us an idea of how many he has surrounded himself with. None of these men should be underestimated but we do need to find how many we might be dealing with.

Hopefully, we will get a view of what they are in case there are more turned humans that we are unaware of with him. There are a few remote viewers that could attempt to see what the doc is up to and what is around him but might not be concrete since the future is always changing, especially when we know." Waiting a moment since Charlie looked deep in thought as he listened to me explain.

It hadn't taken long to describe the weapons the Doc would have in his possession. Also, the fighting style was discussed in detail so that everyone would understand the way he had been when I was taught by him. He may have added to it as the years and his experience changed.

"By any chance do you have anything from the days of your training with the doc? Weaponry or something that he would have touched himself or belonged to him?" It looked like Charlie was forming an idea.

Opening my jacket, I had a pocket inside that carried my cash and anything small and important. I pulled out a small, red-colored fabric piece that had the initials D & H on it. The letters were supposed to remind us of our connection and brotherhood and what our single mission was. We could also identify ourselves with other demon hunters with the small fabric badge. I used it to deter any hunters when they would come across me. I found I never had to explain a thing once they saw the badge. Most wore it however since I left, I kept it in my pocket, forgetting it had been there until now. Holding it only for a moment. I handed it over to Charlie, curious why he wanted it.

Charlie went over to the door and opened it, only leaning out not hearing a word come from him, he must have spoken lightly enough for the one he wanted to hear him. Not someone who I thought he would be calling but Luna came in through the door behind him.

Soon as the door was closed, he had her stand in front of the table. Placing a glass bowl in front of her. The young girl stood in front of it quietly fixated on whatever she saw in the water. Then from her pocket, she pulled out a black liquid that she had in a vile. Still intent on whatever she was watching she poured the liquid in making the water black. As she stared into the water Charlie stood beside her waiting for her to write something down.

Charlie had laid parchment paper with a quill beside it with the intent of Luna using psychography. In a matter of minutes, her hand reached for the quill writing at a rather furious speed.

Then she stopped abruptly and folded the paper with what she wrote on the inside cover. Charlie whispered something only for her ears and she let herself out of the house.

Next had been Grace, she came in right after Luna left. I assumed Luna must have let her know she was needed. Luna had not touched the cloth piece. However, as soon as Grace came into the room, she took the small piece from Charlie. Placing it in the palm of one hand she placed her other hand directly over it cupping it. Standing perfectly still with her eyes closed. Absolutely no movement from her except occasionally her hand would slide a little on the torn badge.

The same action as Luna, she wrote with the quill pen on a piece of parchment and as fast as she wrote what her visions were, she folded the paper over, put the quill down, and walked out of the room as soon as she was done.

Charlie took both pieces of paper and laid them out next to each other comparing the two unique visions. I stood next to Charlie and looked at both. Luna had drawn pictures whereas Grace wrote down mostly words. Luna had seen a large square building that looked like an institution or another asylum. This shouldn't surprise me since I knew he had more than one and in several other locations. It almost looked like an oil painting the way Luna had drawn it out. There were only four humans outside and oddly enough it looked like the doctor was sitting on the steps staring directly at us. It was eerie as if he knew but then maybe he has a way of watching us without us knowing. Just the same as we were of him now.

The next person to come in had been Lewis. They had talked to each other in low tones. Something I assumed vampires and other species could do with each other. Sadly, for my human ears, I did not pick up that well when speech was so low. Even with my gift. I never knew if I was fully human or had any form of immortality, however, I wasn't eager to find out. But I knew it was a possibility during the fight it might happen. When the doc first trained me, I was always prepared mentally to die. Not talking for too long as soon as Lewis got to the door, he changed into his wolf form and took off with three other owls circling overhead.

"I asked him to scout out an area. From the pictures, I can only guess where this is. And that won't be far from where we are now. Once he gets back, we should hopefully have a better idea of how many there are. Either way, I would assume the best time to attack would be in the morning since he would expect a nighttime attack. If he's in the Forrest there should be enough coverage for many of us. At least out here with the fight, it won't matter who notices that we are not merely human. For the sun vulnerable vampires, there will be enough shade to protect them from harm.

From the picture Luna had drawn it looked like Doc planned on attacking us up here. It might be why he is looking at us, in Luna's other picture because he is now aware there are more of us than usual and has temporarily halted their attack. Their plan of surprise for us has been changed.

Everyone sat around the fire pit outside waiting for instructions or rather how they would be involved and be able to help. Both Charlie and I talked at length before assembling everyone in one area.

Darnell had been sitting on the side observing everyone, shaking his head he stood and directed his question toward Charlie.

"I get that we are here to kill the doctor. But there are several here that have never had to fight before, like the half breeds and then you have the opposite extreme that has battled other demons or hunters. There are so many of us and it's pretty much going to be a slaughter, then why so many?" Crossing his arms in front of him, showing he felt there was more to this. Or at least hoping there had to be so he would be ready.

"As you said, it is going to be a slaughter, the fight will be over rather quickly. The only problem we might have is if the doctor has any other creatures that are dumb enough to fight with him. We don't want to underestimate humans. They have been trained and many are successful. They have observed our skills and learned how to use those against us. They may be human, but they can be rather crafty when they have to be, never underestimate the determination of a human." Charlie never changed the tone of his voice. Other than the fact it still sounded slightly sad.

Another person had been standing next to Darnell who stood looking at him, and then quickly slapped him with one hand.

"It's going to be like slapping a bug off your face, or if you will a little slap fight except it will look worse for them, its pointless with so many of us." Smiling the two started slapping at each other goofing off until one hit the other sending him flying back.

Their goofing off turned into rough play with a few others joining in. Charlie shook his head as the group goofed off.

"What are you doing with the kids and the meat bag? Can't help but notice there are some." Darnell hadn't been the only one wondering.

"They will be staying here, right now there is no sense in including Luna if there isn't a need, and the little ones, there's no need in explaining that one. Grant will be staying behind to watch them. He won't be able to fight he's just human." After Charlie had said that he wished he could have worded it differently not to make Grant feel like an oddball or as if being human was not worth anything, after all, part of this fight was to protect other humans.

"It's okay I should probably get used to it if this is going to be my new type of family. No offense taken." Grant was taking it rather well but then he also looked like he was feeling comfortable with the present company and being the only full-fledged human here.

"I want to go with; I can fight just as well as anyone else. I could help a lot, especially with what I could do." As Luna said this, Darnell went to push her back out of the group.

Anticipating the move, she adjusted her stance and moved quickly to his side. Almost watching it like a movie she watched the clips as they played out before they happened and kept adjusting where she stood to either move back or forward even running behind another person who wound up getting grabbed instead. Keeping one step ahead of Darnell until he gave up trying to catch her simply smiling at her shaking his head walking away.

"Worst case scenario you will be here to help protect, or rather help Grant protect the little ones and get them out of here if something bad happens." Wanting Luna to feel important and trying not to cut Grant down again Charlie tried to make it sound important that they stay behind.

Not that it would be needed. No one else seemed to buy the story but agreed with it anyway.

"Don't worry you won't be on your own. I wish there were something more I could do, but someone has to watch the kids." Grant was trying to be friendly to get Luna out of her depressed mood.

"I get why you can't go but your human, and the babies are even stronger than you." Sighing Luna gave up and went over to the bench in front of the house and sat down rather forcefully.

Several hours passed when the owl finally flew back even though he didn't make the most of graceful entrances landing flat on his face as he transformed. Only being grazed had been enough to disrupt his change. Now walking over to Charlie, he didn't look too pleased.

"They know we're coming. No one is outside that I can see. I wouldn't feel safe trying to break in to get to them. We're going to have to find a way of flushing them out if they are in there. There may be another building nearby that they are occupying. One up north of it only looks like a square building with one large tunnel leading to several other tunnels. I'm not sure how but I'm hoping someone will have an idea. According to Lewis, there are at least forty with us, we should be able to handle it." At this point, Lewis took over the conversation when the owl explained all he could.

"They only have what looks like three creatures with them that are not human. I could look in only one window and who knows since they know about us that could be a setup letting us see only that? Or those could be his sacrifices while he attacks from behind. It's a large building and from the smaller creatures in the area, there are many manmade tunnels underground."

Obscured Darkness

Lewis shook his head trying to figure out the situation. Even though he had seen it himself he could not believe it. How did they find out so soon?

Everyone had been watching Andrew to see what his reaction would be. He had the most experience with what the doc was like, and what his fighting style would be with the way he would have trained his troops.

"I can only guess that the lady in black saw us coming. She is rather unusual and very powerful. If she is anywhere near, we will have a problem even if the humans are not a problem. Some of them have been trained rather well; sadly, many of them have fought in another form. It's called a dreamscape. It's something that the lady in black controls. She had enchanted crystals that were imbued with very strong magic. Those of us that had been strong enough or clever enough went after the creatures outside of the dreamscape or those who for some reason she could not pull in. My mind didn't work that way so she couldn't pull me in. I've heard from others who have trained inside and what goes on. If for some reason you get pulled in, the humans will be equal to you, don't underestimate their strength. However, if you get pulled in then your body will be vulnerable out here." Trying to keep it blunt but letting them know how serious it was, this had been better than holding anything back.

Many of the others were looking around at each other; some looked more worried than others. Many however looked more anxious to just get it over. At least one feeling everyone shared. No one looked forward to killing humans even evil ones. Trying to think of the best possible solution Demetrius stood up and came out to the center where only Andrew and Charlie had been standing.

"I have an idea, not a gift I get to use too often. Mainly because it takes so much energy and I'm weak immediately after. I might get nailed by someone after I do it, but I could flush them out if they're in the tunnels or if not, at least they would run from the building since it can be creepy. Just give me a few minutes and I'll have everyone out." Smiling almost an evil smile Demetrius seemed pretty sure of himself.

"So far it sounds like the best offer we have if you can do it. Then we will form a ring at least and hopefully cover as much as we can, we can spread out however not too far in case we need to help each other out. We will have two go with you to protect you when you do your thing. Andrew will be within distance to handle the humans that come out and hopefully corral them. Our main goal is the doc. Even though we don't exactly need weapons most of us are strong enough some will be in close contact and are half-human or a creature with no fighting gifts. So, we do have weapons for you. Dinah had been gathering them up, they've been put by the tree so if you need one now is the time to find what you can work with." Not many but a few went over picking up axes, swords, and knives to fight with.

Nichole placed a blanket on the floor in the cottage for the twins. Lucian and Rose were laid down on the blanket with Claire's son Jacob. Grant and Luna were going to be staying behind to watch the kids keeping them safe while everyone else left. No one had been worried about how many humans there might be, except now no one could get over the idea the lady in black might be there. She was well known and many rumors floated about her. Not a surprise she hooked up with the doc. But then it was a curious thing, as powerful and dangerous as she was on her own then why would she want to be around the one person who might be able to kill her?

Chapter Thirteen
The Fight

Organizing hadn't taken too long, with everyone already here, no one coming and going. Taking up a count most had been very confident. Even more, had been curious just how Demetrius was going to flush them out. As soon as everyone was given instructions, we started to travel across the land to the asylum they were holed up in. There hadn't been much to prepare with. Some had fought before being caught in wars on witchcraft, others caught in the center of demon hunting or other senseless attacks. Everyone kept close in case we had a surprise attack, no one jumped out of the bushes or came as a surprise. We hoped we would have sensed them.

While we made our way, Luna had been back at the cottage giving Grant a play-by-play of what was going on. Not that there was anything to report other than the fact that we were traveling rather quickly, some hitching rides while others were simply moving at their speed. It had taken Lewis a while to run there the first time. Even with our speed it still took a bit. Also, many of our watchers or rather future sight members were scouting for any hidden traps that might have been on the ground. Most of us hardly touched the ground as we moved swiftly. If an average human had seen the sight of us, I'm sure we would have given them a heart attack or made them feel like their world was over. I had to admit our large group looked rather impressive. Too bad we were here for this reason only and not a happier one.

Narrowing in on the place, we stopped so many feet from the property where the building was located. Upon the hill looking down, there wasn't anyone outside. The place looked deserted and for all we knew, it could have been by now. Most eyes were on Demetrious as he went down the side of the hill and walked along the stream that went past the large building. From where we were standing it looked rather depressing for being an asylum other than the fact it had the lake to look at and the trees. It wasn't a real asylum; it was a disguise for other humans if they were to see it. Amazing humans seemed to think this was an appropriate facility even for their kind.

Demetrious stopped out by the water; it looked like he was sizing up the land in front of him and the way the water flowed. The stream had been flowing rather fast. Stepping outside of the stream he started making some rather strong strikes with his fist toward the ground. It had only taken two strong blows as if he were splitting the earth in half. The crack had only been the size of his hand width; however, the crack from it went straight out ahead of him. Not too deep but deep enough to make a dent in the ground, strong enough to divert some of the water. Even from where we stood, we had to be careful. Now we knew why he wanted us standing back. The ground shook like it would in an aftershock. The new opening now started filling in with water as it flowed toward the building, the water started to make the opening wider as it rushed through.

Now he was making his way toward the building itself, as he made it halfway two others joined him to protect him in case anyone came out while he was up there. So far no one had come out of the building. Some of us were wondering if anyone had been in there anymore. As they stood guard, I came much closer planning on holding them in a ring of fire if possible. The creatures would make it out however it would be easier to isolate the humans better this way.

Watching the water flow some of us thought we could have flooded the place. Most of us were strong. Had this been the gift he rarely used? Then we saw it and all of us were amazed. One more gift we were all envious of now. Several in the group had never seen but had heard rumors of this before, perhaps from those with gifts of shading who were more familiar with it, this was different. He just materialized into the building. The other two who had been walking with him now started running back as he had told them. Up from the hill they were not sure what was going on. I was already far enough back as the other two joined me in watching but remaining close.

Demetrious walked along the inside of the wall with his chemistry mixing with the building. Then as he hit the center of the building almost like an explosion, he blew the building apart exposing many of the occupants inside. The tunnels soon flooded causing the rest to either risk leaving through the flooded tunnels or coming back out through the front or back doors of the building. Most of the dedicated demon hunters came out to fight, while several were seen fleeing. We chose to spare and let those leave. We wished more made the same choice as they had.

I scanned the area, trying to see if I could spot the doc. Before they left each person had been put in a group. Not that they were expected to stay in those groups but at least it would be easier to tell them what direction to first head off in. The demon hunters who wore all black looked the most menacing. We would have been shaken if they had been vampires, but then we didn't know what secrets they held if it meant the doctor getting what he wanted.

At least no one spotted the lady in black in their group as the demon hunters held their battle-axes ready to fight, while it looked like the newer smaller recruits were behind them. Then like a heavy anchor, my heart sank. I found her. Not something I wanted to see. Now, this would make it difficult. She could wipe half of us if she wanted to and we were not as coordinated as she would be, not that she needed to or would use the help of humans. I couldn't get over the look on her face. She looked rather anxious. As strong and experienced a fighter why would she look so anxious? I knew she could take me out in a second.

Looking around the area to try and find what might be making her react that way nothing seemed out of the ordinary. Only a few feet behind her standing in the doorway was the notorious doc. He was choosing to participate in the fight. I couldn't figure it out but something about him seemed different. Both Charlie and Anthony's groups were to go after the doctor. Two other groups were to handle the Lady in black or at least keep her busy until we could all help when available. The lesser experienced would go after the humans. Even without experience, we have all fought our prey at some point.

The humans formed their battle cry, running towards us with their weapons ready. Our groups greatly increased when the shades spawned duplicates of themselves. Some stayed in their original forms,' and others morphed into some impressive-looking creatures. The battle had now begun. The first group clashed with the humans. It hardly seemed fair as they went down so quickly. As planned, I threw a wind of fire around the humans trying to group them up and slow the potential of their fighting down so that we might spare a few if they still chose to leave or if they attacked still, it would mean their death.

As I assumed, they were using many of the doc's favorite weapons. The Francesca axe along with the Gladius and Celtic swords. So far, no Hun bows except those had been best used if they were fleeing or racing on the back of a horse. So far none of them ran fast enough to need one for accuracy.

Then I saw something I didn't think I would see. The doctor went back inside the crumbled building as the lady in black, shot off and away from everyone. Why didn't she stay and fight? Why did she leave him unguarded? It didn't feel right almost as if we walked into a trap. The feeling was correct.

The lady in black left to kill the deserters. Both she and the doc had been a little too self-confident. Her only downfall had been underestimating the others. She brought her warring group. Most were pure vampires. She believed that only pure vampires should exist if anyone had a gift. Behind the demon hunters, the vampires had been hidden until now, thankfully not too many. However, knowing how skilled she was I was sure they would have been trained well. Each group did as well as they could as they came across them. Not leaving for them I joined in the fight as well, shooting down the hill as quickly as I could. Seeing Nichole almost get wiped I crashed into the vampire that had landed on her back. Shooting large volts of fire through his system leaving blackened scars from the light that started to disfigure his body. He had left a huge gash mark on Nichole's back as he was flung off her. It had been easy to see who had died so far because of the blood everywhere.

A few humans were leaning against what was left of the building. We could only assume they had gone into the dreamscape pulling a few of ours in with them. Trying to protect those whose bodies would be left unguarded on the outside we moved them quickly to the side hoping it might be enough protection for them while they battled inside.

You could see owls flying overhead just out of reach dive-bombing. I wouldn't have thought their talons would have been that beneficial for a fight, however, theirs were razor sharp they would put rather sharp and deep gashes that after a few strikes it would split an arm or leg off with only three strikes to the same spot. Others transformed into wolves and even black fog. The doc's special creatures, his vampires had a hard time fighting the fog. Something they couldn't exactly get a hold of. The fog would roll around them blanketing them. Making it impossible to move or breathe, making them vulnerable to others' attacks.

As the vampire would lunge to attack, they would shoot through the fog's circle until they circled them again frustrating them with their fighting technique. Each used their gift the best they could. Occasionally the wind would pick up or a flash of fire would shoot across. Even I had to be careful with my fire because it would still go a long distance; I had to be careful not to hit any of our fellow friends or family by accident.

The vampires on the other side fought just as hard, each being rather cunning, getting out of the way or out of a hold. Using spikes on their clothing to fight back against the fog. It sounded nothing like a traditional war. It sounded and looked like the most violent storm to hit the earth in one small area. At times we had to steady our feet to keep from falling. The ground would shake rather violently even though we knew who was doing that.

At times everyone was moving so fast. I could see the occasional arm swing by, or an axe come crashing down. So much had been a blur. I had to concentrate to make sure we did not attack our own. Luna and Grant had seen the whole situation before we had, with Luna replaying the events still to Grant. They felt horrified not being able to tell us, even more so by one of the visions Luna had shown Grant.

As the fight went on now, much longer than we had planned with the other vampires, I wondered what they hoped to get out of it, or maybe the doc changed his plans with the vampires. Maybe he now wanted to control them rather than just eradicate us all. Even though from all the training and seeing the madness in his mind, it would be difficult to believe he would ever change. With the Lady in black and her army, it took much longer than we planned. As we began in the morning light, it was now dark with barely the moon showing through the clouds above.

Claire had gone around the side of the building. Only one vampire stood in her way. As he swept up to her, she would dodge his move just as fast. Keeping his full attention on her and occasionally letting him think he almost grabbed a hold of her she pulled an easy trick.

Demetrious came up from behind quickly and materialized into his body then exploded out from the inside as the vampire littered his body everywhere. Giving each other a quick smile, Claire made her way into the building as Demetrious went back to the group outside to help.

Following down the only paths that were still open, one door half-opened she peaked in; there was a light down at the bottom. Taking one step at a time being careful in case the doctor came to her or someone else might have. Nichole and Anthony followed behind her not wanting to leave Claire alone. The stairs led to a tunnel, where there had been no other rooms. The walls were crumbled from the effects of Demetrious. It helped that the building was old giving his gift a bit of help. Water now leaked in the cracks flooding the bottom of the tunnels and the lower they went the more water soaked into them, walking carefully as they could trying not to make much noise while in the water. They could only guess he used this exit to escape, eventually the steps began to lead upward out of the water. Following down the corridor reaching the end, it stopped on the opposite hill.

The entire fight could be seen from here except no doc or lady in black nearby. Feeling sick they had gotten away. The three started working their way back down the hill until a loud crash sounded. The doc had hurled himself into Anthony knocking him down the rest of the hill, but still no sign of the lady in black. Anthony thrust his back up throwing the doc backward. He was stronger than we had known. It felt so strange for a moment, the doc was checking his pockets when he first attacked. Why would he be worried if Anthony carried anything on him? What was he looking for?

Now he was enclosed by all three. Not moving an inch. Looking out the sides of his eyes, he barreled towards Claire trying to knock her off her feet hoping for her to be the weak part of their circle. Jumping up into the air she spun over him with such force she did a back kick into his back as he passed her, slightly throwing him onto the ground.

Not seeing where it appeared as he turned and pulled from the grass a large axe swinging it with ease, stepping back from him and avoiding the blade. As quickly as the axe appeared the doctor slipped down into the grass and disappeared. Both Nichole and Anthony slipped under the ground. The ground vibrated more, more likely caused by Demetrious out fighting the others. Hitting the ground with a force, it had knocked the wind out of Nichole for a moment as she fell through the hole. Looking around she didn't see Anthony anywhere. Neither did she see the doctor, at least she was relieved not to be alone with him except now she worried that Anthony might be. There was no light and no way to see. Feeling out at the wall she could feel both dirt and gravel. Assuming this might have been a tunnel, standing and trying to feel her way she felt it end. There seemed to be no way out.

Anthony landed in the same tunnel with the doctor, and he could see him as he ran down the narrow tunnel. He was so strong why was he running? He was this war leader afraid of nothing, everything that existed should shake uncontrollably when in contact with him, and yet he was running? Something about that didn't seem right. Splashing water on his way, it led away from the hill but went directly under where everyone had been fighting. Chasing after him, he made a quick move turning around and swinging the axe again. As he did, he slightly clipped Anthony's shoulder taking a chunk from it. As the axe swung back, Anthony plowed directly into his stomach knocking him into the wall shattering it, more of the top of the tunnel fell in showing the light from the outside. Anthony being injured had a huge gash in his shoulder which was bleeding a lot now.

Slamming into the side caused the tunnel to cave in separating Anthony from the doc. The axe was now stuck in the middle of the dirt wall that formed between them. Buried under all the dirt it should have bee impossible to locate or pull except the doc pulled his axe back out. Anthony pulled himself out of the tunnel looking up the hill trying to find Nichole; he could see Claire standing near where Nichole had fallen in. Claire was still trying to find her. Moving in time as another vampire from the outside came sweeping in at her, rolling to the side, another creature attacked it knocking it away from her.

The doc jumped back into the tunnel soon as Anthony climbed out, then he kept running along the submerged tunnel. Not needing to breathe with the water filling it in more now. The tunnel led beneath the original stream. Coming up on the other side behind the tree assuming no one followed him, seeing everyone on the battlefield still. Turning to run again to leave the area, he was caught off guard.

Grant dropped out of the tree, landing on the cold hard doc. As he landed, he pierced a Celtic sword right through the shoulder blade down through his side just missing his heart, not that it should have been beating except it was, even with human hearing, Grant could hear its unmistakable beat. Flinching he knocked Grant into a tree knocking him unconscious. As he turned to kill him, Andrew hadn't been very far watching the fighting as he crossed the water to pull the energy from the air, creating a strong wind whipping around the doc, turning it into a strong blaze. At least he could still attack before Andrew was there to help Grant, encircling him and closing in with the fire. The doc stepped out of the fire. His clothing burned as he still tried to walk away. Catching up to him. Andrew grabbed him from behind and twisted his neck, separating it so that the spine showed through the skin.

Checking on Grant to make sure he was okay. Odd human, guessing Luna told him exactly where he needed to be. I knew he wanted to help but being mortal, he would have been taken out immediately as the others had. Leaving him lying by the tree, he was safer over here than back by the battlefield. At least I had to admit the doc would have gotten away if Grant hadn't slowed him down. We would have had to search for him again. At least this way our goal was accomplished. I couldn't help but feel it was too easy this way. Only two vampires still stood on the field. They were not attacking as much now as they were avoiding being attacked themselves. I carried the doc over to the rest of the group. As soon as they saw his limp body, they ran off in a flash of light for the woods. Dropping the doctor off in the center of the field, most of the bodies tended to blend in with each other.

Sadly, our side saw a few causalities as well. No fatalities, just a lot of casualties that we knew of for now. The vampires had been the only reason our side had any injuries at all, even though I still had that nagging feeling they were only playing with us. Possibly testing us out or for other reasons. Leaving many of the humans and the other side in a pile, burning what remained of them. Most of us had been exhausted from the fight. Demetrious tried working on the ground getting the water to reroute itself back downstream in the direction it originally had gone.

Claire still stood at the hole where Nichole had fallen through. Finding the exact soft spot, she dropped down into it trying to find her. Not being able to see she felt around the sides, making a splash sound as soon as she entered, trying not to make too much noise so she could hear Nichole. She came to the same dead end as Nichole had. Feeling around, it hadn't felt like there could be an exit. Claire stood at the area they fell in, so she didn't come back out that way. There had to be another direction out. Feeling along the wall there was a small hole that might have been larger. Guessing it had caved in, Claire climbed out heading off to get Demetrious to help open the hole more.

Nichole couldn't remember too much other than she had been standing searching for a way out or a way to Anthony. Instead, she felt a hand reach for hers. Taking it, she had been pulled rather forcefully through the smallest hole in the dirt.

Feeling slightly knocked out she could feel herself being dragged. No one she knew would have dragged her like this let alone held her wrist so tight. As soon as she could see a little, she realized she was in another tunnel. There must have been so many. Trying to pull back she saw the figure turn. It was the lady in black.

Taking a deep breath, she whipped her hand back as the lady was ready to attack. As she sprung at her, Nichole dove for the ground. The water on the ground made the ground slippery causing Nichole to slide past the lady as she went overhead. Nichole jumped up and ran. The lady caught up to her and grabbing her by the shoulders as she threw her into the wall.

"Where is the stone? Where did Charlie put it?" The Lady almost looked delirious with anger as she asked.

"We don't have any stones and I highly doubt he has anything you want." Not sure what she was searching for, all of Nichole's pockets had been turned out.

"I'll make you pay for lying. I've seen him with it as well as you." The ground continued to shake from Demetrious started to cause tremors.

Throwing a punch at Nichole she rolled out of the way as her hand thrust through the stone wall. As she pulled it back Nichole attacked her from the back. Trying to snap her neck, the lady slammed herself back shoving Nichole into the wall behind her, Knocking Nichole off herself. Whipping around. The lady grabbed hold of Nichole as she bit her on the shoulder. As she did Nichole slammed her fist down cracking the ribs and taking a chunk out of the lady in black.

Howling in pain the lady broke through the ceiling of the tunnel as more of it collapsed around them. Fleeing, she left Nichole laying there with the venom spreading through the rest of her human body, fighting against the natural venom that she had been born with. The burning fire was intense enough that she could barely move or even think rationally, Nichole tried to climb out of the hole leaving where the lady had. Hoping she wasn't hanging around waiting for her. As she cleared the top, she couldn't make out any of the surrounding areas. Her eyesight blurred. Her mouth felt as if it was wired shut. Dragging herself along the ground she could feel the shrubs around her. Hoping to hide and not let the vampires or the lady find her she hoped to live long enough for Anthony or Charlie to find her. She could feel not only tremors shooting through the ground, but after a while, she couldn't tell if it was the ground anymore or her own body convulsing. Blood began to pour from her mouth as she lay there in pain from the venom now leaving no part of her human existence alive. Choking now as she struggled to breathe wondering if she was finally going to expire this way. From hearing the stories of the doc and how he would add venom to those who were half-breeds and they would perish before his very eyes.

Chapter Fourteen
Not Quite Dead

The battle barely seemed fair. Sadly, with so many human lives lost no victory could ever feel deserved after today. Lives were lost on both sides. As the last of the very few humans from the opposing side fled Charlie and Anthony searched for Nichole. At one point during the battle, she disappeared. There were so many bodies on the ground and so much blood it was hard to tell one scent from another on the battlefield. Searching in the center there had been no sign of Nichole, they had to be quick as others started to burn the bodies. Then branching out where the battle led. It went out rather far from the center. By a huge piece of brush, Nichole lay there covered with blood. Her heartbeat barely beating, almost on its last beats, her human side would soon be dead. The venom from her body was spreading taking over what it had yet not claimed. Anthony picked her up in his arms and raced to their home with Charlie following.

The wounds were healing in front of their very eyes. Wiping off the blood as best as he could. Anthony waited patiently to hear her voice speak to him to know she was alright. Pacing the floor until Charlie took Anthony by the shoulders and directed him to sit down.

"She's going to be okay, its not easy but we need to wait for her body to allow her to awake. Once she does, she won't be sleeping anymore. The dead need no rest." Standing in the corner now waiting, Charlie had been much better and more patient than Anthony ever felt he would be. Claire had been watching Rose and Lucian with her son Jacob.

Claire and Grant had been sitting near the lake not far from the house while some of the others were in the house either healing or waiting for Nichole to awake. Not many stayed around preferring to head back to their own homes and console their families who worried while they were gone. Otherwise, many of the loners were simply on their way again.

Lucian had been restless and bored sitting still. Grant stood with him walking along the edge of the lake occasionally letting Lucian feel the water with his tiny hand. Claire continued to sit on the log with Rose and Jacob.

"I worry about what would happen if I were ever gone. I don't ever want you to be alone. I'm not always with my sister and there won't always be someone here to protect you, but if you have someone to call on if you need help, at least two can fight better than one. Jacob, I am giving both you and Rose a gift." Chanting a charm rhythmically under her breath white smoke circled both Rose and Jacob, as she finished the smoke absorbed into both Rose and Jacob.

Charlotte and Andrew eventually left with Claire and Grant planning on catching up to them later. They decided to spend some time in the Caribbean.

Nichole, after lying motionless for several hours began to mumble a few words, as soon as there had been movement from her, both Charlie and Anthony were at her side. Dinah had taken both Rose and Lucian to her room when Claire and Grant left. Nichole was now sitting up and feeling better than she ever had. Even at that moment, she noticed something was completely different. Certain senses of hers that had been impaired as a human were much clearer. Not even feeling the need to lay or sit down she swiftly got up to a standing position faster than normal for her. Surprising to her how quickly her body reacted to it. Her senses were heightened and were even clearer.

Now looking at Anthony the look of confusion had shown on her face. She could hear voices even more clearly of those who were speaking in other areas. She could hear Dinah speaking to her children in the other room even though she could tell she was only whispering to them under her breath. She could hear the thoughts of others that were not even speaking. Something she had never been able to do before. The last thing she could remember had been getting attacked, bitten, and dragging herself away from the lady in black to try and heal or get out of the range before she finished her off.

"I'm not human, anymore. Am I? My beautiful snow-white hair is different, if anything I thought I would lose coloring, not gain it?" Looking at Anthony for an answer not that he was sure how to explain it to her.

"No dear. You're not. That part died in the battle but you're going to be okay. At least with the look and hair, it all gives new meaning to the word "stone-cold fox." Anthony tried to comfort her as much as possible holding her in his arms, smiling at her.

"The change in hair color is unusual for a vampire. Usually, it doesn't change, or it can change to pure white. Your hair was already white except now you have highlights, another color showing through, a light crème red. I don't think its stained from the blood. But as Anthony said I am sure you're fine now. At least the venom didn't kill you entirely as we were worried it might." Charlie stood to the side still but spoke as he usually did with a calm yet assertive voice.

Then something she wasn't too sure of, a bright flash of a picture that had been as clear as day in front of her. Looking at the others no one else reacted to it. They had not seen the scene that played out for her, another thing that hadn't happened to her before. She now could see visions and this one scared her popping in with no explanation. She saw the mangled body of the man in black, the doctor who the whole fight had been set to kill. Not to kill the others but to kill him and stop him. She was fearful their goal had not been accomplished.

Watching the figure of a woman dressed all in black lace, even her face, she could barely see since it had been as black as night. She watched as the woman hovered over him and bit him. Not sure if he was alive enough for it to work, she saw the woman take off with him. Why would she be biting him if he were already a vampire?

She could see them again at what looked like a later time with the surroundings being nothing she had ever seen before. Instead of being dead, he walked alongside the body that was dead like him. He was struggling to take something from a female gypsy. Not getting what he wanted, the woman ran with the lady in black following after her. Staring at the picture she could still see the expression from Charlie and Anthony as they wondered what she was reacting to.

"Are you sure we killed him? Did anyone make sure his body was dead?" Looking from Charlie to Anthony hoping one of them had the answer.

"Yes, we are sure he's dead. His heartbeat stopped and the vampire part of him died. We attacked and surprisingly for a human. Grant was rather quick thinking. Even though it was not smart for him to join in the fight being he risked more of himself than the rest of us fighting out there. Why?" Charlie was curious why she would want proof. He had seen him lying there with nothing left in him. His head and neck were mangled to the side. Remembering how he heard no heartbeat at all from the human side.

"Just in case, I guess we can check again. I don't look forward to looking through the many mangled bodies, but it wouldn't be good if we left him out there even with a shred of a chance of coming back. Anthony, come with me and Nichole you go ahead and spend time with the kids. We will be back soon. We need to look immediately before the rest of the bodies are buried by the others."

As the others left thinking the battle had been complete. Some heading home, others taking off places to relax after such a horrific fight. We went after him and started this fight, but he had been waging a war on us for centuries, killing off and torturing many for years so when any doubts crept into our minds that we shouldn't have done this, we think of those who were tortured and killed by his hands. It had to stop.

Down in the center of the whole mess a lone woman still searched in the mangled and mutilated bodies on the ground, black hair as night. Smooth black smoky skin with matching eyes. Soon no one would have recognized her from her former self. Shoving body parts away, searching in the deepest of piles. She heard a heartbeat barely recognizable beating as she moved people off the sound until she came to the very object she had been searching for. Badly wounded the body had been badly mangled, missing an arm and leg. The neck was badly twisted but not severed from the spine.

The human side, the barely-there, part of it that lingered this long still struggled to hold on. The vampire side survived the vicious attacks better than anyone would have thought that it would. Leaving half the body withered and permanently destroyed. It seemed like the vampire half of his body was keeping his human heart ticking even though most of his body was lifeless and should have been dead. Instead, they kept each other alive, even though his human heart was soon to die beating weaker by the moment. Leaning over the body she slid the black curly hair over the forehead. Leaning into his neck she bit him, holding him while her venom rushed through him. At least he accomplished their goal and she kept part of her promise.

Hearing voices, she did not want to be discovered for sticking around trying to save him. Scooping him up in her arms, she shot off in a flash with him to her castle to watch over him, or if he were not to live, she swore she would avenge his death. She knew she would have at least two shots at this. If the first died. She would have the second one left. She hoped his human heart would stop beating so that others around would no longer hear it. Hoping no one would notice and kill off what had been left.

Chapter Fifteen
Going Into Hiding

After not finding the body. The family decided to move far away. Somewhere they would not be suspected of living. Before leaving, they sent the message to anyone who had been left behind still that the doctor's body was missing. They hoped he was dead since with their own eyes they saw and killed him. No one after could sense him or see him in visions assuming he was dead. However, to be safe, they wanted to move the family away from their home choosing now to be the time to relocate again, moving to the tropical jungle of all places. The family remained, staying there for several years. At least this way they had no one around to watch their family never age.

An unfamiliar occurrence shocked the family and a few family members who were around or would visit from time to time, Lucian had been a full vampire but somehow grew. They expected him to stay the same for the rest of his existence or someday wither away as some had. Somewhere in his system no matter how small there had to be something living in him almost human. The family expected to raise him as an infant or at least watch as his mind grew and body stayed the same, they were extremely fortunate. Shocked by his progress they were even more shocked with Rose. Century after century passed as they lived in their home while the children grew. Rose grew however she never showed signs of being a vampire. Not that she might not have had some in her system somewhere, otherwise she would have lived out a human's years and passed away. She was never the same as another vampire or the rest of the family. Rose had grown much faster than Lucian had.

As toddlers, Lucian would race around the house and even though Rose was taller than him, she still crawled and didn't seem interested in walking yet. She preferred knocking things onto the floor as Lucian would smash or tear apart whatever landed on the floor.

Lucian had built a fort in the tree, very elaborate and even decorated inside the way he said his own home would be someday. The structure was rather secure for a child building it with no experience. He would shoot up and down the barely made steps, leaving it this way so no one else could make it up unless he chose for them to. Sadly, when Rose would try and climb up, she would trip on a half-broken stick and fall hitting the ground with a thud.

Racing between the two was never equal. Lucian would be half into another city while Rose was still not that far from the beginning starting area. Other times just looking at the lake she would trip over her own feet falling headfirst into the water as Lucian would race to save her. From the time they could both walk Lucian had taken on the duty of protecting his sister.

Camping one night in the woods both Lucian and Rose were sleeping in their tent on the ground watching the stars even trying to count as many as they could. There had been a small deer of some kind near Rose. The animals were never afraid of her, however, they steered clear of Lucian fearing for their life. One night as they were lying out there and Rose had been petting one of the animals, it shrieked in horror and ran off. Scaring Rose, she looked around her. Lucian never far from her had been at her side in an instant. Worried what might scare an animal away from her. The answer showed itself, a creature launched itself at Rose. The ground shook with force as Lucian launched himself between Rose and the creature. A vampire tracked her human scent trying to kill her.

Yelling to his sister to run for home, Rose ran home screaming on the way home while Lucian finished off the vampire. Even for being young Lucian was rather talented at outwitting others, he was also fortunate that the vampire hadn't been that skilled or devious. As Anthony and Nichole tried to catch up to him to protect their son and daughter, they found Lucian hardly needed the help. He had already taken care of it.

Always feeling worried when there would be an attack on her life. They tended to live where other vampires lived, except it was never safe having Rose there. Anthony could fend for himself. He was much stronger than Rose ever would be. There had been three other attacks when the family decided to move away again. The last one had been the final deciding factor. The family hoped to move to an area with less threat for Rose, hopefully, a lesser chance of other vampires being around stalking humans. One tracker made his choice. Just like some did not want those to live with special gifts, others felt there should be no less than a pure-bred vampire. Feeling there was something wrong if the venom didn't take over the body.

Obscured Darkness

Settling on a tropical island, the family settled in. We had lived here before except, at that time the only demon who posed a threat had been one who followed us here after one of our countless moves. When I was twelve, we lived here for about two years. For most, that would have been twenty years ago but for me, as the somewhat human in the family, it felt like yesterday. I aged to a certain point except I hadn't died yet. The only non-human thing I did. Almost like living animals' years compared to humans only this time I looked a younger age than normal. At least I had something going for me.

Still too young for jobs we spent a lot of time at the beach. Lucian had been strong enough to watch over me as mom and dad would try and blend in for the time as best they could. Not that mom left the house too much. She painted a lot which is where I learned to paint so well. Having to be more careful than normal. Lucian picked up on a scent that wasn't human, so my parents watched over me more than normal again. We had this would be a place I could fit in a while and feel human. Not that I complained to my family, it was hard when I was the only one like myself. I didn't quite fit in the human world but then I didn't fit into the world of vampires and special creatures either. Both tolerated me for now as I did with them.

After several showers of rain, the scent hadn't come back and Lucian and I had gone back to spending time on the beach again. Lucian started teaching me how to swim. It rained a little this morning leaving it darker out, except once it cleared up, Lucian made his way for the house and stayed there. Watching out the window, I had wanted to go back to the beach. If I could have, I would have stayed there all day or even lived on the beach. The years seemed to pass quickly. I had only one close call since we had moved here which made it the safest for me so far.

Usually, only Anthony or I went out during the day in the sunlight. My family usually stayed indoors. None regretted it since most preferred the moonlight. Both Lucian and I had our first summer jobs there. Lucian worked at a butcher shop. The boss was surprised he would rather work at night and alone than work during the day. He certainly didn't mind since Lucian finished far more than the other employees had. It had been almost as if he had four workers there. And for Lucian, he had all the blood he wanted and no one to watch.

I worked in a little floral shop during the day. As evening would come, Lucian would pick me up and drop me off at home making sure I would safely get there since he never wanted me walking home alone at night.

One morning I felt better than I usually did almost optimistic. Being picked up by Rhema my boss. She lived up on the other side of the hill from me. I walked into the shop flipping the open sign. There wasn't much to get ready this morning. Pulling out baby's breath and roses and making a few of the arrangements, not many customers had come in this morning. Then one gentleman came in.

"I have to admit something. I have been going by this floral shop for the last three years and every day I see you working here you are always smiling. I can't help it, but it makes my day go so much better when I see you and before I chicken out and don't do it, I want to ask you out for dinner." Speaking rather quickly rushing through the words nervously it showed quite well on his face. Smiling back at him I could feel a bundle of butterflies in my stomach.

"Dinner would be nice." I felt a wave of nervousness trying to cover it with a smile, if he felt anything like I did, then his heart must have skipped a beat also.

"I'm Davian by the way. I'll pick you up at your place. I've seen you outside, so I'll be there to get you tonight around eight in the evening? Is that a good time for you?" Watching for my reaction as I continued to smile at him, I had never gone out on a date before. This would be the first human thing I had done let alone with another human. Not that I could tell him that. At least mom would be happy since she was always disappointed that I didn't try and enjoy more of my human side.

"I'm Rose, eight works, and I'll be waiting for you." As I said that he walked out of the store and I watched as he left.

Only working a half-day today, we closed earlier for my boss's anniversary. I didn't feel like getting a ride. I was so excited. I wanted to work off some of it, so I chose to walk home. Besides, I had plenty of time. On the way home I thought about what I wanted to wear and how to mess with my hair. This was going to be fun but then at the same time, I was nervous. How would it go? Would I behave right? I didn't even make friends would I know what to talk to him about? I was used to talking with Rehma but that felt different. I had so many thoughts running through my mind that getting home seemed faster than I realized. I had been so occupied that I didn't even notice my family had been looking out the window as I came up to the door.

"Rose, is everything alright? Why are you walking home, I could have come and picked you up?" Anthony was worried as I walked in.

"Dad, everything is fine. The shop closed early because Rhema and her husband are celebrating their anniversary. It was such a nice sunny and hot day. I wanted to walk home. Besides, I have some girl stuff to talk to mom about." I could hardly stop smiling. Mom had been standing in the living room and walked over as I said I needed to talk to her.

Lucian looked worried but trusted that at least mom would

find out what it was. I took mom by the hand and walked to my bedroom. I was the only one with a bed to sleep in.

I walked over to my closet and opened it up to reveal many of my dresses, something I didn't wear much but at least owned. I would finally have a reason for wearing them. Mom looked on wondering what I was doing as I pulled out a few dresses.

"Which one should I wear? I was asked out on a date for the first time and I said yes. I figured you would be happy since it's the first human thing I have done and who knows, I might even like it. I just don't know which to wear?" Nichole lit up in smiles.

She always wanted to dress me up. Mom had always been very girly and dressed very feminine. Picking out the frost blue sundress with the strappy shoes, she felt this looked better. Helping me with my makeup and hair. I was amazed at how I looked.

"How well do you know this boy that you're dating? Is he picking you up or are you meeting somewhere? I should probably speak with Lucian, so he doesn't shadow you. I want you to be as human as possible. You're different than the rest of the family and I don't want you to miss out." She looked at me with concern.

"Mom. I have never felt like I have missed out. I love my life. But this will be nice to do something different. I hope I don't mess it up." Mom could hear the worry in my voice.

"Don't worry, as beautiful and sweet as you are, there is no way you could ever mess this up. Just relax and have fun." Mom walked out of the room to speak with Lucian.

I could picture how that was going to go since he worried so much about me. Knowing Lucian, he would have had the guy inspected and thoroughly checked out before I went on the date which is why, I was glad the date had been set before he could do that.

Obscured Darkness

It had been a good thing that I used the walk to eat up the time since I still waited for a while before it was time for Davian to pick me up. He pulled up in his Ford Model T. It looked spectacular, even though my brother had the same car just with a few alterations. It was rather exciting when the car was first invented. It was hard for my family to explain why horses were afraid of them or why they didn't like riding. Walking up to the door he knocked. Even though we knew long before his car was close to the house, we had to wait till he pulled up to the house. Lucian agreed to sit on the couch and act human instead of giving him the third degree. But just like a protective brother he had to get a few words in. As I was walking out, he said loud enough for the human ears.

"Make sure you have her back before ten pm." Then he closed the door as he walked away.

Sometimes I felt like Lucian was more my father and Anthony was more relaxed with me since he knew just how protective Lucian was. At times he also had to remind Lucian that he wasn't my father, giving him a light slap on the back of the head after his comment to us.

"Do you need to be back by ten?" Davian was curious enough to ask which was understandable.

"No, I can stay out as late as I want. That's just my brother being overly protective." As he opened the door for me, I scooped the back of my dress so it wouldn't get caught in the door. Sitting patiently as he walked around the outside of the car. Then we were off for the evening.

We drove close to the ocean ridge. A cute little diner was tucked in the woods with a little walk-out balcony slightly over the water. We chose to eat outside to enjoy the weather. It was such a beautiful night. The moon illuminated the ocean. Before dinner, he handed me a rose.

"I'm sure you probably get tired of flowers since you work around them all day. But I couldn't help it when I saw this perfect rose, I thought of you." As he handed the single rose to me, his hand slightly slid softly up the side of my hand, the warmth from his skin felt nice.

We talked for a while about work and the island and he explained why he moved here. I avoided the real reason we moved here by saying we relocated here to relax. I didn't want to tell him where we came from, or he would wonder why we couldn't relax there. I found he came from a rather large family. He had been born and grew up here finally choosing to move back. It must be nice to be able to stay in the same place for that long.

The evening went on well, finding we had a few things in common. It was nice speaking with another human, one at least I had more in common with. It appears he traveled almost as much as I had. The only difference is that he came back to the same place, and he didn't have to leave because someone wanted to make a lunch out of him.

After dinner, we went for a stroll along the beach. Sadly, as we walked, I would find the only loose stick on the beach sand as I tripped over it, Davian caught me before I hit the ground.

As we walked Davian reached for my hand. I wasn't used to holding someone's hand. It was rather nice. I hoped I wasn't disappointing him since I didn't know what was expected on the date. He seemed happy or at least polite enough not to complain.

"This evening has been nice. I just feel like I monopolized the conversation. I tend to talk a lot when I get nervous. I still don't know very much about you. How do you like living on the island?"

"I love it. The waterfalls and the sunsets here are wonderful.

I love the weather, what's not to be happy with? I even enjoy my job. I haven't been around long enough yet to make new friends. You're my first date since I've been here." Not wanting to tell him he was my first date ever.

Leaning into him a little, it was nice having someone to walk with at my pace. But I couldn't help but feel like I was betraying someone. The first date was far too soon to make any concrete decisions.

"I have something I want to show you then. It's not far up the coast here, we can walk there. It's beautiful. It's one of the places I go to think or relax." Holding my hand, we walked along the water's edge.

Eventually, we came to the area where the tall grass started to take over and the side of the water separated more as rock formed and we went up an elevated cliffside. Walking for a while the cliff became even higher. Then the trees replaced the high grass. As we went further, I began to wonder just how much further we were going to walk. Then as we walked a little further, the spot he wanted to show came into view. A small waterfall dropped into a wading pool and a small stream from it made its way over the side joining the ocean in the most amazing waterfall. I could see why he would want to be here.

Guiding me with his hand on my back. We walked up to the little waterfall. There were a few large rocks up near where you could feel the light mist spray. We sat on one and enjoyed the water cooling us off. Sadly, there was not much moonlight that reached through the woods, even though we could see from where we were at. We didn't even have to say very much to each other. It was just nice sitting there. The only thing that seemed to slightly interrupt my evening had been the light noise that I heard. My date didn't notice but from personal experience I knew Lucian followed us out here and no doubt since it was dark, he was keeping an eye on me.

"Can I see you again tomorrow? Perhaps earlier in the day?"

"I normally work till four o'clock except the shop is closed for three days; my boss is gone on a mini-vacation. So, any time would be fine. It would be nice to see you again. This evening was very nice."

"Maybe have a picnic at noon? I could show you more of the island since you haven't had much of a chance to explore it. Being a local. I know of some great places to check out. I'll pick you up again. Just wear something comfortable since we will be climbing a little." Smiling at me he must have thought this would be a great thing. Sadly, he didn't know what I was like when I tried to climb.

"It's getting pretty late and we should try and get back if there's going to be any moonlight at all." Sadly, as I went to get up, I slipped off the rock and fell right into the wading pool below the waterfall.

At least I didn't have too far to fall in this one and it wasn't very deep. Hopping down as quickly as he could, getting his pant legs and shoes wet. He helped me stand with the water swirling around my feet. The shoes I wore looked great but not great for balancing in the water.

"Maybe the climbing isn't exactly a very good idea? Don't worry there's plenty to do." Helping me along I shivered a little.

Without saying a word, he took his jacket off and placed it over my shoulders. Being wet didn't help but the jacket helped block the light breeze that chilled me. The walk back felt even longer, eventually, we made it back.

As he dropped me off, he was such a gentleman as he walked me to my door, kissing me lightly on the cheek and saying goodnight. It was a perfect ending to a beautiful day. I waved goodbye as I watched him drive away. Opening the door my family had been waiting in the living room. I had forgotten to give Davian his jacket back. I shut the door and gave an excited squeal and just as I did, I slipped off my feet and fell against the door, and hit the floor with a thud. I couldn't help but laugh. I laughed so hard my sides started hurting. My family must have thought I was nuts or at least that had been the expression they were showing. They must have been surprised when they saw me come in sopping wet, other than Lucian who had been spying on us.

"Are we to assume the evening had gone alright?" Nichole came over and helped me get back on my feet.

The expression on her face she wasn't exactly sure how to take it. Even Lucian who would have known me best seemed confused; apparently, he left before I fell in wanting to get home first.

"Leave it up to sis to be herself and still get a kick out of the evening." Lucian went outside now that Davian had left.

"The evening went great even though I fell several times and even fell in the wading pool. He still wants to see me! I'm off to bed, we are having a picnic tomorrow and then he's showing me around on the island." Giving both mom and dad a hug, I went up to my bedroom.

I fell asleep fast. But then I had one of my usual dreams, a person who I had created in my sleep. After having a date, I wasn't surprised to dream about him.

In the dream, we talked about our families, and what we liked to do. We would hike, explore caves and even go swimming with each other. There had been one time when I woke up sopping wet from rain in my dream, which always surprised me, but I never shared this with anyone. I didn't want anyone to know I was also going nuts since we couldn't see a traditional doctor. My friend and I chased each other in fields or wherever we happened to be. We even climbed up a pile of hay that had been rolled and stacked. I had fallen between the two stacks. Trying to climb out I even used my head, arms, and legs to press against it until I was high enough that my imaginary friend could help me out. We had been more than just best friends. The last time I had seen him I was nineteen and he was eighteen.

Then one day he told me he could not see me again, that because things had changed it was not safe for us anymore. Now when I dreamed about him it had been about memories of us together. Then I realized I felt like I was betraying him. I felt both sad and strange for feeling the way I had. I didn't want to tell anyone, but I hoped I would just outgrow it if it was possible. I had fallen in love with him.

Shifting my position, I tried to think of something else and fell asleep again. It wasn't easy but I tried to focus on what tomorrow might be like as I dreamed about Davian. The morning had finally come.

Getting up, I went to the store picking up a few things for our picnic, came home, and packed it. Dressed in comfortable walking shoes and even wore a long skirt with long stockings made of cotton underneath, along with a short-sleeve shirt.

Mom seemed happy as she must have driven dad batty about the details of our date. I told her since she was waiting this morning to find out more. She would have asked me last night, but she had seen how tired I was. Mom always wanted me to sample human life since I was human and sadly moved around so much and lived the life of a vampire. She was always worried that I didn't have friends and the other things that most humans depended on or craved. I was always happy. I didn't know I was supposedly missing anything. How could I if I had never done any of those things? The only thing I wished I had been able to do would be to walk alone at night or be able to stay in one place long enough.

Watching out the large picture window I watched for any signs of the car coming. Sighing I could tell I was driving everyone else nuts. Probably because they knew they would hear the car's engine miles away and I had been waiting for it. Not that I had the benefit of hearing the way they did. Even so, I figured if they could pace back and forth, I can do the same for a different reason. They must not have wanted to ruin my excitement since not once did they tell me to stop and try to tell me when he would get there.

As soon as I heard his car, I said goodbye to everyone and stepped outside. The car pulled up close to the house as I walked out to the passenger seat. Leaning across he opened the door and took the picnic basket from me as I hoisted myself into the car. Taking off for the other side of the island, he parked near the beach. Taking out a large blanket we placed it on the sand and had our lunch.

I thought he looked cute when he ate, after a while, we went swimming. I had my bathing suit underneath all my clothes. It had felt good getting wet except I was getting overheated, I liked the clothes I picked but I dressed to warm. I thought I would be colder like the night before when I got wet, which wasn't the same. Our date wasn't quite what I expected but then we went out to the reef and tried to see as much of it as we could. It looked beautiful. Drying off as we walked along the beach, we talked about his childhood some more. His family had a wood-cutting mill. Not here, however in another country. He chose to live here because it had been his home from childhood and was very relaxing for him.

I had only told him about part of the last place we were at, just that the tropical heat was way too hot and the creatures were not exactly safe, it's why we had moved. I couldn't tell him it was because they were vampires who wanted my blood and nothing more. He would have thought I lost my mind. At point much less people believed in vampires.

After walking for a while, we went jumping off the cliff intentionally into the water. First, he would jump that way he would make sure I would make it back to the surface of the water. He showed me many of the plants that were native to the island as well as some of the animals in the woods.

Several paths we took around always seemed to lead to an amazing place. We even checked out the museum and the tiny local zoo, I always had so much fun. I couldn't wait to see him again, we had finally been dating for a few months now. This time when he left me off at my place, he kissed me on the lips. As I waved goodbye as I usually did, I always felt sad when he left. Except I felt I was waving goodbye to a friend and not a boyfriend.

This time when I came in my family acted very differently. Lucian did not seem so happy as he stood quietly staring out the window.

"We need to talk with you about something important. It seems you have been seeing Davian a lot and you are getting serious. We wanted to make sure you're not preventing yourself from getting closer because you can't exactly have him here because of us. Someday he might be trusted but for now, it's too early to tell. You're old enough to be living on your own and we want to give you this house as a gift. We want you to continue living a normal human life. We are also giving you a number we can get reached by. Your father and I decided we wanted to move back near Grandpa Charlie, however since you have started putting roots down, we didn't want to make you move again. We will miss you and love you but so far this place seems to be very safe for you. We see how happy you are here; this doesn't have to be permanent if you're not happy. But I think it will be a good thing for you to be a little more independent of us. Just so that we don't have a long-drawn-out goodbye we are leaving tonight. You know we don't waste time. But if you even slightly need us, then call us. We won't be too far."

As mom told me this I stood in shock, now I understood why Lucian was staring out the window. I knew there was no way he would agree to this. Somehow mom and dad must have made him agree not to argue about it let alone show me his face, I would be able to read his expression. Even without seeing his face, I could see his arms crossed in front of him showing he was not in favor of leaving me behind.

And as they said they did not stick around. As I found it was more for my mother's sake than my own, even though they felt this was the best choice for me it was even harder for her to leave me.

Hugging mom and dad before they left was hard. It was difficult enough to register all that happened today. I watched as they left. Lucian stuck around with permission from mom and dad so that he would not leave his job without either a replacement or a warning that he was moving away. They were not happy to lose him but were hospitable to him as he left on his last day of work. They had even given him a going away party, not that he could get into it. Lucian never wanted to leave let alone to leave me. I didn't want Lucian or my parents to leave me. Then it was even harder telling my twin brother goodbye. The one I depended on the most.

"If you need me, you know how fast I am. I can be here no matter what I am doing. Call me for any reason it doesn't matter. I'm always available for you sis. I'll never be too far away." Hugging me I watched as he left.

Rebekah McClew

I didn't want to cry till I knew he would be far enough out of hearing distance. Otherwise, it would have made it even harder for him to leave. Then I broke down crying. Why did I have to be different? I felt like my insides were going to tear out. I cried so hard I had fallen asleep on the floor near the door.

To pass time when normally I would have spent it with my family, I set up an art room of my own. I became very obsessed with my painting. I even started selling them. I had to leave working the floral shop to sell more on a full-time basis. I was still doing something I enjoyed but this way I could get lost in it. Mother had been taught by grandpa and he had been taught by his mother. I missed my family more than I thought I would. Once they left, I became very closed off.

They might have thought in theory this was the best choice, but I couldn't see a positive benefit. There wasn't a night I didn't cry myself to sleep. I never told Davian. He seemed happy to be spending more time with me. He even stayed in the guest room that used to be my parents' room. I insisted on not sharing the same bed unless we were married.

Since Lucian and my parents left, the town had grown quite a lot. I started getting a lot of comments on the fact that I seemed to be aging well. On one of the days I waited outside of the art gallery, Davian planned on picking me up except he was running late. For a small island, it shouldn't have taken him this long.

I have never had to wait on him; he was always there when he said he was going to be. Eventually he pulled up with his car. I could see he had something planned. A picnic basket and blanket on the middle of the seat. He said he had a surprise for me. Not much surprised me anymore however I figured he could always try.

"I know you've been depressed since your family has been

gone. I've been working more and you've been wonderful and haven't complained once but I want to make it up to you."

"Where are we going? That way I know what to wear?" I was curious since he was taking the items out of the car. Odd if it's something nearby that he wanted to show me. Not much around here. I had been wearing a basic skirt and blousy shirt. At times I wore something appropriate if I knew we were going to climb on a rock or something.

"What you're wearing is perfect. It's going to be quite a walk from here. I would take the car down there but it would just get stuck in the sand so we can leave it here. We'll get our exercise in today." With everything in hand, I held his available hand as we walked toward the lake.

I didn't mind walking except for any unusual bump or root in the path. I found myself tripping over it. The brush had grown up in this area. I used to go down to the lake a lot but then Lucian used to make a path for me making it safer to travel through. The area had also been rocky since the edge of the lake was more of a drop from the cliff. If you went straight out and to the right, you would eventually end up at a beautiful beach. I didn't spend much time in the woods since usually my experience in them hadn't been too good.

I wish Davian had been more of a conversationalist. At first, things had been nice getting to know each other except now we don't speak much. He usually watches me paint while he reads a book. I know not everything is going to be exciting all the time; however, it's sad when I am excited when he leaves. Davian had started to stay with me but then after a while, he was working more and decided to stay at his place since it was in town. I had a feeling it was other reasons I was just glad to have a reason for him to leave.

I had to admit after being in the house for so many days

even if it was with Davian, it was nice to get out for a while. We made it to the cliff as we went left and not in the direction I was expecting. There was a small stream in this direction that would go over the cliff and join the ocean.

"We are almost there; I wanted to take this way since there are so many trees and rocks coming up the other way, much easier to get there from this side." Trying to reassure me that he knew where he was going, I just followed.

I had to admit I was curious now where he was heading to. As we went further up the cliff, then we came to the stream that I had seen up here before with him except it had been the furthest, we would usually go. We followed along the small stream until it had gotten thicker. Then I started wondering if he was going to show me the cave. Lucian and I had been in there many times then I realized it was.

"This place is great, but I wanted to show it to you. A friend of mine showed this to me a little while ago." He stuttered on the word friend.

I assumed more than likely it was probably a girl who showed him the cave. We went into the opening and followed the path. Just as the light started getting dark in the cave we stopped. Apparently, he hadn't wanted to go any further.

"I thought this would be nice and a little different than what we normally do. We can sit here; it gets too dark down lower. But isn't this nice? Besides, I must admit I know I haven't been around too much, so I wanted to make up for that. I felt bad leaving you alone so much lately." He had gestured around the cave with his hand, sitting on his blanket now Davian started laying out our lunch.

As we ate the sky had become slightly darker and started to drizzle. I never did like storms but at least this looked like it might be something that would pass over. At least we were inside.

"It's very sweet of you, this is nice." Not that I wanted to admit I had been here before.

Pretending to see this place for the first time seemed to be making him rather happy that he had something I supposedly hadn't seen before. I hadn't made any effort to come here again after the episode with the Witch. I had played around the cave when I was much younger. A Witch had been casting a spell on the cave when I had stopped and seen her. She had something she wanted to show me. She said it would explain why she was casting a spell on the place. I never did learn what it was except she said good luck as she pushed me down the tunnel.

I had been around the age of twelve which translated into human years I would have been 84. Regardless of how long I had been around I was still klutzy and acted like a kid. When that horrible situation happened Lucian as usual had to save me from it. However, it has been a very long time since that happened. At least I had guessed by now the Witch would have long since passed away being human herself.

Sitting and eating with Davian. I still felt strange being here almost unsafe. But then it was odd. The glowing light that came from the end of the tunnel glowed more than it usually did. Before I could only see it as I had been near it. Odd it's glowing out this far.

After eating I stood out of curiosity and stared more into the cave. Walking back just a bit before Davian caught my attention.

"Don't go too far back there is a drop-off back there. It would take a while to get you out of there if you fell in. I'm going to stay here since I don't like the dark. Just think this place used to be filled with jewels. Some of the stories about this place are even more unusual. That it is either haunted or that at one time demons and angels fought in here. Can you believe such stories? It's so funny someone actually would believe in them but either way, they make the place sound romantic if you're into having your ear tickled like that." Shaking his head, he laughed to himself as he found it humorous. Good thing he doesn't know my family or our history.

Walking back not too far, close enough to see that the hole had been made larger since the last time I had been in here, probably from those who didn't like the claustrophobic feel of such a small hole. The slope looked a lot steeper than I remembered but then when I first came across it, I found it the hard way by falling in. Stepping back a little, the water from the outside started to come into the cave.

"I hate to say it, but we are going to get a little wet, or at least our feet are going to. It's pouring a little more outside, I don't remember the weather looking bad before we left. Maybe you should come back here so you don't fall. The floor is getting slippery." I could see him watching out the front of the cave observing the weather.

As I stepped back a little more trying to walk slowly since the floor was very slippery. Nasty when moss and shale get wet, not much to catch too.

Turning when I felt I had been far enough away from the end. I went to catch up to Davian which was the worst mistake I could have made. Tripping over my damn foot I wound up slipping back and he just stood there and watched in horror as I fell. Not even trying to catch me since he was more worried about falling in himself. Sliding down, there had been a curve in the cave, trying to grab the corner of the cave wall didn't help either. It had been so glossy coated with wet moss my fingers slipped off with no hope of slowing down. Finally, in the end, I hit the bottom with a thud as I hit my head against the wall. I could hear Davian yelling at me except I was in so much pain, and the wind was knocked out of me that I couldn't respond right away. Then the last of his words trailed off as he yelled, that he was going to get help. Then I didn't hear his voice anymore after that.

Breath-taking as this place looked, I was still astonished by it. I didn't like the idea of being trapped down here. Lucian could get in and out with no problems, however, I had no chance even if I tried. My head was throbbing, putting my hand on the back of my head. I could feel a huge lump forming. If I had been a vampire, I would have put a huge hole in the wall of the cave. The immortality part of my life sucked as well as being human. I know I have family who are half-breeds like I am, and they don't deal with this. They could get out except they have gifts. I would be happy if I were not so clumsy or at least strong. My head wouldn't be throbbing so badly.

Trying to get to my feet didn't prove very effective either. Feeling dizzy as I stood up, I decided to sit on the ground. The water that now came down the tunnel of the cave joined the little stream in the center down here and went out the far end. Sitting against the wall I wouldn't get too wet over here. Sighing to myself I wondered how long it was going to take him to get help?

The ground had been so smooth I slid myself along the floor over to the little waterfall that formed the stream in the center. Staring at the water felt relaxing. Not sure why I hadn't seen it before. I could see a red glint coming from the center of the water. How did that get there? I wasn't sure if I wanted to find out what it was. The ground was pure white. I wasn't sure what the red color would be coming from.

Sadly, being as curious as I am, I leaned forward and slid my hand into the cool water. The ground inside felt so silky smooth. A nice smooth basin that the water after time had formed as it hit the ground. Sliding my hand over the red glint it felt bumpy. Almost as if something were coming out of the ground. I could feel the red glint it was hard but felt like it was a separate piece. Almost as if it were being pushed up. At the thought of it coming out of the water, I leaped back. The first feeling had been panic. What if something was still left in here? Would Lucian hear me from here? He would think I was crazy for coming back here without him.

Not taking my eyes off the red glint it seemed to shine even more. I could even hear a scratching sound as if the ground were sliding against itself. Now I was panicked and sadly no way out. As I slid further away from it there had been bubbles now forming around it. Then I saw the red glint shoot out of the ground and into the air. For a split second, it looked like a ring, a rather strange thing to see. The sound stopped and the water was running smoothly again. The red glint now lay inside of the water. I wanted to know if this thing was going to come and get me or if I had to worry about it. Either way, if something bad was going to happen I wanted to get it over.

Leaning forward just a little I felt my way into the water. Trying to be careful not to get my hand back in the hole where it came out, I picked up the red glint. As I raised it out of the water, I could see some of the salt had encrusted itself around it almost making it look like a ruby coming out of a small rock. As I rubbed the stone the salt began to crumble away. I held it out in front of me in disbelief. It looked like a wedding ring. White gold with diamonds in a teardrop shape with a red ruby in the center. It reminded me of my mother's ring. I doubted it was her ring. When Lucian and I had been a couple of months old, her ring disappeared, and dad bought her another ring. Mom loved it but always said it wasn't the same.

Wiping it off on my shirt I placed it on my finger. A perfect fit. I wonder how this got down here let alone stuck in the cave. Reaching back into the water to feel where it had popped out of, I couldn't find the hole anymore. The entire basin had been smooth almost as if the rocky bump had never been there. Maybe I hit my head harder than I thought? Staring at the ring I couldn't get over how beautiful it was. I know I would be heartbroken if I lost something like this. It had to have come from somewhere. Not that it hurt at all. I could feel a slight tingling or bubbly feeling from the ring before it stopped.

Running my finger over the red stone I stared at it. I could have sworn I had seen my face in the reflection but then I looked closer. It didn't look like me. Feeling a little shocked I couldn't get over exactly what I was seeing in it. A girl standing holding out the ring was smiling. She was dressed in earlier-period clothing. It was almost as if she was handing it to me. Maybe this place had been bewitched and wasn't just a story? It felt so comfortable having the ring on. Keeping the ring I sat and waited for Davian to bring help.

Soon I heard several voices yelling down at me. I didn't hear Davian's voice at all however I did recognize the other voices. Yelling back to them to let them know I was okay. The first person slid down the slippery tunnel and stopped as he came close to the ground with me. Letting go of the rope he walked over to me. Helping me get up I was so sore. I didn't realize it until I walked that I had a limp. Lying on his back while I was on his chest, he held onto me tight as several people pulled the rope upward.

"Too bad for the romantic picnic, Davian told us he was trying to give you a romantic surprise. But don't feel embarrassed you're not the only one who had fallen in here. Not too much longer the town is planning on closing this place up. We will all feel safer about it when the opening is closed." Still holding me tight as we slid up the tunnel, once we could get on our feet, he still helped escort me out.

As we made it out of the tunnel I looked around for Davian. I didn't see him anywhere.

"Davian was hyperventilating when he came into town looking for help so we had him stay at the tavern. We will bring you back into town. The doctor is out here to check you out to make sure you're alright." Walking over, there had been a man with a bag in his hand. I showed him the lump on my head.

He checked my pulse and seemed to think I was okay. Sadly, after today's incident, I didn't see very much of Davian again. He even started acting very strange. Either way, I didn't want to see him. I couldn't stop thinking abou tit. If it had been me, I would have waited for him to come out of the cave, I would not have sent another person and then avoid them for a few days. Our last time together had been a very short date, even though I still wore the ring. Since I found it, I didn't take it off.

After not hearing from him for a while we were supposed to go to his sister's wedding. Going to town and meeting him where we agreed. I had decided after the wedding I would let him know how I was feeling. That it wasn't working and that I planned on moving. I wanted to start over.

"Where is he; he should have been here by now?" Looking down at my watch realizing I had been standing there for over three hours now, standing near a bench but unwilling to sit down next to the smelly man that was sitting there.

Not moving or swaying just standing still watching both sides of the street. Growing more impatient waiting for the ride, he had known to expect me here we had spoken just this morning.

Out of the blue, I felt a tap on my shoulder and a young man's voice spoke behind me.

Obscured Darkness

"Do you want to go to dinner with me?" The voice coming from the young gentleman from behind me waiting for my answer certainly had the audacity.

"Why, do you make it a habit of picking up strangers from the street and asking them out?" Looking at the young man with no change in voice or stance, glancing up and down at him sizing him up trying to figure out what he wanted or was trying to do.

"I saw you from my bar; I couldn't help it I had to ask you out. I'm a nice guy if you give me a chance. Besides, I have an awesome job and I'm loaded. I could show you a wonderful time." He seemed assured this ploy or common line would work.

"Do I look interested? Do you think you're that important that someone waiting out here had to be here because they were waiting for you to pop the question of dinner? Just a bit sad, I don't care if you're rich and you can save telling me because I don't care. I don't pretend to care very well either. I was waiting for a ride and he was late. He's either found a chick and is nailing her and forgot about me or as I like to think he was held up by gunpoint and shot to death, and that's why he isn't here to pick me up. The last thing I need from anyone is money, I have all I need. Let alone someone that I don't even know just on a whim asking me out." I knew it wasn't this person's fault that he was late but then it was even sadder that it didn't bother me too much that he might have been with someone else.

At this point, I knew without a doubt, that I didn't want to date Davian anymore. We were great friends, and we had a lot of fun, but there just was nothing for us. It was like hanging out with my friend. It was sad when I could count to when Davian would kiss me to the point it was over. The more time I spent with him the more I had thought about the one I had fallen in love with in my dreams. I decided that the person I wanted to date or be with would give me the same feelings. I wanted what I dreamed about and I didn't feel bad for waiting for it. This wasn't working.

Davian's office wasn't very far from the art gallery. I walked down the street to his office. I assumed the secretary must have been out on a lunch break. I wanted to surprise him since I heard his voice in his office. Opening the door slowly and peeking in I saw all I needed to see. I no longer felt bad for him that I was going to break up with him. His hands were already busy with his secretary and for who knows how long?

Closing the door, I no longer felt I needed to give him an explanation of why I was leaving. Packing my belongings and stuffing as much as I could into the car my brother left behind for me, I took off for the ship. At least I showed up on time. The ship heading out was leaving soon, grabbing a ticket from the booth I was ready to leave. Loading my car in the lower area I stood at the top near the rail watching as land floated away. Usually, if I traveled on the water, it had always been with my father. But this time I figured if they wanted me to be independent and more human then I would find a place and settle in myself.

Not sure where I wanted to be, I moved around a little. I hadn't realized how much time passed. Lucian had come to check on me and saw that all my things were packed and gone. Checking at Davian's house he saw that he was already with someone else. Lucian wasn't sure to expect me heartbroken over this, or if I would be alright however one thing, he knew is that he didn't like the idea of me traveling on my own.

After finding me he found a place of his own close by, as he had promised, he would always be nearby. I moved several times, going through several jobs. This is when I had run into

Obscured Darkness

Joanie again, one of the rare friends that I would have in my life. Even mom and dad accepted Lucian moving around with me since I was still living on my own.

Chapter Sixteen
Searching for the Humans
(During Jacobs Lifetime)

Claire had given both Lucian and Rose a goodbye kiss before her and Grant would take off with Jacob. The two had decided to leave for the Caribbean. Not a place she had ever been to, but then it had been mostly because of the sunlight. She felt it would be beautiful during the moonlight.

Jacob seemed to love Grant. Grant even treated him like he was his very own son spending a lot of time playing and talking to him. He seemed to hang on his every word. Settling into a little cabin the family decided to stay here for a while or at least until they would have to move again. Staying in an area where there were not very many others. Always pretending to speak a foreign language that way others would not even bother trying to speak with them.

Only occasionally there was a very kindhearted person who would try and communicate with them or would coo over Jacob and how cute he was. He grew rather quickly. More at a human rate rather than slow like the vampire family. At least he wasn't stuck being a physical baby for the rest of his life. The human part of him helped a lot. Charlotte and Andrew joined their mother's household for a little while.

One of the mornings Jacob had been playing out in the sand, Grant taught him to build a sandcastle. Not ever feeling afraid of anything, the storm didn't seem to bother Jacob that the weather turned severe. Figuring this would be a good time for him to take a nap, Grant took Jacob inside to put him in his bed. Jacob already started to yawn; he had spent all day out in the sun and playing with the water.

Grant had even felt tired himself. After setting Lucian in his crib Grant walked into the living room to see Claire working on a book. She had finally finished it. It only took a few weeks; she had explained that because of the gift she gave to both Rose and Jacob that someday they might need it. The book was about old family spells and history from the beginning of the change right down to the battle. She even included Rose's family history as well as Grants.

"From a vision, I see in the future. I know they will need it. I have charmed it so that it will only present itself when either of them needs it. This will protect them when we are unable to. They will know how much we loved them and that our promise to protect them will even survive our final death. I love you very much however there are things in my visions, I don't know how they will happen or how it's controlled. However, I know there is little to safeguard ourselves. I am so sorry to have gotten you involved. Even to death, I shall love you."

Grant knew there were many visions that Claire would have, however, she did not speak of them hoping it would be better not to fear the future since there would be very little, they could do other than to hope for the best. Spending more time together they watched as the sunset came. The moonlight shone through the window as Grant retired to bed and Claire sat up finishing up her enchantments on the book.

It hadn't been too long when Grant had fallen asleep to find something that shocked him. At first, he thought he was locked in a bad dream. He thought this until he had seen Claire drawn there standing next to him telling him this was not a dream; they were pulled here by these two people.

There was a woman and a man. The man was of an impressive size and the woman very petite. Both dressed entirely in black with no part of their skin showing. Only for a split second, the dark-figured couple had been standing behind Grant.

"I am making you pay for leaving me in this condition. I can no longer move around; because of you, I am trapped in my body unable to wake. I shall haunt every creature in their dreams or draw them to me. I will fulfill my destiny as a demon hunter no matter who gets in the way. As for you, even though you are nothing more than a human you sided with those horrible things. You deserve death as much as they do." His voice boomed loudly shaking the ground as if causing a small earthquake. As Grant looked around them, he saw Claire laying on the floor crushed to death.

Having such an intense urge to wake from this nightmare Grant hoped this was not what Claire had been telling him about. Forcing himself out of his nightmare, as he would normally have jolted himself from a regular nightmare, Grant ran from the bedroom into the living room only to see a swirl of red smoke in the air where he had last seen Claire standing. Running into Jacobs's room to check on him he could see he was still sleeping contently in his pram. Grabbing a few things and shoving them hastily into a burlap sack, he carefully took Jacob out hoping not to wake him and left the house. He might just get far enough away to save his son.

Grant would have taken Jacob back to the rest of the family or at least to the other vampires hoping for protection. Except Claire did all the navigating. He never once knew where they were or how to get in touch with them. Grant would have taken the book that Claire worked so hard on except it already vanished. No horse around since they usually traveled with Claire. They had planned on getting something for him to move around on so he wouldn't have to depend on Claire all the time. Walking as fast as he could staying awake not risking being pulled in again, he went south trying to stay in the sun hoping this might give them some sort of protection.

After a few hours, Jacob had woken up with a curious look on his face. Grant assumed he was probably wondering where his mother had been. Trying to stay calm hoping he wouldn't start crying. He seemed more interested in the things around him and what Grant was doing. Only stopping a few times to rest, he kept walking. Following along the coast had been a little easier. It was more likely that he would come across a town or something. Eventually, he did. There was a large ship sailing out with cargo and passengers. Not worried about where it was heading Grant wanted on it hoping that outdistancing the area, might prevent them from getting ahold of him or Jacob. Preferring to stay out on the deck with the many chairs laid out for passengers. Grant stayed awake the best he could. He had been curious why they could pull Claire in while she was awake, yet they haven't pulled him in yet?

His head was already throbbing with a headache even though he associated it with not sleeping and being stressed out trying to get away from killers who killed his wife and his child's mother. Trying to protect them from creatures he had no chance against. The spray of the salty water or the cool breeze kept him awake. Occasionally slipping into sleep but not long enough he would jolt himself awake hoping for almost anything at this point that was good.

As a human with no special gifts or background with special human creatures, being exposed to so many creatures around him wondering now, would he notice the difference if he were to see or speak to one? Would the difference be hard to tell? Before Claire, he had no idea any of this ever existed, and now, he was running from it, and worse yet if he were to tell anyone they would think he was either crazy or risk having demon hunters alerted to where he was. Jacob was getting quite a bit of attention from the ladies on the deck. Especially when he told them his mother passed away. Sparing them from the truth he simply chose to tell them she died from an illness and he was leaving to join the family to help him raise the baby. What he was hoping for had been to run into someone familiar or off to his old home where it all started. After two nights of not sleeping Grant was tired enough, he could no longer control his nodding off. One of the ladies on the deck held Jacob once his father fell asleep.

Feeling restful he thought of Claire and saw her walking toward him in his dream. He was so happy to see her and started feeling it must have just been a nightmare and when he woke it would be all over and he could explain to her how terrible it had been, then as the figure had come closer the face changed completely. It was another woman someone he did not recognize other than she was dressed in the same colors as the person who killed Claire. Turning to run he realized he didn't have Jacob in his hands. Panicking about where his son was, he couldn't run in any direction. Either the one woman was waiting for him in one direction or the man in the other. Thankful for being on the sea, a gust of salty water woke him back to reality and out of the dreamscape.

Looking around to the side the lady sat in the chair beside him holding Jacob and peacefully talking to him. At least she was unaware of what was going on around them. He could see she had wrapped Jacob in another blanket probably assuming he was having problems staying warm with the breeze now being cold outside blowing on him. If she only knew the truth. At least his skin coloring and heartbeat helped from giving away what part of him was not human. Being grateful for the woman holding him he took Jacob back in his arms feeling a little better hoping Jacob would be safe with him. After one more day at sea, they departed from the boat. Still nice and sunny the weather seemed to change quite a bit. Grant had taken some money with them and bought a horse hoping to ride for a while rather than walk. It would get them further and faster. He felt they didn't control him as well and waking from the last dreamscape hadn't hurt as much as the first time. Hoping his assumption had been correct they kept trying to flee.

Almost too afraid to stop, after almost ten days of straight traveling and doing odd jobs for food for the two of them and the horse Grant was able to purchase, Grant knew he was getting worn out.

Over the next several months' Grant hoped the ones they ran from had given up or could not find them. Sleeping restfully now feeling his son was finally safe. Hiring a nanny to care for Jacob while he worked, spending all the time he could with him when he was home. Not sure how much he would remember but teaching him about sadly the little he knew of his own son's mother, His gift mainly trying to give him a normal life the best he could.

Only a year passed after Claire died. Jacob was growing rather quickly and the nanny was complaining about his growth. Hiring a new nanny to fill in to keep things calm and quiet. Grant felt things were falling into place, feeling comfortable raising him. One night after working a little later than normal Grant had come home to find Jacob frustrated. The nanny explained he was like that all day. No matter what she did she could not console him. This particular nanny had known there was a difference about Jacob however she never complained and kept silent about it. Hoping that he was now at home to care for him he carried him holding him close hoping to relax him. It had been as if Jacob did not want to be put down, he held on rather tight and it was painful for Grant. As little as Jacob was, he was so much stronger than Grant already.

Tired Grant took Jacob to bed with him. Laying down hoping he might be able to relax and sleep when he had Jacob with finally nodded off releasing his grip a little, Jacob fell asleep. Then finally Grant fell asleep for what would be the last time. Finding himself back in the same dreamscape this time he was not able to snap himself out of. There was nothing exterior to pull him out either. At this point, he hoped to distract them long enough that they might forget he had Jacob. Hoping they had no interest in an infant not that he knew how Jacob would care for himself other than the nanny coming back the next day to care for him or worse case, find him a home. Anything she could do would be better than leaving him in the open just to be killed.

Doing whatever he could at least to save Jacob he thought wildly searching for a way out for him. Trying to run had been pointless; throwing Jacob hoping he might get away he threw him into the bushes hoping they might conceal him. Grant realized at the last moment that the man in black, the doctor was not indeed dead. In a matter of a second, before Grant could even do anything, he had been killed by him. It had been so quick that he felt no pain. Looking into the bush the lady reached in and pulled Jacob out.

"Do you wish to kill him or use him? I can't tell if he is human or a half-breed?" The woman's voice was so much fainter than the man's voice had been.

"It would be much sweeter to use the son to do my work that his father seemed to be willing to die going against. How fitting that he works for me now. Take him from the dreamscape and take him to Elston. He is our strongest demon hunter; he will do quite well at raising and training him.

As the demon hunter recoiled back into his own comatose body. The woman took Jacob from the dreamscape, tucking him under her arm with him on his back looking up at her she shot off in the direction of Elston, the town which had been named after its founder. Racing through the forest, swamps, and flatlands until she reached the edge of her destination, she accepted the fact that she worked for a demon hunter and that he viewed her as one as well. Knowing full well that when he completed his purpose that they would both die, at least that had been his word, now that he was in the physical state he was in, she didn't share her plans. If she were the only one surviving, no one could stop her. She knew the secrets he learned as well as the stone she hunted for.

At the far edge of town, a huge castle loomed over the whole town. It could be seen from such a long distance and even further with her eyesight. Being careful not to break his ruse or let others know that she was a demon, she walked on the outskirt of town. Just in case someone were to see her she was careful never to walk too fast even though she would have been there by now. Walking always infuriated her having to blend in with mere mortals, a life she was glad to put behind her. Feeling if she were the only demon, she could do whatever she wanted. She would destroy anything that would get in her path. Drink the blood of anyone she wished without consequences. She knew many of the docs secrets, but even in a coma state, he held information out on her that she needed. She was extremely venomous with anger knowing he would trust a duplicate of himself with the information and not her. It had been the only reason she protected him.

As soon as she had what she wanted. The stone, she would finish off the doc and his imposters. Finally walking up the long winding path far enough out of the range of human eyes she shot in a hurry to the front door. Before she did the door opened in anticipation of her. He had not sensed her, he had merely been waiting for her since the demon hunter reached him in his dreams.

"Katherine, I have been waiting for you, what is this mission that is so important that the leader wants me to fulfill? He said he was drained and that you would explain his mission. What is it? Do I need to leave right away?" He had been excited; his gear lay sprawled across the floor of the main room as he tried to decide what weapons he might need depending on what demon he was about to hunt.

"Elston, this is not, as exciting as you may think. The leader does regard you as his strongest fighter, his best demon hunter, which is why he assigns this pain to you. In revenge for the actions of a mortal betraying humankind, he has taken his human son to be raised and trained as a demon hunter. He has appointed you to take over this mission." Even though

Katherine explained this she also said it in a rather sarcastic teasing tone, the great one being saddled with an infant. This was to be looked at as a step up but to both, it was degrading to lesser than death.

Taking the child out that she had tucked under her arm, covered in a blanket, Jacob looked around with wide eyes. He was too afraid to cry with these strangers. He never made a sound. Calling for one of the servants in the house, a young woman came with an apron on.

"Geneva, this little one is your responsibility now; I have no time to be weighed down with this. Take it away and raise it. Do whatever with it; just keep it out of my way. I have important responsibilities to attend to. Sorry Katherine, I must get going. I will be gone for many nights tracking so I do not know when I will be back. You're welcome to stay until you are ready to leave. Just do not touch my workers or I will hunt you down regardless of the pact that you have with the leader. You are still a worthless demon." With that, he grabbed a few of the weapons on the floor, packed them in animal skin, and slung it over his shoulder.

He was a rather huge muscular man who did not hide his skin. No shirt and only wearing cotton slacks for easier movement. Pushing past Katherine, he dropped Jacob into the arms of Geneva and left.

Most of the time Jacob played with Geneva's other children, not even growing up in the castle, to make sure he stayed out of the way, he lived with her family in their humble little cottage home. Growing up Jacob felt he had several brothers and sisters. Even though later as he grew older, he found that they were not blood-related. However, Geneva was very much a loving mother to him. Something he would never have received if Elston raised him or if the lead demon hunter killed him. Geneva had the understanding that a demon killed Jacobs's parents and she felt sorry for the little one not having a family. Trying even harder to make sure he felt he had one now. She had no idea how correct she was that a demon killed his family and that he was not that far from her own family or that Jacob had a special gift waiting inside of him.

Celebrating birthday parties, family celebrations, and many other town events, Jacob was brought along and raised as one of her own in every way. Trips to the lake to swim, teaching him how to play games, her husband Lloyd had bonded with the small boy. Just spending a few minutes with him it was easy to connect to him. As he grew older a natural calm reserve and demure attitude took over.

One of the days his family had gone to church his mother hoped he would come, after a while he just felt he was wasting his time there. Never feeling comfortable almost as if eyes were tearing into his skin, there were many gifts and abilities he had he knew the rest of his family did not. Keeping these silent so that he would not scare anyone, even though he held the secret with his mother, she loved him so much she did not want anything to happen to him. Teaching him to keep his secrets silent, she had only found out when she saw him running along the beach at a rather fast clip. Stopping him making sure no one saw him, she had a long talk about being safe to him.

As his family left for church, Jacob chose to walk along the beach as he had every morning, skipping stones along the top of the water not paying attention to the cool breeze wafting in from the lake. Sitting on the sand watching the waves come up.

"I see you enjoy the water as much as I do. I probably should be in church with my family, but I can't stand sitting in those old hard pews listening to something I don't agree with, anything interesting in the water. You're watching it rather intently."

Even though she did not know him she walked over naturally as if she had known him for years sitting down next to Jacob.

"Nothing exciting, I just like sitting here, it allows me to sift through my thoughts. Sort of hard to do when you have a large loud family around you all the time. Sort of the only time I get to be myself or away from them." She leaned against him, not flinching Jacob accepted it.

She almost felt like another sister to him only quieter. She took something out of her pocket, it was wrapped in paper. Taking it out she handed him a piece. Just sitting there next to each other you would have assumed they were longtime friends.

"Would you like to hang out tomorrow? I have to help my family but maybe later in the evening if you're not busy?" Sitting there nonchalantly looking out at the water not in a hurry for an answer.

"Sure, I would be great. I'll meet you here." Both sitting there rather content not saying anything other than to enjoy the nice breeze blowing in across the water.

"Sorry to cut this short. My family must be back. I can hear my mother calling. I'll see you here again tomorrow only later."

She looked around for anyone that might have been calling me. The look on her face was of confusion.

"I didn't hear anyone. How do you know it was your mother or that she was calling? Are you one of them?" Not looking shocked at all she looked more curious or even a little excited.

Standing still I couldn't believe I let something that simple slip. I had never given thought to what I would do if someone found out. I must have given her some idea that I felt stuck.

"Don't worry, it's not as if I plan on telling anyone. Besides, it shall ruin all I have planned for tomorrow. There's nothing wrong with having a few secrets between friends. You should probably get going." Jumping up from her sitting position she hugged me and then skipped away in the direction she originally walked from. Smiling as she left, I couldn't help but feel she was a bit odd, but I was happy that I would see her again tomorrow.

If no one were around or in sight range. I raced as fast as I could to the clearing, stopping just before the woods. The cottage was very close, not many steps away from the woods which separated the cottage from the beach. It was always nice living this close to the water. Except in the winter when the cold harsh winds would chill the small cottage. I could see some of the kids goofing off and playing in the yard still wearing their fancy Sunday clothing.

"Have a nice day at the beach sweetie?" It was nice that mom never pushed me to come to the church with them. She respected my space as much as possible. Geneva stayed outside to watch the children play. At times I had to remind myself that she was an adult. At times she played as childishly as the kids had. At least she still knew how to have fun.

"Yeah, it was nice, a little different since I just made a new friend. We are going to hang out again tomorrow later after she is done helping her family."

"A lady? By chance do I know her? Is the young lady single?" Geneva could not hide the excitement in her eyes. Not only had I spoken with a girl, I was letting her know I was looking forward to seeing her again perked her curiosity.

"I don't know. I didn't ask." Which is true I hadn't and it certainly didn't come up? I hadn't thought about that fact as being important.

"What is she like? Do you know anything about her family?" She was hoping to find out what kind of conversation I would have had with her.

Obscured Darkness

"I don't know, we didn't talk about her family. Mostly she was just quiet." As I talked, I walked into my bedroom which I shared with two of my other older brothers. Both were outside goofing around.

"Is she interested in you?" Geneva continued her questions as she sat down in the only chair in the room. I laid back putting my hands behind my head and resting on my bed.

"I don't know, but she must like me somewhat, she asked to hang out tomorrow." Shrugging my shoulders to show I wasn't sure.

Not that I wanted to analyze it. I wanted to accept it as it came. It was nice having a friend my age and the fact she figured out my secret without my telling her. The fact she acted like it didn't seem to bother her and she barely knew me.

My own family didn't know about my gifts other than my mother. Besides, the kids here were much older and almost ready to move out or getting married soon. The young ones were too small to play with. With them, if I were to play with them, I had to be so careful.

I had to use so much caution, after all, it's not like I wanted to say, "hey mom, I was tossing the ball with Johnny and accidentally ripped his hand clean off." There were some games I didn't play with them at all because it was too much of a risk. Even with the older ones.

"Do you know anything about this girl? How about her name? Maybe I've heard of her? How old is she?" Geneva stood up looking like she had given up on getting any answers.

"I'm sorry but I don't know her name, it didn't come up but then I didn't introduce myself either. We just sat and watched the water mostly. I do know she likes muffins. Maybe I'll bring some for her tomorrow? I assume she's my age, at least she looked close enough to it and I'm seventeen."

"Your hopeless, hopefully, tomorrow will go better? "As she

said this, she left my room closing the door and leaving me to myself.

Chapter Seventeen
Two to Love

I laid back for several hours remembering what it had been like sitting on the beach sand. The way she leaned against me felt so natural. I couldn't wait until tomorrow to find out what she had planned. This would be the first time I looked forward to something of interest. Sadly, I would have to endure hunting in the morning with my father and two older brothers.

I couldn't sleep so instead of replaying the short day over and over in my memory. I walked quietly into the kitchen. I found I was not the only one who couldn't get sleep. Geneva had been in the kitchen messing around with the flour and the fresh eggs from the chicken coop.

"I thought your new friend would enjoy these fresh muffins since you said she seemed to like them. I wanted to help you out a little." As much time that Geneva spent with her family, at social gatherings, and cleaning homes for others, she always found the time to do those special things for her family, especially since she was human and had no extra gifts to help her along.

Other than the fact she was so loving and a hard worker. I had no idea how she managed it all. I felt she was far more gifted than I had ever been.

"I hope I didn't wake you, I wanted to surprise you with these. I don't get to see you get this excited too often." Geneva looked so sweet as she smiled at me.

"I was already awake. I just couldn't sleep. Guess you could say I'm more excited about my day than I thought I was going to be. I was coming out here to make muffins myself, I see you beat me to it. Anything I can help you with?" I felt guilty that I didn't show more appreciation for my mother very often, hiding my secret sort of made me quieter and much more withdrawn.

It was easier to avoid than deal with others and explain why I couldn't participate in certain activities.

"I just have to bake it now. You can help me clean up if you want to." Picking up the muffins Geneva placed them in the stone hearth at the corner of the kitchen.

As she placed it in there, I wiped down the counter with a damp cloth and put the dishes in the sink. It hadn't taken much to clean off the mixing bowl she used. At least I could do that since she does so much for me.

"I think while they bake, I'm going to pull out my paints." Walking over to my mom I gave her a light hug even though it felt rather firm to her, "I don't say it enough but thank you, mom. After having a mother as great as you, it's difficult to get excited about anything else. Everything else pales in comparison." Giving me a playful slap on the back she knew I was sucking up to her.

Obscured Darkness

"Okay that's enough manure, go paint and I'll finish up here." Not that there was much left other than to wait.

I had built a small shed outside, with two windows to let in the air and sunshine. Taking out my canvas and oil paints, I never used brushes, so my hands tended to get messy. There were certain scenes I tended to paint as well as a familiar face. Not that I had ever met her or been to any of these places I painted. However, I knew every line on her face, the way she smiled, and almost to the point I could hear her laugh. Even at night, I would dream about her. Mother worried that maybe I was obsessed over this fictional woman so much that it turned my interest off any other woman. I couldn't help it. I knew her name, her scent, and even her dreams. I just wished she were real. I had already fallen in love with her. As usual, I painted her face again.

For the first time, I started to feel guilty as if I were doing something wrong, betraying the woman I loved. How could I do such an injustice to her? Maybe mom was right, I was putting too much interest in her.

Putting down the half-completed picture of her, I washed my hands in the rain barrel that I built to the side of the shack. Leaving I went to prepare my bow and arrows for the hunt. It would not be that much longer before the others would be awake.

My father and brothers preferred using muskets. I liked my bow compared to the loud sound and the reloading time of the gun. It was interesting watching the ritual they would go through getting ready for the hunt, both mentally and physically. Each had what was supposed to be a lucky charm with them. A rabbit's foot is a very old superstition. One I was happy not to have to follow myself. After all, what made it lucky since it brought the rabbit to its demise? Or was it that they could kill a pathetic defenseless rabbit?

We would sit for hours in different locations waiting for an animal to appear. At times there would be herds or scarcely anything at all. As I would get bored, I would draw a picture in the dirt or make stick houses. It helped me to go off on my own. My brothers and father still liked to stick together more so they would not accidentally shoot each other. On the other hand, I used the excuse that I had to have a clear shot before I could shoot, that way no risk of injuring a person. However, today I felt the effects of feeling tired. Leaning against a tree with the bushes shading the ground. I slumped down to take a quick nap. I must have slept a little longer than I wanted to. I could hear my father calling for me in the distance and the sun was beginning to crest over the trees.

Grabbing my bow and arrows. I jumped quickly to my feet. Unlike the rest of my family, I could cheat, standing perfectly still listening for any rustling around, smelling for the odor of the surrounding animals. Mulling over the option of several different ones until I hit the scent I wanted. Nothing stood a chance when I went hunting, a quick whoosh of wind was all they noticed. Just as I caught up to the poor deer it never had a chance to get away. Grabbing it by the neck, I snapped it. Dying instantly, I shot an arrow into the neck just for the benefit of my family, that way it would look like I hunted with the bow or they might have questioned it.

Holding it now in my arms while the bow hung around my neck and the arrows in their sheath slung over my shoulder. I ran back towards the voices. Now that I was within walking distance I slowed as I was now close enough. As soon as they did see me, I heard the excitement of bravo from my brothers and father.

They didn't have any luck this morning. We walked back to

the house as my brothers did their best to help me carry the large deer back, not that I needed it. I pretended since it made them feel part of it even more. It helped with the bonding and I knew it made my father happy.

"The fearless hunter has done it again. Never lets us down." Dad told mom proudly as he passed her standing in the doorway of the house now heading out to the shed with my brothers to get ready to prepare the deer. Mom was giving me that, I know what you did look. Smiling at her as I snuck off to my room. I was hoping they wouldn't mind that I wasn't sticking around. After I changed my clothes and rushed out of the house.

I noticed only mom had seen that I was leaving, the others were too busy with the dead deer. Before I could forget mom handed me a bag with the muffins she baked last night. Kissing mom on the cheek I left for the beach.

I knew I was getting there early, not that I minded waiting. It gave me time to relax and mull things over in my head. The sun had been out at full strength so the breeze from the water felt good. I sat there for several hours even getting lost in my thoughts at times. Oddly enough I started to wonder what Rose was doing. The girl from my dreams, then I reminded myself to stay in reality. I did begin to worry that I was being stood up. I knew she had plans with her family and would come later.

I let out a deep sigh of disappointment feeling sure that I had been stood up, standing up still holding the paper bag with the muffins. I stood there watching as the sunset and the moon would have been the only source of light to guide me home. Not wanting to get there right away. I started walking back slowly, deliberately taking slow steps. Guess I just hoped she would show. Then at the last, I heard it.

"Can you hear me? Please still be there." I didn't see her as I ran back to the spot on the beach where we first met at. Even with my good eyesight, she was much further than what I could see. I could pick up on the scent as the wind carried it from quite a way away.

"I'm lost, if you can find me, I would appreciate it, I don't want to sleep in the woods tonight, it's sort of creepy in here." As she continued to talk, I followed the direction of her voice.

Sadly, the human side of me impaired my eyes in the dark so badly that I took out a few trees as I tracked her. Once she stopped talking, I could hear her breath, and when she sat down on the ground the leaves made a rustling sound beneath her. Her scent was stronger as I was getting closer. Being careful not to take her out like I had the trees. I walked more slowly now.

"Can you hear me? I would call you by your name except I don't think we ever covered that part?" Hoping she would talk more since the wind swirled around here in the woods. It was hard to sense the exact direction.

"Can't you see in the dark? My name is Abbey, what's yours?" She sounded kind of surprised as she said her name.

It's when she realized at that moment, neither of us shared something as basic as our names.

"My name is Jacob; I am part human so unfortunately because of that I can't see in the dark that well." Feeling around in the dark, I could see a darker figure sitting on the ground. Her scent permeated the small area.

"Reach your hand up and I'll lead you to the beach, at least the moonlight has it lit there." As she reached up, I took her hand and helped her up off the ground slowly leading her to the small patch of light that barely came through the trees. As we emerged both could see the water in the distance.

"I'm sorry I was so late. Our family had bad news or I would have been here earlier. I didn't realize how late it was until I was about halfway here and the sun set so quickly." Walking into the clearing, still holding hands we walked along the water.

"That's okay; I was about to head home until you called me. When you're ready to go home I'll help you get there safely. There are nasty things out in the woods. I don't want you running into. If there is anything I can do to help you, or your family out just tell me."

"It's just my fiancée, not much anyone can do, he's dead, probably buried by now. Not sure how they handle it?" She smiled and pulled at my hand to walk a little faster.

"Wow..... he passed on? Are you sure you're, okay?" She had a fiancée.

I was curious why she didn't say anything yesterday about it. We didn't say much about anything personal. Trying to keep up. I started wondering if she was trying to occupy herself or just not think about the heartbreak? She didn't seem that affected by it. Was I reading her wrong?"

"Yeah, I'm fine it's not like I knew him. My father thought he would be a good match, so he pre-arranged it. Mom arranged the previous one. Both have died in the same war. My guess is they should stop picking men that are going off to war and we wouldn't have this problem. Besides, I told them it's god's way of telling them I should be able to pick who I want. I'm guessing you have several waiting for you unless its prearranged also." Abbey kept watching the water as we walked never looking at me.

"Guess I can't argue with that. I never thought about being married. No one has ever talked to me about it before. Is there someone you want to be with?" Her warm hand still in mine felt nice as we casually strolled along the water's edge.

"There's no one, I like you, but I just don't think it's in that way. I would like to just be on my own, but my father says it's not safe; neither does it look good for a girl to live alone. They think it's unnatural that I do not wish to be with anyone. My mother keeps reminding me how she had her first baby at my age. Do you think it's strange I don't want any? Besides, I don't always feel good so how could I take care of someone if I don't feel well?" Letting go of my hand she reached into the water to pull out a shiny black stone. It had the look of either blackened ash or an old smooth lava stone.

"I've never had anyone tell me I had to do something. It's always been an option. Even though I don't care for hunting it's not required but I know it helps my family. I don't think you should ever do anything you don't want to. But what do you mean you don't feel good at times?" We both stopped. Abbey looked more at her stone as I looked at her concerned.

"It's nothing serious. I feel sick but then the doctor comes and uses leaches. I usually feel weak for a few days after but then I'm fine again. Probably another reason my father wants me to marry so I won't be alone when I get sick. But let's not talk about that, it's depressing you. Let's walk the other way if we walk far enough, we will end up at my aunt's home. I told my parents that's where I was going. They would pitch a fit if they knew I was hanging out with a boy. I wanted to have fun today, but I had to stay and pretend to grieve. Hard when you don't know the person. I'm sure father is already working on picking another suitor." As she looked at me, she rolled her eyes at that last part.

"If we had been here earlier, what would you have planned?" Even though it wasn't happening yet, I was still curious about what she would have planned for us today.

"There's a cave near here that I like to explore. There are some shiny stones and I like to collect them. I thought you might like to see it. I think it's too dark now. I'll point it out when we walk past it." Looking disappointed she kept walking.

"Just a second, stay here and I'll be right back, it won't take long." Not worried that she saw me take off at lightning speed, I rushed to my art shack to grab my two oil lamps. On the way back I hit two more trees. Dad always blamed the animals, if he only knew the truth. Just the idea seemed funny to me. As I told Abbey I would not be too long. I had been right; it didn't take me very long. Not that I wanted to risk leaving her alone at night.

"Climb up on my back, I'm about to give you a fun ride. Just hold on tight." Smiling at her I swung her up on my back she held on around my neck, her legs around my waist.

Holding her hands as I ran, she let out a squeal of excitement even laughing at times as we sped along. This I could get used to not having to hide my gifts and just be myself. The run was cut short as I had to slow down since we were almost near the cave. It wasn't far from the beach as we made our way through a few trees. We crossed a stream from a tiny waterfall and kept going back behind it. Just as it started getting dark, I could see the cave. If you didn't go behind the waterfall you would never know it was here.

Both lanterns were still held in my one hand. I took one and lit it handing it to Abbey, then the second I lit and held myself. As we walked in Abbey led the way. Down in the cave there were two tunnels. Choosing the one on the right she kept walking down. The descent wasn't too steep until we went further in. The descent declined a lot as Abbey started walking sideways to keep her footing and not slip. About another mile down the tunnel straightened out more. With the lanterns, we could see well enough. As she told me this was an impressive place. The jewels started to sparkle even from a distance.

"See this one, I love the red ones they are so bright and

beautiful. There are a lot more down further, but I only found those because I fell. I couldn't get out, but my father knows I like coming here. I promised him I wouldn't go any further than this anymore. This tunnel is much safer, the other we passed by, its only fourteen steps before you come to a steep slope and it ends up in the same spot, the tunnel we are in is just a huge half circle. I bet there's even more past this wall of rock. The wooden tracks were once used to bring out materials from here. But since the cave-in, they don't mess with this one. More than half the men died, not from the cave-in but the disease after. They thought it was a curse. I don't believe in curses. See this large white one? I know my mom would love it; except it's stuck in there pretty good. Are you strong? I only know the rumors I've heard about vampires."

"I'm strong but I've never tested how strong I am, never had the chance to. I know I can take out trees by accident. Guess I could try." As I told her about the trees she laughed. Her laugh sounded so sweet.

I stared at the rock wall aiming to punch through it alongside the white shining stone. Hitting it with all the force I had my hand went straight through it almost like butter. I was up to my elbow. Scooping my hand, I pulled hard, and a chunk of rock came out with the stone. Breaking the white stone loose from the rock. I handed it to Abbey.

"Now you have your beautiful stone, even though it sharply pales in comparison to you." We looked around a little longer before we decided to leave. We sat at the mouth of the cave for a while talking before I took her to her aunt's home.

"My aunt is going to be surprised you got this out. I won't tell her how, but this is great. We both tried to get it out before."

"Will she be up this late? I don't want to have you walk too far alone; I can hide in the woods and stay close enough in case you need me?"

"You don't have to worry about my aunt. She's very open-minded, besides she's a little different. She lives on her own, but most don't like going to her. She makes medicines. Father calls her a witch doctor. She reads people's futures and past with bones and other things. Not human bones but chicken and such. The bones are from those who died naturally. She feels if you kill something to use pieces from it, that it taints it or cast a negative effect. I don't understand how it works but she can also read palms. She's not here for too long, soon she will probably take off again, she lives like a gypsy. I wish I could go with her; my father would never allow it." Sighing, she continued to inspect the stone.

Then looking like she had a thought occur to her she looked at me.

"If your family doesn't know about your gifts then am I the first to know? Am I your first friend?" She looked a little surprised.

"With my gifts, it's sort of hard-to-find friends. There are too many things I can't do, or I would expose myself. So yes, you're my first physical real-life friend. Besides my mom, you're the only other one who knows about my gift"

"Do you have nonphysical friends? Odd you put it that way?" Laughing out loud, she found the concept interesting.

I wasn't sure if she would understand it. I knew how my mother understood it, first time I told her she thought I was dreaming about a crush or a girl I must have seen at some time. But she was never happy when I intentionally tried to search for her in my dreams.

"It's hard to explain. There is this girl that I have dreamed about for as long as I can remember. I have very strong memories from a very young age. One I couldn't see too well, and I never wanted to tell my mother, I saw my parents get killed, at least in my dreams these people must have been my parents. Sadly because of human eyes, I couldn't see the demon well enough because of the dark clouds around him. But this girl feels so real. She has been sort of my friend as I grew up. I still see her at times now. We just hang out and she is just like me, so I don't hold back at all. I don't have to worry about hurting her. I know her so well she is just as real as anyone in my family. But I realize I must sound crazy." Looking down not wanting to see if she thought I was, I wasn't sure if I could handle hearing her confirm it.

"If she's real enough to you then that's good enough. I don't think you're silly or strange. There are a lot of things we assume are not real because we don't have solid proof, but it doesn't mean it's not. Some still don't believe in vampires, they think it's an excuse to cover up for humans' misdeeds." Shaking her head to emphasize her point showing she didn't approve but agreed with me.

"When did you find out you were a vampire? Or have you always been one? Is the rest of your family? I thought vampires couldn't get pregnant since their bodies were dead and all or am I mistaken? Sorry, I'm asking so many questions, but I've never known a vampire before?" Sitting Abbey was still inspecting and looking over the stone they retrieved, she was so happy to be able to give it to her mother soon.

"So far I'm the only one like myself in my family. That I learned a long time ago. I've watched the others, no one else does what I can. I wish I knew other vampires also then I would finally know if I truly were one or not. It's been my secret with my mom. She taught me to be human and to be normal. I don't know much about vampires myself. It's not hereditary so I don't know how it happened. I thought my parents were mine until I was older. Mom thought I could handle knowing later. A demon killed them and I was left to die. So, she took care of me. Someone gave me to her to raise. She cleaned their home and kept the other staff in order. According to legends and stories, I fit most descriptions, but I don't crave blood but if I do drink it, it doesn't repulse me. I've only drunk the blood of deer since they're so plentiful. I'm careful not to let my mother know. I've never attempted drinking blood from a human. I don't think I'm a vampire since my skin is still smooth, I can bleed and I have a heartbeat. Mom thinks the venom only affected me a little however it happened to me."

"I've always been curious how many more vampires are out there." Leaning against me I felt the heat coming off her body.

She shivered a little as she leaned against me. My skin was cool but not as frozen cold as a corpse or some legends let people believe. But then it could be because I was a little different?

"Maybe we should get you to your aunt's home before you get sick, it is getting colder out tonight." Both standing up she raised her arms smiling.

I knew immediately what she was hoping for. Pulling her up onto my back quickly we raced back to her aunts' home. No one would be up at this hour so we could sneak close enough. As we reached just a few steps in front of the cottage, Abbey slid down off my back. Hugging me and thanking me for the stone she turned and walked to the door. Before she disappeared, she waved and said she would see me tomorrow here at the cottage. Her aunt always had a way of knowing who she was with and would be asking questions, it would be better if she was able to meet me.

Stepping back away from the house. I raced almost all the way home. No one had been up in the morning yet; it was still too early. This morning mom had to go to work and dad would be leaving for the same. The oldest of my brothers Darrin and Odair usually joined him as they sold their goods at the marketplace. Usually, when everyone was gone, I took care of the three little ones. After sleeping for a few hours, I was awoken by Rohan jumping on top of me being excited that it was morning already. Not far behind him were both Vivian and Jared. The oldest two girls were living with Geneva's aunt before their wedding date. They planned a double wedding to save on money. They had been the only two in the family that I never bonded with. I painted a personal portrait for each of the girls with their prospective husbands and gave it to them ahead of time. It had been the only time that Merlene or Lacena seemed to notice I lived.

Later, I found out why they left me alone. At times I wondered if they figured it out or if Lloyd or even my older brothers Darrin and Odair knew also? One night before Lacena moved out she came into my room and sat on my bed.

"I wanted to thank you for the portrait. The house is already built, and we hung it above the fireplace in the living room. You should sell your art, you could do quite well. I always knew you were gifted, even extra gifted. I just didn't know how to treat you. I'm sorry I was never closer. Before she left, being careful, she hugged me as if she thought she could break or injure me.

"If you ever need help or a place to hide if anyone finds out, you're welcome to come home to me." With that, she walked out of the cottage and so far, has been the last time I have seen her.

Taking the little ones out to the living room they had their assignments. Both boys were supposed to work on reading. Vivian however was expected to work on her piano. As the boys studied, I would work with Vivian playing alongside her. The boys would sound out the words or read them next to us. We made it a bit of a game for them to sing along with the music.

Obscured Darkness

Then as they would finish, I would have the boys play the piano and give Vivian a chance to read also.

This was something special that mom agreed on and had been my secret bonding with my younger siblings to give them a chance at something outside of what was expected of them. I found Rohan to be natural with playing the piano even coming up with his notes. Vivian had her talent; she was already reading at two levels higher than her younger brothers and needed very little help.

After the kids worked on their assignments for a while, I took them out in time for mother to be walking home. I couldn't tell if she was happy or upset. As the kids were occupied. I walked quickly to catch up to her. Pulling out of her pocket she handed me a shiny white letter.

"I know it's supposed to be a privilege but it's just not safe. Unfortunately, since he is the one who gave you to me, he could take you away, so I don't have any say. I don't know what he wants but just be careful." Not saying another word or stopping to play with the kids, I could tell she was upset as she walked straight into the cottage holding back what looked to be tears.

Stopping where I stood, I unfolded the letter to read it. Inside written in gold letters had been instructions. Not an invite or request. It was a requirement.

Jacob,

You are expected early in the morning, there are important matters that need to be tended to. Clear any plans. If you fail to appear there will be consequences not just for you, but for your family as well.

www.ingramcontent.com/pod-product-compliance
Lightning Source LLC
Chambersburg PA
CBHW070811180626
46818CB00001B/208